PASSION'S PRISONER

"Let me go—please."

Antoinette's cries of protest rose and died beneath the fierce pressure of Ramón's mouth.

"Why do you shrink when I touch you?"

"Because when you look at me I know you are only seeing another woman to kiss and make love to, or to abuse as the mood takes you—as revenge against your wife."

"With you it is different. You have to believe that."

"I can't. I won't. I can't even trust my own feelings anymore. . . . Oh, please, let me go." But Ramón had no intention of letting her go. The icicle was melting. She was flesh and blood now. Instead of releasing her he caught her chin firmly with his fingers and turned her face up to his, his eyes blazing.

"So you are not afraid of me, *chica*, but of yourself. That pleases me," he murmured.

PASSION'S PRISONER

(formerly titled Val Verde)

JUDITH POLLEY

A DELL BOOK

Published by
DELL PUBLISHING CO., INC.
1 Dag Hammarskjold Plaza
New York, N.Y. 10017

ISBN: 0-440-19357-5

Reprinted by arrangement with Delacorte Press
Printed in the United States of America
First Dell printing—June 1978

PASSION'S
PRISONER

ONE

As she came up onto the deck of the ship that had brought her from France, Antoinette Dubec wondered if she had not been a little mad to leave the safety and comfort of the château near Versailles to come to this strange country of Mexico. From where she stood, Veracruz seemed little more than a collection of adobe buildings surrounded by sand dunes and scrub. The name meant "True Cross." The occupying French army had also named it "Frenchman's Grave" because of the prevalence of yellow fever and malaria that had claimed so many victims. It was situated on the tierra caliente, the coastal region, where it was always hot and unhealthy. It was the first stop on her long journey to Mexico City.

Her blue eyes, bright with anticipation, searched the quayside, but there was no sign of her father or any uniformed figure that might have been sent to meet her. Surely he had received her last letter, posted over a week ago in Texas. Quelling a momentary fear at being stranded alone in a strange land, she followed the young Negro boy acting as her porter down the gangplank toward dry land. It was a relief to leave the ship. The journey had not been a pleasant one. A storm the second night out had given her mal de mer, and then, just as she was feeling better, more passengers embarked at the last port of call, and from then on her sleep was continually disturbed by a howling baby outside her cabin. The mother of the child had spent the trip on deck along with numerous other peasants too poor to pay for cabin space. Antoinette had found most of the accommodations occupied by Southern families from the United States. The internal war had been over almost a year, but still they were leaving their homes to seek refuge in a new country. She preferred the quiet-spoken Southerners to the more brash people from the North and wished them well in their new life, inwardly marveling at their courage in dragging up established roots to begin again.

It was well past noon, and the quayside and the town beyond were deserted as people shut up their shops and businesses or simply sought the nearest shady spot and took their siesta. The sun blazed down on the white silk parasol Antoinette held over her head. Already she was growing exceedingly warm, and without the umbrella she suspected her skin would begin to burn. The little Negro boy struggling with the first of her trunks managed to squeeze past the two men talking at the bottom of the gangplank, but Antoinette had no intention of being forced to follow suit and came to a halt behind the soldier leaning nonchalantly against the wooden rail and completely blocking her path.

"Excuse me, monsieur."

The man turned, and Antoinette found herself looking into a hard yet attractive face, deeply tanned by the fierce Mexican sun. His uniform and the insignia on the collar of his tunic told her he was a major in the Mexican Chasseurs. He stood straight and tall with the air of a man born to command. From beneath black brows equally black eyes surveyed the elegantly groomed woman before him. Although he could not have stared at her for more than a few seconds, she could have sworn that in that short time, with one sweeping glance that started at the top of her shining red hair and swept down over the crisp white lace-trimmed blouse to the neat leather shoes just visible beneath the hem of her crinoline skirt, he mentally registered every detail of her appearance. He came to attention and gave a short bow before stepping back and allowing her to pass without a word.

The boy had deposited her trunk on the ground and

gone back for the rest. Antoinette waited patiently while he trudged to and fro with the remainder of her luggage. Most of the other passengers had disembarked earlier that morning, and she was virtually the only person, apart from the two men behind her, who was not asleep. Several Negroes and Mexicans sprawled out in the sparse shade of packing cases piled three and four high, the former stripped to the waist, their black bodies gleaming with sweat in the sun, the latter hunched inside colorful serapes, their faces shaded from the heat by their huge straw sombreros. Not one animal or person moved anywhere along the length and breadth of the quay—nor beyond in the town where more figures reclined in doorways and shady alleyways. There was not one whisper of wind to stir the dust on the sun-baked road and relieve the intense heat. As the last of her cases arrived, Antoinette looked around for a carriage to take her to the nearest hotel, where she could wait for her father in comfort. She felt she would melt if she did not have a bath and a change of clothes.

"A carriage, señorita?" The Negro boy's face split into a wide grin at her request, and he shrugged his shoulders. "It is siesta—it is too hot to work. In one hour, maybe two, I go and find one for you."

An hour to wait in the blazing sun! She would rather walk, although that thought was almost as distasteful. Shading her eyes, she peered toward the town.

"Where is the nearest hotel?"

The boy pointed down the street, where a sun haze shimmered above the pavements, but was not more explicit. His grin widened as she picked up a small hand valise.

"You walk, señorita?"

"No, the señorita does not walk." The Mexican officer was at Antoinette's side, although she had heard no sound to inform her of his presence. She darted a swift glance over her shoulder to find his companion had gone on board and they were alone. There followed a rapid exchange in Spanish, which she did not understand, a

9

silver coin changed hands, and then the boy turned and ran in the direction of the warehouses that dominated the landscape. "Felipe is a young rogue, but he will come back with a carriage—even if he has to steal one."

"After being well bribed," Antoinette answered, annoyed that she had not realized the boy was probably half starved and would render any service if paid well enough.

"Felipe has four brothers and two sisters all younger than himself," the officer returned, a cool edge to his voice, and she felt herself coloring beneath his steely gaze. "Forgive me if I have taken too much upon myself, but I was under the impression you were anxious to get out of this heat." The strong voice matched the man. It was a voice used to issuing orders, accustomed to obedience.

"I am," Antoinette said quickly, suddenly afraid he too might disappear and leave her stranded. "Please forgive my brusqueness; I suppose I am finding all this rather strange," and she waved a hand in the direction of the sleeping figures a few yards away. "There should have been someone here to meet me, but he has obviously been delayed. Is there a hotel nearby where I can wait?"

"I'm afraid you will find the hotels in Veracruz are nothing like those in Paris, but at least you will be out of the sun." Dark eyes swept down to her ringless left hand. "The person you are expecting—he is a man?"

"My father. He is coming from Mexico City. Are you stationed there?"

"I am. Permit me to introduce myself. Major Ramón Ruy Chávez. And you, señorita?"

"My name is Antoinette Dubec. My father is General Adolphe Dubec. He has command of a French troop in the capital. . . ." Her companion stared at her in silence and so intently that she heard herself protesting, "Major Chávez, why do you look at me so strangely? Is something wrong?"

"Forgive me, now it is I who am taken aback. I am acquainted with the general, but—well—I had no idea you would look like this. He has always referred to you

10

as his 'little girl.' I had visions of you as being nine or ten years old."

"Dear Papa, does he still call me that?" Antoinette returned with a smile. "Ours is an army family, Major. Most of my relatives and my brother and father have dedicated themselves to army careers. Alas, many are dead now, which is why I have come to join Papa. We are too much apart, and he is all I have in the world. I want to be with him, not hundreds of miles away on my own. I have seen him only once in the last two years. It is little wonder he still thinks of me as a child."

A carriage rumbled slowly out of a side street and halted before them. Felipe jumped from beside the swarthy driver, who grumbled and protested at being made to labor under such conditions as he began to load Antoinette's luggage.

"If you will allow me to escort you to a hotel, it might save you further irritating delays," Ramón Chávez said quietly.

"Thank you, Major. You are most kind," Antoinette answered gratefully, and gave him her hand to help her into the carriage. His grasp was firm, his long, tapered fingers unexpectedly cool against her own hot skin. This was no ordinary soldier, she told herself as she relaxed in a corner, but a man of breeding who would be more at home in the court of the Emperor than in barracks. With those dark eyes, which possessed an almost wicked gleam, there would be many women among the wives and daughters of the European officers who would find him dangerously attractive. Yet somehow she sensed he was an unknown quantity.

The carriage moved off at a slow pace, but she did not mind now that she was in the shade. She raised tentative fingers to her cheeks, wondering if they were as red as her hair.

"You will grow accustomed to our climate—if you remain for any length of time," the major remarked. She had the odd feeling he did not want her to stay, but refrained from any comment. When he had found her

11

suitable accommodations he could consider his duty discharged and go his own way. Perhaps she was not as open with her smiles as other women of his acquaintance, or willing to repay what she had taken to be an act of kindness with more than simple gratitude. "Here we are."

The carriage stopped, and Ramón Chávez got out and helped her down. He led her into a building at the end of the street. It was deserted, but in less than a moment his authoritative tones had brought a man hurrying from a back room. Antoinette looked about her with some apprehension. The place was clean but shabby, with well-worn furniture and paint peeling from the walls. It was unbearably stuffy. She wondered how long she would have to wait for her father and how she would cope once she was alone. She did not particularly like her companion, but at least he spoke the language and was capable of dealing with these impassive strangers who glanced at her out of the corners of their eyes and smiled without meaning it. Her father's colorful letters had led her to believe the Mexican people were of a cheerful, easygoing nature, ready to welcome newcomers to their country. Was she wrong in her assumption that they resented her, both as an outsider and a Frenchwoman?

"I have made arrangements for you to be made as comfortable as conditions here permit." Ramón Chávez led her upstairs and along a narrow corridor to a door at the far end. He opened it and stood back to allow her to enter. Antoinette stared at the large brass bed with a crucifix hanging on the wall behind it, the chest of drawers with a book propped beneath one of the broken legs, the washstand in the far corner, and wished herself at home in the comfort of her own pretty pink bedroom. Then she put the image out of her mind and turned to the silent man in the doorway.

"Thank you for your help, Major Chávez, I am sure I shall be able to manage now. I must detain you from your duties no longer."

"I am not leaving for the capital until the morning. My

room is opposite, should you require further assistance."

"I am sure I will not," Antoinette replied firmly. Crossing to the window, she opened it wide and waited for him to go, but he did not move. Her blue eyes widened as he stepped into the room and closed the door behind him. "I thought I had made it quite clear I no longer require you, monsieur."

It was the way she would have spoken to a disobedient servant at home, and she saw the handsome features darken in anger.

"There is something you must know." He was ill at ease. She watched a tiny vein throb at one temple as he struggled for words and was seized with a terrible feeling of foreboding. When he spoke his voice was unexpectedly kind, as if to try to soften the terrible hurt he was about to inflict on her. "There is no easy way to deliver bad news. It is best broken quickly, and that has always been my way. I beg your forgiveness now for any extra pain my frankness brings. General Adolphe Dubec, your father, was killed in action two weeks ago."

Antoinette was stunned, but still the dreadful words went around in her head. Her father killed! It was not possible.

"Drink this." Ramón Chávez was holding a glass against her lips. She swallowed a little of the contents and immediately began to cough violently as the fiery liquid burned her throat. She was sitting on the edge of the bed, clinging to the brass rails she had grabbed to prevent herself from falling when the first waves of faintness swept over her. "You will be all right now, just sit quietly for a few moments." He stepped back, replacing the silver flask inside his tunic.

"How—how did it happen? Do you know?"

"Sí, but surely the details will only bring more pain."

"I am used to pain." Antoinette raised her head to look at him. A tiny red curl had broken loose from her chignon to tumble across her ashen cheek, and huge tears trembled in the depths of her eyes. The urge to weep was overwhelming, but she fought against it and won.

13

Later she could grieve in private. "Six years ago my mother was killed in a riding accident. Robert, my brother, died last year. My father remained at home for one month after the funeral and then returned here to Mexico. I have not seen him since. There is nothing you can tell me about pain, monsieur."

"I am sorry. I will tell you all I can, but it is very little. Your father and his men were ambushed. He was among the casualties."

"Ambushed! By whom? Bandits?"

"Juaristas." Ramón Chávez' mouth tightened into a bleak line. "Rebels, if you prefer."

"Rebels." Antoinette's eyes searched his face. "I thought they were no longer a danger—that they had been stopped."

"Not at all. Benito Juárez has returned to Mexico, and his following increases daily. His men are supplied with arms and ammunition from across the American border, and already there have been well-planned attacks on smaller towns loyal to Maximilian and the French."

"How is it that you, a Mexican, are not loyal to Juárez?" Antoinette could not restrain the question. Her words were met with a haughty stare.

"That is scarcely a question for you—a stranger in my country—to ask. I am a Mexican, as you point out, and my first loyalty is to Mexico. If you are feeling better, señorita, I will bid you adiós. I have much to do before I leave in the morning."

Antoinette rose to her feet as he spun around on his heel. Then, as abruptly, he halted and looked back at her with a deep frown.

"The boat does not sail until tomorrow evening. Do you wish me to arrange a return passage?"

"Return?" For a moment she did not understand.

"There is nothing for you here." The words were not meant unkindly, but they cut through her like a knife. "It is unthinkable for you to remain here alone—and without friends."

14

"You have made your point, Major. My father is dead, and so there is no reason for me to stay, but I will make up my own mind, thank you."

"Very well. The final decision must of course be yours. Good-bye then, Señorita Dubec. Vaya con Dios."

The room was dark with shadows, for Antoinette had not bothered to light the oil lamp on the chest of drawers. She lay outstretched on the bed, still stunned, but drained of all tears after many long hours of weeping. Gradually, as the shadows lengthened around the room, she began to compose herself and take stock of her situation. She had always been levelheaded and extremely self-reliant, so it was natural that after the first flood of grief receded common sense began to prevail. She could not stay in Veracruz, and there was no reason for her to continue her journey to Mexico City. She would go home again, to the house in Paris and her many friends. It would be better there than at the château where every room held some memory. After the death of her lovely, vivacious mother she had taken over the running of both the château and the townhouse. At eighteen she was acting as hostess to her brother's and father's army friends, attending balls and soirées in her mother's stead. There were frequent visits to court, and once, with her father, she remembered meeting Maximilian and Carlota at their home at Miramar. It had been a huge task for such a young woman, but she had a natural talent for organization and luckily a good head for business, which enabled her to carry on in her father's place when he went off on another campaign.

Wearily climbing off the bed, she lighted the lamp before the light failed completely. A huge moth swooped through the open window and flitted around the flickering flame. Quickly she pulled the faded red curtains, noticing as she did so that the hotel was situated directly opposite a cantina. She glimpsed Negroes and uniformed soldiers among the copper-faced Mexicans crowding

15

through the door. The sound of laughter floated across the street, and the strains of a melancholy guitar made her feel tearful again.

Her luggage was piled in one corner. She found some night attire in one trunk and began to undress. After a refreshing wash she slipped into a loose wrap and began to brush the tangles from her hair, grimacing at the pale reflection staring back at her from the mirror. The room was exceedingly stuffy, and she longed to take a walk, but was afraid to venture out into the street alone. She knew she was still too distressed to sleep (not that the noise from outside would allow her much rest), but the thought of remaining closeted in the tiny room until morning depressed her. And then she remembered she had passed a dining room on the way upstairs. She was about to search through her luggage for a dress when there came a knock on the door and it opened to admit a buxom Mexican woman carrying a tray.

"The señorita is awake—that is good. I have brought you food," she said cheerfully, and set it down on the small table beside the bed. Until that moment Antoinette had not realized how hungry she was. "I have brought enchiladas and mole poblano and the best red wine in the house. The major said you were to have only the best."

"Do you mean Major Chávez?" Antoinette asked, astonished.

"Sí. He left orders to let you sleep until dark and then to bring you a meal. Is everything to your liking, señorita?"

Antoinette smiled into the woman's expectant face and nodded, grateful for this sudden show of hospitality. Alone once more, she sat down and tentatively tried the enchiladas, which she discovered were maize pancakes filled with chicken and chilis. The second plate was piled high with sliced chicken covered by a thick spicy sauce that tasted strongly of garlic and onions and was too highly seasoned for her to finish. A glass of the rough red wine put out the fire in her throat.

After the meal, which she had to admit was not

16

unpleasant and very filling, although not her usual fare, she decided it was only good manners to seek out Major Ramón Chávez and thank him for his unexpected kindness. His action had surprised her and made her bitterly regret the rude way she had spoken to him.

As she stepped out of her room, she heard raucous laughter from the dining room below and was glad it had not been necessary for her to eat there after all. Crossing to the room across the hall, she knocked at the door and waited. There was no reply and no sound from within. She turned and walked quickly to the head of the stairs. Below her the room was packed with Mexicans and soldiers, some instantly recognizable as French in their red-and-blue uniforms. There were women here also— black-haired, bright-eyed women wearing heavy gold earrings, colorful skirts, and bright rebozos over white blouses that exposed bare brown arms. They were drinking at the tables or dancing, and some were reclining against uniformed chests in such a way as to show more than a modest expanse of suntanned leg. Antoinette knew the scene should not have disturbed her as it did—she who knew better than most how hard fighting men chose to relax. Her father had preferred drink, her brother the company of beautiful women—neither was so very different from the men downstairs. The air was thick with cigar smoke that began to irritate her throat. She was about to turn away when she saw him. He was at a corner table, his chair tipped back on two legs against the wall, his dark eyes narrowed against the smoke haze to watch one of the women climbing onto a table to dance. His tunic had been discarded, and his white shirt was open to the waist. A silver medallion on a long chain stood out against the dark hairs on his chest as he leaned forward to refill the empty glass he held. He looked tired—and lonely—and at that moment Major Ramón Chávez of the Mexican Chasseurs looked very drunk. As she watched he stretched out a hand and caught the arm of an attractive girl, pulling her down onto his lap. Antoinette turned away as the two figures became entwined in a fierce embrace. She was embarrassed, disillusioned. He was not a man of breeding after all,-just a man, and a man of the worst kind—dangerously attractive, sensuous, and obviously accustomed to taking his pleasures where he found them. She found the knowledge oddly disturbing.

At eight o'clock the following morning Antoinette came downstairs. She wore a plain traveling dress of blue linen, and her hair was hidden out of sight beneath a bonnet of a matching color. In one gloved hand she carried a parasol, in the other her overnight bag containing her jewel case and her necessities. She was still pale, but her eyes were clear and resolute. She had decided to continue on her journey to Mexico City; it was necessary for her peace of mind.

"Good morning, señorita." Ramón Chávez stood in the curtained doorway of the dining room. "I did not expect to see you again before I left."

"Nor I you, Major," Antoinette returned coolly. He looked none the worse for an excessive amount of tequila. His smile was friendly, but she chose to ignore it, unable to forget the way he had kissed the Mexican girl—he would have smiled at her the same way. His uniform was immaculate, the sword at his side highly polished, as were his high leather boots.

"I have just had breakfast. Would you care for some?"

"Thank you, no," she returned with a shake of her head.

"Some coffee then?"

"Yes, that would be nice."

They sat down in the deserted dining room. The major called to someone out of sight in a back room, and a moment later they were served two large cups of steaming black coffee.

"I was afraid you might have been too distressed to eat last night, but María tells me you managed to get through most of your meal," the major said quietly. "It was simple fare, of course, not what you are used to, but I hope it sufficed."

Antoinette's eyes challenged him across the table.

"What am I used to, monsieur?"

"You are obviously a woman of considerable means, accustomed to servants and a fine house, not the likes of this." He motioned to their surroundings with a tight smile. "Your father was very proud of the family link with—who was it now—Josephine, Napoleon's ex-wife. She was a kinswoman, I believe?"

"A very distant one. Yes, my father was proud of the link. It could have opened many doors for him at one time, but he chose not to exploit the opportunity. He was that kind of man. Did—did you know him well?"

"Better than most, I think." The answer was noncommittal, and she was disappointed at his obvious reluctance to be drawn into conversation on the subject. "What will you do now, I mean when you return to France? Have you someone to stay with?"

Antoinette sipped her coffee and thought of Aunt Sophie in Paris. She would be welcome there or with her married cousin Gabrielle in Rouen, but she contemplated the idea for a brief moment only. No, she was going to Mexico City to see for herself the kind of men who had killed her father and to be sure that his murderers were brought to justice.

"I am not going home, Major Chávez, I have changed my mind."

"Dios. You don't intend to remain in Veracruz?" He looked at her in astonishment.

"No, I am going to the capital."

"Are you out of your mind?" The anger in his voice brought a flush of annoyance to her cheeks.

"I assure you I am not and I do not understand your objection. I see no reason why I cannot stay in the capital for a few weeks."

"Alone? Do you know anyone there?"

"No, but . . ."

"Where will you stay?"

"In my father's house. He wrote he had rented a small place in the San Ángel district. I can go there. I will not change my mind, Major, and if you will not be of service to me, then I will manage alone. I am quite capable."

"And stubborn." Ramón Chávez rose slowly to his feet, staring down at her grimly. He was making it apparent he did not agree with her decision, but she knew there was nothing he could do about it. "How do you propose to travel?"

"By train."

"From here to the capital it is almost three hundred miles. There are fifty miles of track laid down by the French, but after that you will have to travel by coach." His voice was heavy with sarcasm. "The latter part of the journey will take perhaps four or five days, less if the coach doesn't break a wheel or you aren't attacked by bandits."

"Don't you mean Juaristas?" Antoinette asked coldly. She had not considered the journey at all, and it sounded frightening, but not wanting him to see her alarm, she rose to her feet and began to pull on her gloves.

"There are both in the mountains," the major told her as he followed her out of the room.

"I thought you were on your way back to Mexico City," she said meaningfully.

The sun-bronzed face turned in her direction was suddenly hard and uncompromising.

"I have a duty to see my men safely back to their wives and families, señorita. If we are attacked they will react with the experience gained from many years of strict training. I have no fear they will scream or faint or throw a fit of hysterics. I regret I do not have time to play nursemaid to such tantrums."

"Monsieur, you are insulting," Antoinette gasped, her cheeks flaming.

"I am a realist."

"And I am quite capable of looking after myself, whatever you may believe. Tell me, Major, are you only averse to Frenchwomen? If I were a pretty Mexican girl, like the one you were with last night, would you offer me your protection?"

Her scorn stung him. A deep flush darkened his neck and cheeks as he realized she had seen him drunk, then a contemptuous smile twisted his mouth.

"Jealousy does not become you, but you have proved a woman is ruled by emotion—as I tried to stress just now —and totally unsuited to the hardships of the journey. Take my advice and go home, señorita. Adiós."

Antoinette watched him stride outside to where two mounted Mexican troopers were waiting with a spare horse. Ramón Chávez swung himself onto the back of the huge black stallion with the ease of a man who had spent many hours in the saddle, and indicated they should leave. He did not look back in her direction, and she turned away, blinking back hot tears. Jealousy indeed! Antoinette Dubec, who had been courted by gentlemen of nobility and rank, jealous of the attentions of a low-born soldier to a peasant girl! She would show him she was no helpless female, no slave to his arrogant male ego. Calling for the Mexican woman, María, Antoinette ordered her luggage to be brought down.

The train was crowded. She squeezed into a tiny space between two enormous women, both loaded down with shopping satchels brimming over with vegetables. Men with fierce black mustaches, who, she noticed, had taken the best seats next to the open windows, immediately went to sleep, ignoring the women, many of whom were clutching young babies or holding tightly to the hands of raggedly dressed, barefoot children, who were forced to sit or stand in the aisle.

The smell was overwhelming—garlic, tobacco, smoke, and sweat—and the hubbub of voices threatened to deafen her. She tried to reach into her pocket for a handkerchief, but was too firmly wedged to move. Another passenger carrying a live pig passed by and knocked her bonnet at a ridiculous angle. She sat fuming inwardly as a dirty-faced Indian boy opposite grinned at her discomfort.

"Excuse me, señorita." A young officer pushed his way

to her side. "Compliments of Major Chávez, will you come with me? You will be less uncomfortable in another compartment," he added as she stared at him inquiringly.

She needed no further encouragement. He moved ahead of her, ordering people out of the way, pushing them to one side when they did not move, and opened the door to another carriage. Antoinette paused on the threshold as a score or more heads turned to look at her. It was full of soldiers—and at the far end Ramón Chávez stood waiting for her beside an empty seat. It was a blessed relief to sink into it, despite the curious eyes that followed her every move. It was better not to think of the implication they had drawn from the action of their commanding officer. Pulling off her bonnet, she allowed her hair to fall about her shoulders, and with a sigh, rested her head against the back of the seat. After a moment she looked across at the silent figure reclining opposite. He had removed his shako, and she could see that his hair was thick and black.

"Whatever your reason for changing your mind, I am grateful," she said quietly.

He produced a long cigarillo, inquired if she would mind if he smoked, and when she shook her head, proceeded to light it.

"I feel I am under some obligation after the distressing news I brought you," came the infuriatingly indifferent reply. She stared out of the window to avoid the mockery in his eyes. He had acted out of a sense of duty rather than friendship. In a sense she was relieved. He looked far too dangerous to be anything so casual as a friend.

As the hours slipped by she became absorbed by the panoramic scenery flashing past outside. Gone was the low-lying, unhealthy tierra caliente with its tropical vegetation. They were now nearing the more comfortable tierra templada, where there were fertile valleys and rich agricultural land. She leaned forward eagerly as the train began to slow down, and from the conversation and movement of the soldiers straightening their uniforms, she realized they had come to the end of the track. In the distance loomed huge mountains, some snowcapped, others completely shrouded in mist, while below stretched the cactus ranges of the tierra fría—the "cold country" —and Mexico City.

TWO

The journey from Veracruz had taken a little over two hours, yet already Antoinette felt limp and exhausted, and there was a maddening ache behind her eyes. As she sat up to remove her bonnet a sharp pain tore through her head and she winced. Her discomfort did not escape the sharp eyes of Ramón Chávez, who stood a few feet away supervising the unloading of her luggage. A small cart had been commandeered, piled high with the heavy trunks, and pulled by four troopers to the cantina where she now sat.

"What is it? Are you ill?" he demanded, crossing to her side.

"A headache. Nothing more," Antoinette replied quickly.

"Yes, I think it is more," he said with a fierce frown. With an impersonal gesture he laid a hand against her burning temples, and she heard him mutter an unintelligible oath. "I was afraid this would happen. You have a lion's heart, señorita, but not his body. This has been a long and tiring trip, and you are troubled by your father's death. Come, let me help you. There is a room here where you can rest."

Unprotesting, Antoinette allowed him to draw her to her feet. Her legs threatened to give way beneath her, but the strength of Chávez' arms kept her upright. She blinked back hot tears as she looked up into his brown face.

"I—I'm sorry." It sounded terribly inadequate. Here she was acting like the weak, emotional women he de-

24

spised, but to her surprise she saw no condemnation in his face. On the contrary his expression was concerned. He led her to a back room, closed the door behind them, and guided her to the nearest chair, onto which she slid with a sigh of relief.

"I suggest you try to sleep for a few hours. I have to see to the needs of my men, but I will leave someone here to watch over you. The coach has been delayed, so there is no hurry. Can I bring you anything?"

"Yes, please, my overnight valise outside."

He fetched it and placed it on the narrow bed that stood against one wall and then paused beside her chair.

"When you love someone deeply it is not possible to put them out of your mind in a few short hours."

"After my brother's death I tried to make myself accept the fact my father could be killed at any time. I wanted to be able to face it in the manner he would expect of me. He was not a hard man, but he hated women to cry over the inevitable," Antoinette said.

"The reality of such a situation is far harder to accept. You will try to sleep, won't you?"

Mutely, Antoinette nodded, and he left her. She could hear his voice outside the closed door as she unfastened the buttons of her dress; then a blissful silence settled over the whole cantina, and she sank down onto the bed, worn out in both mind and body. She fell asleep immediately.

Antoinette awoke to find the room filled with late-afternoon sunshine. The little silver fob watch fastened to her bodice told her it was almost five o'clock and that she had been sleeping soundly for over five hours. The extra rest had restored both her strength and her self-control, and she now felt quite capable of continuing the journey to Mexico City without further displays of weakness before Major Ramón Chávez. What a strange man he was, with his enigmatic face and swiftly changing moods, she thought as she brushed her long hair. Twice in the short time since they first met she had assessed his character and had been proved wrong both times. He had the manners of an officer and a gentleman, yet he ignored protocol to drink with his men. By doing so he had given her a totally wrong impression. Nor was the impression of the completely indifferent soldier a true one. He had been perceptive enough to realize, even before she did, how deeply the death of her father had affected her, and the way he had taken control of the situation showed her he was far from the unfeeling monster she had at first imagined him to be. As she finished tidying her appearance, she heard the sound of men's voices and the braying of mules from the street outside. She saw from the window that the coach had arrived. It looked very old and unreliable, and she reproved herself strongly as her spirits sank. She had been given fair warning about the uncomfortable journey to come, and so it was no use complaining. The alternative was to return to Veracruz, and that she would never do—not until the murderers of her beloved father had been brought to justice and punished.

"Good evening, Major Chávez." She found the Mexican officer outside the door of the cantina, watching two of his men loading a heavy brassbound box into the coach. Antoinette had seen the same box being brought from the train, guarded, then as now, by heavily armed men. Whatever it contained, she thought, must be valuable. "I see my conveyance has arrived. When do we leave?"

A faint smile touched the man's lips as he turned to look at her.

"You have remarkable powers of recovery, señorita. I did not expect to see you again until the morning. Yes, the coach has arrived, but I have been forced to commandeer it for army purposes. I regret you will have to remain here for another two days."

"Because of that?" Antoinette indicated the box, which now lay on the floor of the coach.

"Sí. Arrangements had been made to transport it by other means, but a mysterious fire last night has prevented that."

"I don't see why I have to remain behind," she protested.

26

"What about the other passengers? Are they staying too?"

"You are the only one, and I cannot risk your life by taking you along. I did try to warn you how dangerous this journey might be."

"Why, what does the box contain? Dynamite?"

"No, several months' back pay for Don Maximiliano's soldiers. Customs dues collected from the port of Veracruz. The Emperor is hard-pressed for cash, and the Juaristas know it. If they could lay their hands on this little lot, we would all be in trouble. The arms and ammunition it could buy for them and the dissension its loss would cause among the troops would be a double victory for them."

Antoinette's momentary annoyance vanished as she realized the importance of the money. For a moment she considered the dangers and then said in a very determined tone, "I understand your position, Major Chávez, as I'm sure you understand mine. Will you leave me stranded in this godforsaken place for another two days or perhaps more? What happens if the other coach is delayed? You have no sure way of knowing it is even on its way, have you? Nor that the Juaristas will attack you."

"It is more than a possibility. We have more than a day's ride through rebel-held territory."

"May I suggest I ride in the coach until then, and while we are traveling through this dangerous area you mention, I will ride on horseback with your men. I assure you I am a competent horsewoman and I promise to stay out of the way and do as I am told."

"If I refuse I suppose you will attempt the journey alone," Ramón Chávez said dryly. "I had hoped the thought of staying here for several days might induce you to return to Veracruz, but I see I was wrong. Very well, señorita, you may accompany us, and I will do all I can to ensure a safe journey, but if we are attacked, I will hold you to your promise of obedience. Can you be ready to leave as soon as you have eaten?"

"I am ready now. I am not hungry."

"I insist." The major took her firmly by the arm and led her back inside. "We will be traveling throughout the night. You will need a meal and a hot drink to sustain you. I also suggest that if you have a riding habit, you change into it before we leave."

The table in the main room of the cantina was laid with two places, but Ramón Chávez did not sit down with her and left her after hastily swallowing a cup of coffee. Antoinette ate only two of the cheese pancakes brought to her by a stoic-faced Indian woman—and a little bread. The thought of the coach ride throughout the night forced her to drink all of the hot coffee, despite its bitterness.

An hour later, as she was repacking her valise, the young captain she had met on the train came with some men to collect her luggage.

"I have put some warm blankets in the coach, señorita," he said, with a friendly smile.

"That was most thoughtful of you," Antoinette returned. "Thank you."

"It is the major who deserves your thanks."

"I'm afraid I am being rather troublesome to him. Do you think the Juaristas may attack us?"

"You must not be afraid, señorita, you will be well protected. Can I be of further assistance?"

"No, I am ready now. Yes, wait, Captain, perhaps you can. Did you know my father, General Dubec?"

The soldier looked at her in surprise.

"Of course. He was my commanding officer."

"But I thought Major Chávez . . ."

"When most of the French troops withdrew from my country, those that were left were amalgamated with Mexican units. The general's regiment was joined with a cavalry troop under Major Chávez. We all knew your father, señorita, and respected him both as a soldier and a man. It has been a great loss for you."

"I find Major Chávez a difficult man to understand," Antoinette said, deciding to change the subject.

The last of her trunks were removed from the room, but the young man appeared in no great hurry to follow and lingered to accompany her from the cantina.

28

"Very few men understand him, women never do. He is a man who prefers his own company."

"That was not the impression he gave me last night," Antoinette said quietly. They were almost at the door of the coach where Ramón Chávez was standing. A few feet away a trooper held the reins of his horse. The rest of the Chasseurs were mounted in a column of two's, patiently waiting.

"You saw him?" The captain was momentarily embarrassed. "Most men have the need to seek solace from a bottle or a woman sometime in their lives. Believe me, señorita, to see the major drunk is a rare sight. As for the girl, I doubt if he was even aware of her—as a woman, I mean."

"You are very loyal."

"There are those of us who have much to thank the major for," came the sincere reply, and she had no chance to question him further, for they were within earshot of his superior. With a polite bow he left her.

Ramón Chávez' dark eyes searched her face for a moment, then swept down over her green riding habit. The long jacket, buttoned to her neck, was shaped to accentuate her small waist before flaring out at her hips. The calf-length skirt was divided, enabling her to ride in comfort. Knee-length boots and dark gloves completed the ensemble. Her hair, secured in two thick plaits, was tied at the nape of her neck by a yellow ribbon. She looked very young and fragile.

"Qué hermosa! It has been a long time since I have seen a woman dressed so elegantly."

"I have heard that Empress Carlota is most fashion conscious," Antoinette replied, taken aback by his declaration.

"Unfortunately she is not in the best of health."

"Don't Mexican ladies like to ride?"

"In their carriages, protected from the sun and admiring the scenery through the windows—yes, they do."

"My father used to tell me I rode like a man," Antoinette

29

said as she suddenly thought of him, buried somewhere in this heartless country he had tried to serve.

"Come, it is time to leave. I hope you are prepared for an uncomfortable journey."

Antoinette nodded, clasped his outstretched hand, and climbed up into the coach. On the seat were two brightly patterned blankets. She spread one where she was to sit and arranged the other one over her legs. Ramón Chávez swung into his silver-mounted saddle, holding a wicked-looking bullwhip, which was coiled around the pommel, and gave the order to move out. Slowly the coach rattled down the street, away from the train, which was ready to return to Veracruz, past the few wooden shacks scattered around the waystation, toward open country. Antoinette's eyes were drawn once again to the snow-capped peaks in the far distance. Her journey to the capital was proceeding once more.

Throughout the night the coach rumbled on its slow, monotonous way. Enveloped in the large homespun blankets, Antoinette grew almost used to the bumpy, bone-jarring ride and even managed to make herself quite comfortable by supporting her legs on the opposite side and her head against the back of the well-worn leather seat. She thought rest would be impossible, but as the night lengthened she dozed intermittently and by dawn had managed to sleep for several hours. They stopped for two hours at midday, and she was brought a plate of bread and sliced pieces of spiced sausage and a cup of red wine. From the window she could see the soldiers had nothing better than plain bread and wondered if she again had Ramón Chávez to thank for these extra comforts.

Antoinette was relieved when, several hours after dusk, the coach was pulled into a grassy gully and halted for the night. She climbed out stiffly and wandered up and down to restore the circulation to her cramped limbs, while around her the troopers began to unload their mounts and light small fires to cook an evening meal. Soon the air was filled with the delightful smell of bacon and onions and aromatic spices. The major appeared as she relaxed in the coach and stood by the open door staring at the half-full plate on the seat beside her.

"You have hardly touched your food."

"I'm not very hungry."

"Has the journey upset you?"

"No, I am just not used to such rich food."

"You will find things more to your liking in Mexico City. It is quite a civilized place now. The French left much behind them."

Antoinette was glad of the darkness of the coach, which hid the fierce color the mockery in his voice brought to her cheeks.

"You don't like the French, do you, Major?"

"They are tolerable, which is more than can be said for the Austrians."

"Yet you serve one," she said quickly, and then could have bitten off her tongue for such thoughtlessness.

Major Chávez stepped back, and the light from a nearby fire showed his face to be a mask of contempt. "I serve my country in the best way I can, señorita, fighting to save my people from destroying themselves. Perhaps I would appear more romantic to you if I rode for Juárez at the head of a band of peons, but that is not my way. It is getting late, and I have my rounds to make, so if you will excuse me, buenas noches."

He had been swallowed up in the darkness before Antoinette could think of a reply, and she huddled in the corner of the seat, regretting the bitterness of the short encounter.

The fires gradually died away, and apart from the sentries, the camp slept. The dull call of a night bird was the only sound to break the silence as she closed her eyes and tried to sleep. She awoke stiff and cold just after midnight to hear the murmur of voices somewhere outside. One fire still burned several yards away, and in the half-light she saw a tall figure beneath a tree and could just make out the hawklike profile of Ramón Chávez. His companion was not visible, and as she stepped down from

31

the coach, he turned and came back to the fire. There was no one behind him.

"Do you wish for something, señorita?" He poured himself a cup of coffee before turning to face her. Without knowing why, she felt like an intruder, and the coldness in his manner did not ease her discomfort.

"I would like a cup of coffee if there is any left." Hesitantly she moved nearer the fire. "I am very cold."

"Come closer then and drink this." He handed her his own cup and stood with hands on hips, watching her as she drank the hot liquid. His eyes narrowed suddenly.

"How long have you been awake?"

"Only a few moments. I thought I heard voices."

"I was making an inspection of the guards to be sure they were not asleep."

Antoinette returned the cup, which he refilled for himself. She knew she should return to the coach, but the warmth of the fire invited her to remain and perhaps try to make a friendly peace with this untouchable man. After all, they would be traveling together for another two, perhaps three, days. It was unthinkable to fight with him after all he had done for her.

"Tomorrow one of my men will ride in the coach, and you will take his horse," the major said. "Is that understood?"

"If you think it necessary."

"I do. We are almost into the mountains. Can you handle a pistol?"

"My brother taught me, but I prefer not to."

"As you wish. Don't you want to go back to sleep?"

Antoinette looked back toward the shadowy outline of the coach and then at the flames and shook her head.

"May I stay where it is warm?" And then on the far side of the fire she saw a prepared bedroll and realized this was where he intended to spend the night.

With a half smile he waved a hand in that direction.

"Make yourself comfortable."

"But you . . ." she protested. "Really, I couldn't. . . ."

"Nonsense."

As she sat down on the bedroll, he walked quickly across to the coach, returning with the blankets from it. Fashioning one into a rough pillow for her head, he draped the other around her shoulders. As he bent over her, his bronzed face was close to hers. She felt his warm breath on her cheek and closed her eyes to shut out the vivid memory of the Mexican girl in the cantina in Veracruz. When she opened them again, he had taken off his pistol belt and sword and was seated a few feet away, watching her as he unfastened his jacket.

"You won't forget, will you?" The bitterness in his voice made her wince inwardly. "Don't be afraid, señorita, you are in no danger from this bête noir."

"I'm sorry. I didn't mean. . . ." Antoinette floundered for words and then gave up. For one mad moment she had been afraid he was going to touch her. Afraid! Was she being entirely honest with herself? Was it fear she felt or an attraction she was trying to ignore? He was not like the young men she had known in France, and she wondered what Aunt Sophie, who always cast a speculative eye over prospective escorts, would make of this handsome Mexican officer. Earlier Antoinette had found herself comparing him to the mountains—strong and tall, with a hard exterior that she guessed might soften for the right woman. What would it take to kindle some interest in those dark eyes and perhaps soften the fierce line of his brow? She had never seen him really smile, and never once had he completely lost his air of indifference. On the occasions she had managed to irritate him (and that seemed to be whenever they were together) the anger or annoyance he felt showed only in his voice. Even that was quick to disappear.

"Forgive me, I didn't mean to . . ." She tried again, but her voice trailed off into silence at the look directed at her. Gathering all her courage, she went on determinedly, "I was shocked, Major Chávez, I admit it. I was tired and upset and I read more into what I saw than took place. I realize that now and I apologize for my foolish behavior—then and now. My father would be ashamed of me."

On the ground between them lay the major's bullwhip —she had noticed it was never far from his side—as well as a sheepskin bag similar to the ones many of the soldiers carried containing either fresh water or wine. Ramón Chávez picked it up and tipped some of the contents into a clean cup. This one, she discovered, held wine the color of honey. He drank slowly, staring doggedly at the fire until she began to wonder if she was to be ignored for the rest of the night.

"I am trying to understand. . . ." she began.

"Is it necessary you should? I don't want or need your understanding and I've made a firm rule never to explain myself to anyone. Explanations so easily turn into excuses, and they disgust me."

"You are a hard man."

"To you perhaps. I am a product of a hard country."

"And it has hardened you." Antoinette replied. He raised his head and looked at her, and she knew he had understood her train of thought. "Don't you ever show your feelings?"

"I don't wear my heart on my sleeve, but contrary to what you believe, I do have one. Slightly the worse for wear, but still intact."

She wondered what he meant by that, but dared not ask. "You have been very kind since we met, but I wish you would not think of yourself as being obligated to care for me because of your friendship with my father."

"That has nothing to do with it. I merely told you that in order to stop you feeling grateful. After the other night you may have misinterpreted my motives."

Antoinette could not help smiling as she looked at the sleeping soldiers all around them—and beyond, four patrolling sentries.

"I think I am quite safe."

"It's strange how wrong our impressions of people can be. When we first met I thought how much you would be at home in the tierra fría—you were so aloof, so cold. The grand lady and the poor soldier."

"Don'tl You make me sound terrible."

"Lo siento! I am sorry, that was not my intention. Looking at you now, I find it difficult to think of you as the same elegant Frenchwoman who stepped off the boat, with a snow-white blouse and a dainty parasol. You have begun to blossom in my country, señorita, and it becomes you."

Antoinette had unbraided her hair before she fell asleep, and it hung past her shoulders, its color deepened by the firelight. Her riding habit, which had been spotless when the journey began, was creased and streaked with dust, and a thick film of dirt covered her boots. She was disheveled but comfortable and she was suddenly at ease.

"Would you be offended if I offered you some wine?" Ramón Chávez was leaning toward her, holding out another cup. His fingers brushed hers as she took it, and she hoped he would think it was the warmth of the fire that had brought a sudden flush of color to her cheeks.

"If there is to be an ambush, do you think it will come soon?" she asked tentatively.

He nodded, staring over her shoulder into the darkness.

"Beyond, the mountains will make perfect cover for an attack. Don't be afraid, my men have orders to take good care of you."

"I don't think I am. It's hard to be afraid with you. You are so—so in control. I think that's what I want to say. You never show anger or alarm, and I've rarely heard you raise your voice even when giving orders. You tell me we will probably be ambushed as calmly and unemotionally as you paid me a compliment just now. It was a compliment, I suppose?"

"Why not? Wine and good company bring out the better side of my nature," came the amused answer.

Again she had the feeling he was laughing at her inability to understand him, but she was determined not to be provoked and allowed it to pass. The heat from the fire and the full-bodied wine were beginning to make her feel sleepy. She had so many questions to ask him, but she knew they would have to wait until tomorrow. If that had been his intention when he gave her the wine, it had been successful. She could hardly keep her eyes open and reluctantly she stretched out on the bedroll. She heard him rise to his feet and a moment later felt the blankets being tucked around her and managed to mutter a sleepy word of thanks. As she drifted away she heard his voice, close to her ear, quiet, reassuring.

"Buenas noches, La Florecita. Sleep well."

When Antoinette awoke the following morning, the camp had already been dismantled, and everyone was making preparations to move out. A soldier brought her a plate of vegetable soup, and she swallowed it quickly, conscious of the hasty preparations going on around her. Afterward she washed her face and hands in a nearby stream, rebraided her hair, and was ready to leave when Captain Pedro Martínez, the young officer who had spoken with her at the cantina, who was Major Chavez's second in command, gave the order to mount. She was brought a gentle-looking bay mare with three white stockings and she was happy to discover that the horse responded instantly to the slightest touch on the reins. Most of the Chasseurs were deployed in front and beside the coach. She rode some way behind it, beside a preoccupied Ramón Chávez, and three more soldiers guarded the rear.

It was a beautiful day, and they were passing through some breathtaking countryside. Antoinette found it hard to believe they might be under constant surveillance from enemy eyes. A pleasant breeze eased the heat toward midday, and she unfastened the top buttons of her jacket to allow the cool air onto her neck.

During a brief rest she found a suitable vantage point and surveyed the scenery. Behind them lay Orizaba at the foot of the highest mountain in Mexico, the Pico de Orizaba. There was always an outline of mountains, snow-capped, cone-shaped peaks, their color changing with every light from blue-gray to drab brown. Tall cactus, which resembled huge organ pipes, stood like silent sentinels in the foreground. Elsewhere, bright flowers pushed their way from behind rocky crevices and boulders to soften and color the harsh landscape. Ahead of them lay the town of Puebla, and after that they would have another eighty miles before reaching the capital. Despite the midday heat, Major Chávez did not order another halt, and Antoinette was glad of the straw sombrero one of the soldiers had given her, which she had pulled well down over her face. When she had volunteered to ride she had completely forgotten the blazing sun, and without protection she knew it could have made her quite ill.

They skirted Puebla, but stopped at a small posada four miles outside the town where Antoinette was able to wash off some of the dirt and grime of the road and have something to eat. She hoped they would stay over for the night, but just as she was settling comfortably into a chair she heard the order to remount and hurried back outside.

"We will make camp by the river," Ramón Chávez told her as they moved off again. "Another uncomfortable night for you, I'm afraid, but you understand why it is necessary."

Taut lines of tiredness beneath his eyes told her he was still worried about an ambush. She nodded, regretting for the first time the way she had almost forced him to act as her escort. Without the extra burden, she suspected he would have driven his men harder and made fewer stops.

"You make a good soldier, señorita. Your father would have been proud of you," he said with sudden, unexpected candor. Such praise instilled new life into her weary body, and she rode the rest of the way as if on a cloud.

The river wound through a plateau of pine and oak trees some eight thousand feet above sea level. She would have loved to immerse herself in the cold water, but had to be content with a sponge bath. Afterward she rested on a blanket beneath a spreading pine and watched the soldiers lighting fires—fewer than usual, she noticed.

The sun was going down as she finished her meal. She checked her watch and found it was almost seven o'clock. There was scarcely any twilight in Mexico; once the sun had disappeared, the light rapidly diminished and night descended suddenly. By the time she had arranged her makeshift bed in the coach the sky was full of stars and she lay watching them until sleep claimed her.

She knew something was wrong the moment she awoke. It was quiet—deathly quiet. No familiar sounds of horses being moved, breakfast being prepared, soldiers chattering idly. As she pushed aside the blankets and sat up, the door was flung open and the barrel of a Springfield rifle froze her against the seat. She almost screamed, but the sight of the unfriendly bearded face behind the weapon froze the scream in her throat.

"Vamos, pronto!"

She knew enough Spanish to respond to his order. She climbed down to see thirty or more heavily armed vaqueros completely encircling the Mexican soldiers, who had been stripped of all weapons and ammunition and rounded up beneath the trees. The bandits were an ill-dressed assortment of young and old men in leather sandals and huge sombreros, yet in each and every pair of eyes was the same look of grim determination. These were not men to be trifled with. Their weapons looked new, and she remembered how Ramón Chávez had told her the rebels were buying smuggled arms from across the border. The bandoliers across their chests were full of bullets. They had come down on the camp in the gray light of dawn, probably before anyone was awake. No doubt the sentries were lying dead or wounded somewhere in the trees. The thought made her shudder.

Ramón Chávez was held securely by two men. A third stood with a cocked pistol at his head. He looked disheveled and bruised and had obviously put up great resistance before being overpowered. The rifle at Antoinette's back prodded her, and she stumbled across to his side, stepping on his bullwhip, which was half buried in the dust, as she did so. She could almost feel his frustration at being unable to get his hands on it.

"Don't be afraid. They won't harm you once they find what they have come for," he muttered, with a quick glance at her pale face.

38

"Would—would you fight if I were not here?" she whispered, dismayed to think her presence might lose him his precious cargo.

"If I had the chance I would do so now, but as you can see we have none. Por Dios, I should have posted more guards. I have no one but myself to blame for this."

"I don't believe you could have done more," Antoinette answered. Beneath her dismayed gaze her trunks were tossed to the ground and broken open, despite her protests. One of the rebels found what they were searching for beneath the driver's seat and handed down the long metal money box. Without bothering to open it they loaded it onto one of the waiting horses. Slowly and carefully they then began to back away, still training their weapons on the soldiers.

One of the vaqueros, a young boy of not more than eighteen, passed Antoinette and stopped, his eyes riveted on her hand. She tried to hide the emerald ring on her little finger, but he caught her wrist and snatched the ring from her. She heard a savage oath from behind her and was pulled backward as Ramón Chávez struck out at the thief. "No—let him take it," she screamed as rebels converged on Chávez from all sides. "It isn't important."

He was deaf to her entreaty. In one smooth motion he scooped his whip up from the ground and swung it at the youngster. Thirty feet of plaited rope snaked out and brought the boy crashing to the ground with a howl of pain. The whip cracked once, twice more, beating back the men who tried to come near, until Chávez was struck down from behind by a rifle butt. Taking advantage of the distraction, the Mexican soldiers broke and ran for their weapons. Antoinette cried out as everyone began firing at once, and she fell to the ground, covering her face with her hands as bullets whined past her ear.

It was over in a few minutes. The Juaristas did not stay to fight. Captain Martínez took a dozen men and pursued them, but returned within an hour with the news that they had disappeared without a trace. These were the same kinds of men who had killed her father,

Antoinette thought bitterly as she followed two soldiers carrying a semiconscious Ramón Chávez to the coach. Cutthroats, cowards, who killed and then ran.

"Lie still, you are bleeding." She knelt at the major's side and pressed a wet cloth against the gash at the side of his head. He ignored her and sat up, stifling a groan of pain and muttering under his breath. It was the closest she had ever come to seeing him lose his composure. She herself was still trembling from the incident and she felt violently sick.

"I shall recover, señorita. I bear a charmed life."

"From that?" She pointed to the medallion dangling outside his torn shirt. Seeing it close up, she discovered it was a beautifully engraved figure of a woman who appeared to be wearing a skirt of writhing, twisting snakes. She had expected a St. Christopher medal or a lucky coin, but not this symbol of paganism.

"Coatlicue, the goddess of life and death." He touched the silver figure almost reverently. "Don't look so stunned. My family roots are as deeply imbedded in Aztec culture as yours are in the Catholic church."

"But you don't really believe in such nonsense?" Antoinette said, drawing back.

"I believe in the wonderful woman who gave it to me and the power of the love she has for me." He looked up at the face that appeared at the window. "How many men did we lose, Martínez?"

"Five dead, including the sentries, another three injured, Major. We wounded two, maybe three, rebels, but they got away."

"Are our men badly hurt?"

"No, they can ride."

"Good, we move out in ten minutes. See to the dead and have the mules made ready. There is no danger now, you can ride in the coach again," he said, turning back to Antoinette. "Is that agreeable?"

"Quite." The quiet of the coach, where she could compose herself before he saw how badly shaken she was, would be a blessing.

"The ring—you said it was not important." He suddenly remembered her desperate effort to prevent a fight.

"It was only a keepsake." It was a blatant lie. The ring was valuable both monetarily and because it had been the last present ever given to her by her father. Yet not even its great sentimental importance would have allowed her to risk Chávez' death in a fight for it. But she could not tell him that, not while Coatlicue's silver form danced and swam before her eyes, the token of a woman whose love was so strong it made him totally fearless of death.

"Señorita." One of the troopers came up to her as she repacked her ransacked trunks, wiping something against his trousers. "Is this what was taken from you?"

In his outstretched hand was her precious ring. She thanked him and slipped it onto her finger and then had to turn quickly away as a sudden rush of tears blurred her vision.

THREE

Just before noon on the following day, the weary, travel-stained cavalcade moved slowly down the dusty road toward the capital. It was still twenty miles away, but that distance was nothing after the miles they had covered. They entered a small village where the coach was halted and the soldiers began to dismount. She peered out of the window curiously.

"Find yourselves some food and drink and be ready to ride out when I return," she heard Ramón Chávez order.

"Where are we?" she called out.

He drew rein before her, wiping a hand across his sweating brow. His mouth was taut with pain, and she knew his head was troubling him.

"The quinta of a good friend of mine is ahead. We will take advantage of his excellent hospitality to rest for a while," he answered, and rode off before she could ask any more questions.

A mile down the road she saw a house set back from cultivated fields where oranges were growing fat in the sun and pretty trees were in flower. Wild oleanders climbed over the encircling wall and around the heavy wooden doors that provided the only entrance. The coach came to a standstill beside a well-kept garden full of multicolored blooms. The air was heavy with their perfume. As she sat drinking in the heavenly aroma, a smartly dressed vaquero came running forward to open the door for her and help her alight. Ramón Chávez dismounted and tossed the reins of his horse to another servant. Then he turned to greet the man coming out of the house.

"Luis! Salud, amigo." The casual greeting told her these two were close friends. "We are hot and tired and sick of trail rations. I am as desperate for a glass of your wonderful brandy as I'm sure Señorita Dubec is for some civilized company," he exclaimed, embracing him warmly.

"You are always welcome, Ramón, you know that. Doubly so when you bring such attractive company for me to entertain." A pair of amused brown eyes fastened on Antoinette until she felt her cheeks begin to burn. He did not look at her in the same way as Ramón Chávez. There was interest here, and he did not mind her seeing it. "Come, introduce me before I die of curiosity."

"Señorita Antoinette Dubec, may I present Don Luis Rafael Santos." Major Chávez performed the introduction with a smile tugging at the corners of his mouth. Antoinette ignored his amusement and extended her hand to the newcomer, who took it in a light grasp and courteously raised her fingers to his lips. He was in his late twenties, younger than his friend, with brown hair to match his eyes and a friendly manner that immediately made her feel at ease.

"I am pleased to meet you, Don Luis." Again that interested gaze fixed on her, making her acutely aware of her appearance. "Major Chávez has spoken of your excellent hospitality. May I take advantage of it to change into some clean clothes?"

"Mi casa es su casa," Luis Santos returned, and took her arm with a smile. "My house is yours."

"And mine too, I hope," Ramón Chávez remarked dryly as he followed them into the house.

They stepped into a long, low-ceilinged room furnished with carved high-backed chairs and a table that dominated the center of the room. There was a great yawning chasm of a fireplace, solid furniture, and many silver ornaments mainly of Spanish-Moorish design.

"But of course, since when have you had to ask for anything you want?" Don Luis said, and laughed as his friend crossed directly to the cut-glass decanter and crystal glasses on a carved-oak sideboard and poured himself a large brandy. He also poured a sherry and gave it to Antoinette. She found it nectar after the bitter coffee she had consumed during the journey.

"Are you on your way to the capital, señorita?" Don Luis asked.

"Yes. I was to have stayed with my father, General Adolphe Dubec, but he—he has been killed by rebels." Antoinette faltered over her answer. Even now, part of her still refused to believe he had really been taken from her.

"I had heard of his death. You have my condolences, señorita. A sad occasion brings you beneath my roof, perhaps the next time will be a happier one. Ramón, what is it? Dios, your head!" He had suddenly caught sight of the major's head wound, which was still red and looked extremely painful.

"He was hurt when we were attacked," Antoinette explained quickly. "He should be resting—and not drinking."

"I think you are right." Don Luis turned from her, calling urgently for servants to come and help Ramón Chávez upstairs. The major declined their help, finished his drink, and reeled unsteadily toward the staircase.

"Let me help you."

He turned sharply on Antoinette as she ran to his side and slipped an arm beneath his. Her blue eyes locked with his and defied their silent command to release him.

"You cannot ride to the capital in this condition," Luis Santos said, following them. "I insist that you remain here overnight. Shall I send to the village for a doctor?"

"For a knock on the head? You will have me taking to my bed next," his friend replied dryly.

"Then think of poor Señorita Dubec," Luis implored him. "You cannot expect her to continue. I am sure she is exhausted."

"She is not as fragile as you would believe, amigo, but

44

very well, I agree. Will you send for Captain Martínez? I must give him new orders."

"Sí, at once. Come, I will help you. Tomás will go to the village after he has shown the señorita to her room." Luis Santos indicated that Antoinette was to follow one of the servants along a long, sun-drenched corridor. "Your luggage will be brought up directly, and I will send one of the women to attend you. I hope you will be comfortable."

"Thank you, Don Luis," Antoinette murmured.

"It is almost siesta. Perhaps after you have rested you would allow me to show you over my domain?"

"That would be very nice."

"Good. Until later then."

Antoinette avoided looking at Ramón Chávez as she turned away, but she was aware of the frown puckering his brows and wondered why Luis Santos' interest in her should disturb him.

She was shown into a sunny room where large windows opened out on to an iron balcony overlooking the patio. In the distance she had her first glimpse of the range of volcanic mountains encircling the valley where Mexico City lay. The snowcapped peak of Popocatepetl ("Smoking Mountain") dominated the landscape. Nearby, its twin, Ixtaccihuatl ("White Lady"), was no less impressive. Cottonwoods and scrub and the now-familiar organ-pipe cactus at the base of the slate-gray mountains gave way to green fields, where Antoinette could see peons working, and the village beyond, where the Chasseurs were no doubt taking full advantage of the unexpected rest. She wanted to hate this country because it had deprived her father of his life, but something inside her would not permit that. Mexico had wooed and won her with its ever-changing hue of colors and magnificent scenery. Cruel and austere one moment, gentle and breathtakingly beautiful the next. It was like a wild animal challenging someone to tame it and love it. It would submit to the gentle hand of a knowledgeable master, but it would never be conquered. Perhaps if Maximilian had been left to his own devices, he might have walked in the shadow of Quetzalcoatl and in time won the respect of the Mexicans who now resented him so strongly, she thought, and felt a momentary twinge of compassion for his failure.

The door closed silently behind her as Tomás departed. A few minutes later he reappeared with two other servants and her luggage. Behind them came a Mexican woman in a spotless white blouse and a blue patterned skirt, who introduced herself as Soledad and said she had been sent to act as Antoinette's maid for the duration of her stay.

"Would the señorita like me to unpack her clothes while she sleeps?"

"Sleep? I don't want to sleep yet," Antoinette protested. "I want to take a bath and then I will show you which trunk to open." She longed for the luxury of hot water and scented soap.

"I will attend to it at once, señorita."

A small dressing room adjoined the main bedroom, and to Antoinette's delight it contained a pastel-colored bath and an assortment of perfumed jars and soothing balms. For over an hour she lingered in rose-scented water, and then Soledad rubbed her dry and smoothed jasmine scent into her skin before slipping a loose robe over her shoulders. She lay down on the bed feeling like a new woman and fell into the most peaceful sleep she had experienced since leaving France.

"Will you wear the white or the pink, señorita?"

Antoinette surveyed the two dresses Soledad had carefully pressed and draped across a chair for her inspection and decided on the white chiffon, which had a low, rounded neckline and full sleeves adorned with tiny white bows and gathered at the wrists. To go with it she chose a rope of pearls and matching earrings. She had not forgotten this was her time of mourning, but out of all the clothes she had brought she had only one black dress—a velvet evening gown, severe in its simplicity and far too formal for this occasion. Apart from that, only her riding habit and the dress she had worn on the train were made of darker materials, but neither could be considered suitable.

The Mexican woman was not as skilled as Antoinette's maid at home when it came to dressing the long red hair, but nevertheless the result was pleasing. Nimble fingers twisted curl after curl into long ringlets combed back from her face and secured at the base of her neck with tortoiseshell combs.

"Who is that, Soledad, Don Luis' wife?" Looking down from the balcony Antoinette could see a woman walking in the garden picking flowers. She caught a glimpse of a haughty profile and a voluptuous figure as the woman spun around to greet someone out of sight on the patio below.

"That is Doña Mercedes, the sister of Don Luis," the woman answered, glancing over her shoulder. "She has just returned from the United States. Her husband was a norteamericano. He was killed in the war."

"I would like to meet her," Antoinette said. "It seems years since I have sat down for a leisurely conversation with anyone."

"Oh, you will. She will want to see the woman Don Ramón has brought to her brother's house."

"Why should the fact I came with Major Chávez interest her?"

Why indeed! Did the answer not lie before her eyes? The two figures below stood close together in the shade of the cyprus trees, Doña Mercedes with her face upturned, arms entwined about the neck of the bronzed man who had just joined her. He was elegant in his dark-green trousers and white frilled shirt—so different from the tired, dusty soldier in whose company she had spent the last few days.

"The Blessed Virgin has answered her prayers," Soledad murmured.

"I don't understand."

"He is her novio—her sweetheart."

So there was someone in his life after all—this was the woman whose love protected him in the name of Coatlicue. A widow of less than a year, already seeking solace in the arms of another man. Antoinette reproved herself for the malice in her thoughts and continued with her toilette.

Mercedes Lucia Santos was very beautiful, and she knew it. She was tall for a woman, taller than either her brother or Antoinette. Jet-black hair framed her sharply defined features, narrow black brows, violet eyes, and full, sensuous mouth, as scarlet as the dress she wore. A heavy gold pendant hung about her slender throat, bracelets coupled her wrists, and a magnificent ruby adorned one of her long, tapered fingers. She had not been dressed this way when Antoinette had seen her in the garden. Was it for the benefit of her guest, she wondered, or perhaps, for Ramón Chávez, who stood at her side, smoking silently while Don Luis performed the necessary introductions. Chávez' pallor had gone, and he appeared relaxed and more amiable than Antoinette had yet seen him.

Mercedes Santos laid a hand on his arm—it was almost a caress—and drew him down beside her on the velvet-covered couch. Don Luis pulled forward a comfortable chair for Antoinette and sat beside her while a servant served coffee in the old Spanish style: black with sweet honey in wafer-thin porcelain cups, accompanied by tiny sugared biscuits and thinly sliced sandwiches.

"My cook has promised to excel herself tonight in your honor," he said, leaning toward Antoinette with a smile. "Your first real Mexican meal must be perfection."

"Do you always confront your guests with such hospitality?" Antoinette asked in genuine surprise.

"We are a hospitable people."

"I would like to have heard my father's answer to that," she replied quickly. She caught a sudden flash of anger in the eyes of Ramón Chávez across the room and regretted the bitterness in her that had given vent to such cruel words. "I am sorry, Don Luis. I did not mean to be rude."

"But you loved your father and wish to see his killers brought to justice. I understand perfectly, Doña Antoinette, but I beg of you, do not judge us all in the same light. I take no sides in this conflict, which is tearing my country apart. I ask only to be left in peace here at the quinta, to care for my home, my lands, and my sister."

"Since when have we sat back and allowed others to do our fighting for us?" The burning gaze of Mercedes Santos centered on her brother. "You are a fool, Luis. We will lose everything if you have your way."

"Which side would you have us take, Mercedes?" There was a cool edge to Luis' voice, but his face had not lost its smile, and Antoinette guessed the subject was a constant source of argument between them. "That of Maximilian or our own people?"

"Maximilian, of course. Would you have us join forces with ignorant peasants and indios? You will be treating them as equals next."

Antoinette heard him mutter in annoyance at her words and then quickly begin to apologize.

"My sister has been too long away from home, Ramón. I hope you will forgive her bad manners."

Ramón Chávez shrugged his shoulders.

"Por nada, amigo. I am used to the illogical workings of a woman's mind."

"Illogical indeed! How you like to play the fatalistic Indian sometimes, Ramón," Mercedes declared, eyes flashing angrily. "You are a landowner in your own right and you are respected by Maximilian and everyone who knows you. Why jeopardize a future in the new Mexico by clinging to the past. You owe nothing to the indios."

"The blood of my mother's people tells me otherwise," Ramón Chávez returned. As he spoke, his eyes flickered across to where Antoinette sat, not understanding the trend of conversation, and they remained on her as he

49

continued. "I am as proud of my father's Spanish ancestry as I am that my grandmother can trace hers back to the same village as La Malinche. I have knowledge of two worlds, two cultures, and can live just as easily in one as in the other."

"But what would you do if you had to choose between them?" Luis asked with a perturbed frown.

"He has chosen, hasn't he?" Mercedes retorted. "He is here, with us, not in the hills with Díaz and his cutthroats."

"The rebels are well armed and organized," Ramón said in a dry tone. "We should no longer dismiss them lightly. Despite all my precautions they descended on us at dawn yesterday, stole the money chest entrusted to my care, and vanished back into the hills without trace. I lost five good men because I too had underestimated their worth."

"Do you think they were El Padrino's men?" Luis asked.

"I doubt it. He concerns himself mainly with the freeing of prisoners. You are neglecting your guest, Luis. She has been sitting with an empty cup for the past ten minutes."

"Forgive me." Luis swung around to Antoinette with an apologetic smile and held out his hand. "Permítame."

"No more for me, thank you," Antoinette answered. "But if you could spare a few minutes to show me over the quinta?"

"I can think of nothing I would rather do. Ramón, will you and Mercedes join us?"

"I think not," Major Chávez returned after a glance into the beautiful, pouting face beside him.

Mercedes helped herself to a sandwich and relaxed back against his arm with a decidedly relieved expression on her features.

"My sister has only just put off mourning," Luis said as he walked with Antoinette between well-ordered flower beds, where a gray-haired peon was busily weeding. In the trees above them two white-tailed doves moved closer together and watched them pass. "Her husband was an American, on the wrong side, unfortunately. He was killed only days before Appomattox. He had no family, and Mercedes hated the way of life in Richmond after the war, so she came home. I'm sure she expected to find nothing had changed. Mexico is like that—the surface always seems to remain untouched, but underneath . . . Ay! As you have seen, there is much violence. Men like Díaz and Juárez have kindled a new flame in the hearts of the people, and they are beginning to rally without considering the terrible consequences to themselves, their families, or their homes. If they are defeated they will have nothing."

"The cost of winning would also be very high, and many more innocent people would die—men like my father who never deliberately did harm to anyone," Antoinette said, and was immediately aware of the intense sympathy in the warm brown eyes that rested on her face. "In his letters he wrote of a growing love for this country. He made it come alive for me—so much so I had to come and be with him and see it for myself."

"He was a man of great understanding. Twice, no, three times, he and several others of Maximilian's officers dined with me here. It was a great sorrow to learn of his death at the hands of El Padrino's men."

El Padrino! That name again. Antoinette looked up with a frown.

"You mentioned this man earlier. Who is he?"

"My dear child, I thought you knew he was the one behind your father's death. He has a force of men in the hills behind the capital. The number has never been accurately recorded because he comes and goes like a shadow on the sun. For months now he has given General Bazaine a considerable headache, but the man is so well protected by those who ride with him, no one has ever betrayed him, either for reward or under torture. He is fast becoming a hero among the peons. They marvel at the audacious schemes he uses to spirit away prisoners from under the very noses of the French. That is why they have named him El Padrino, the 'Godfather.' They think of themselves as children under his protection, able to turn to him whenever one of them needs help. Since he first became known to the authorities about a year ago, the legend has grown, and now his name commands almost as much respect as that of Díaz or Juárez. Personally, there are times when I believe the man is a product of General Bazaine's imagination—a distraction to cover his own countless blunders. The emperor relies on him too much, you know. But for him, there would still be a full force of French soldiers to put these rebels to flight. The flame could be put out before it becomes too strong. Is Ramón taking you to your father's house?"

"Why, yes, I suppose so. With all that has happened, I haven't really given it a thought. I know there is a house. It will be closed now though, won't it?"

"You must ask Ramón, he will know more about it than I do, but if it is, I insist you return here."

"I could not do that," Antoinette returned, but her protest was only halfhearted. It was a nice feeling to know she could return to this peaceful place and be welcome.

"I insist. You cannot stay alone. You must take Soledad with you. She has served my family for many years and will care for you until you can make arrangements of your own. This is Mexico, Doña Antoinette, not France."

"I am quite able to care for myself, I assure you."

"The fact that Ramón allowed you to travel with him is proof of that," Luis returned, "but in my country there are certain proprieties to be observed. A duenna, to accompany you wherever you go, is one. Es la costumbre del país—it is the custom of the country. You will find my people more ready to accept you if you respect such unwritten laws."

"Thank you for your concern, Don Luis, I will remember. Do you think Major Chávez will be well enough to ride tomorrow?"

"I'm sure of it. I don't envy him his report to General

Bazaine. Those two cannot stand to be in the same room together."

"Perhaps if I had a word with the general . . ." Antoinette began, but Luis Santos shook his head.

"Ramón would not wish it. We must hope he can contain his temper."

"I have never seen Major Chávez really angry. I can't even visualize it."

"He is slow to anger, but when he is roused, ay de mí, the man is a devil."

"Have you ever seen him that way?" Antoinette could not suppress the question and pretended to admire some gardenias as Luis looked at her curiously.

"Angry? Sí, many times. But only once did I see him in a murderous rage, and I pray to God I never see it again. Such anger destroys the soul. It was over a woman, of course, but that is his affair and not ours, and why are we talking of Ramón when you have me to tell you my life story?" Tucking Antoinette's arm beneath his, he began to tell her about the quinta as they moved in the direction of the orange groves.

Early next morning Soledad brought Antoinette breakfast in bed and prepared a bath while she ate. Antoinette was reluctant to drag herself out of the comfortable bed, but already it was nine o'clock, and she had promised Ramón Chávez she would be ready in less than half an hour. Her riding habit and traveling dress lay across a chair, freshly laundered. She chose to wear the latter and asked for the other to be put away in her trunk. Yawning, she slid down into the perfumed bath and hoped she would not fall asleep again. The previous evening she had heard the grandfather clock on the stairs strike three times as she entered her bedroom. She had been wined and dined with great panache by Luis Santos and his sister, whose attitude had become more amicable as the evening progressed. Undoubtedly, some of her unfriendliness had softened because of the attentions of

Ramón Chávez, who had not left her side for an instant.

I am as proud of my father's Spanish ancestry as I am that my grandmother can trace hers back to the same village as La Malinche. . . . Ramón Chávez' words haunted Antoinette as she listened to Luis describing the delights of Cuenevaca, one of the favorite resorts of the Emperor and Empress. Her eyes often lingered on the frilled shirt where Coatlicue lay out of sight close against the major's heart. Mercedes Santos' revelation about his Indian blood helped her to understand his fierce pride and his desire to cling to some part of his heritage, to belong to both worlds. It was a feeling she could respect.

Luis escorted Antoinette to the waiting coach, waved aside the hovering servant, and helped her in himself, reminding her of her promise to return to the quinta if the house in the capital proved too lonely.

Mercedes followed Ramón Chávez to his horse and lingered while he mounted and gave orders to Captain Martínez, who was waiting at the head of the Chasseurs. Chávez' manner was impatient, Antoinette noticed, although he held himself in check long enough to lean down and kiss the full red mouth offering itself expectantly. Regardless of her brother's stern expression, Mercedes clung to him for a long moment, then with a soft laugh and a triumphant look in the direction of the coach she turned and ran back into the house amid a flurry of white petticoats.

The house of General Adolphe Dubec stood in the Calle de Comerciantes (the "Street of Merchants") in the San Ángel district on the road leading to Cuenevaca. It was an imposing house of pale-gray stone with two smiling cherubs at either side of the heavy door that led into the open-air patio. In one corner was a fountain that no longer worked and a religious statue, hands closed together in prayer over a vase which now held dead flowers. The upstairs rooms opened on to a balcony that ran all the way around the patio and was connected to the lower floor by a wrought-iron staircase. All the windows were closed and the curtains drawn. Inside, Antoinette found that only three of the rooms had been used by her father—a bedroom, a study full of books and heavy furniture, and a small attic room where she discovered countless charcoal sketches packed neatly away in a box. Her father had always wanted to be a good artist, but a demanding army life had left him little time to indulge the gift he possessed for capturing the essence of people and places and bringing them alive on paper. Ramón Chávez found her kneeling in the empty room, the sketches spread out on the floor around her, her cheeks wet with tears. He went down on one knee beside her, and she heard him mutter an oath as a gentle finger traced the path of a tear.

"Come downstairs, you are not ready for this yet. Soledad has let some light into the place, and it looks quite different. The furnishings are not what you might call luxurious, but if you decide to stay, I'm sure you could improve on them."

"In a moment. I want to put these away first." Antoinette stretched out a hand to gather up the sketches, but he caught her firmly by both wrists and drew her to her feet.

"No, not now. Soledad will do it. Don't come into this room again until you have been here for at least a week. Promise me."

His tone was so authoritative that Antoinette found herself nodding without argument, and she allowed him to propel her downstairs to the drawing room. Soledad had removed the dust covers from the furniture, dusted hastily, and was laying a coffee tray on the table as they entered.

"Will you stay for something to eat or a cup of coffee?" Antoinette asked as Ramón Chávez halted in the doorway.

"Coffee only, thank you, or I shall have dissension in the ranks. Have the señorita's trunks been unloaded, Soledad?"

"Sí, but the señorita has yet to decide which room to have."

"Put everything in the back bedroom, she will come up later and supervise," Ramón ordered, and the woman left them without questioning his instructions. Seeing Antoinette's questioning look, he quickly added, "The front rooms will be too noisy for you, especially at night. The one I spoke of overlooks the courtyard and will be quite pleasant when it is cleaned and aired."

"Have you been here before?"

"Once or twice. Your father and I played chess together. My logical Indian mind found him a worthy opponent. When you have come to terms with what has happened, perhaps you would like to see his grave. It isn't far from here."

Antoinette put down her coffee cup with a jerky motion as her hand suddenly began to tremble. The word "grave" reminded her so vividly of what had happened before her arrival. She wanted to see it, but knew she did not have enough courage yet. In a day or two perhaps . . .

"I will never come to terms with a senseless murder," she said in a low voice.

"He was a soldier. He died doing his duty. He and his men were ambushed, I admit, but men have been ambushed before and fought their way to safety. He—he was unlucky. Luck runs out for us all eventually."

"A strange answer for a man who believes in the power of Coatlicue."

Ramón Chávez swung around, but checked the retort on his lips as he saw the bitterness on her lovely face.

"To understand me, you must also understand my country, and that I suspect you will never be able to do. I will not stay for coffee after all, it is nearly noon and I have an unpleasant report to make out."

"To a man you do not like. Don Luis told me," Antoinette added by way of explanation.

"You are fortunate to have found the friendship of Luis Santos, he is a good man and will be a true friend if you will let him."

And you would not approve of that, Antoinette almost said, and stopped herself just in time. She did not know why he gave her that impression, but she had sensed it since the first moment his friend had shown more than a cursory interest in her.

"Will I see you again?" Hesitantly she followed him to the front door. For days she had relied on his advice, taken comfort from his company despite their somewhat awkward encounters, but only now that he was about to leave did she realize how much she owed him. "There must be some way I can repay your help. When the house is straightened out, perhaps you would dine with me."

"I think not." In the courtyard he turned and looked at her standing beside the silent fountain, and the hard line of his mouth softened slightly. "We shall no doubt encounter each other from time to time, that will be unavoidable, but I do not think it wise that we meet again socially. Try to be happy—such lovely eyes were made for laughter, not tears. Soledad will provide you with all you need. You have this house and Luis' friendship if you desire it, the rest is up to you. Good-bye, Doña Antoinette."

The more informal use of her name was lost on Antoinette as she watched him ride off, dismayed and left empty by his refusal to accept her hospitality. As the sound of horses' hooves on the cobbled streets died away, she took a deep breath, straightened her shoulders, and walked steadily back into the house.

Two weeks later, Soledad almost fell out of the window in surprise when an elegant carriage, drawn by two white horses with plume-decked harnesses, halted before the house. One of the Mexican escorts dismounted and helped out a richly dressed woman whose hair shone like burnished gold in the sunlight.

"Doña Antoinette," she gasped. "It is La Emperatriz Carlota!"

Antoinette flew to the window, unable to believe her ears, and her eyes widened at the sight of the waiting visitor. Marie Charlotte Amélie Augustine Clementine, Empress of Mexico, at her front door! And beside her a familiar uniformed figure whose sun-bronzed features sent a rush of gladness to her heart. She had neither seen nor heard of Ramón Chávez since he had brought her to the house, and now he was below—as escort to the Empress.

"Soledad, go and admit them. No, wait, perhaps I should go myself. Oh, dear, I can't think. . . ." Suddenly all the correct protocol Antoinette had once been able to recite backward fled from her mind, and she raised both hands to her flushed cheeks. Minutes before, she had been in the study, methodically going through the many books there, dusting them and putting them back on the shelves in some kind of order. She wore a dark cotton blouse and woven skirt purchased in the market by Soledad. Her face was pale from staying too long indoors, her pallor accentuated by the bright hair that fell loosely around her shoulders. Her first meeting with Carlota since she had become Empress, and Antoinette looked like a gypsy.

"Señorita, they are waiting. Shall I go while you change?"

"No, it's too late now, I shall have to go as I am," Antoinette said, pushing back her hair, and with Soledad's horrified protests ringing in her ears, she went downstairs—a slender, rather disheveled young woman whose face was flushed with excitement as she swung open the front door to admit her visitors.

The visit of Carlota to the house in the Calle de Comerciantes lasted less than an hour, but the fact that she had gone out of her way to call and express her condolences on the death of Antoinette's father was a heartwarming experience for the young woman. They took tea in the drawing room, and Soledad, who served them, was so nervous she almost dropped the tray of cakes onto the Empress' beautiful velvet gown. At twenty-six Carlota was aging swiftly, but in her face there still lingered a hauntingly fragile beauty. Her dark hair was secured in a smooth chignon beneath a mantilla of exquisite Spanish lace, and her flawless white skin had been carefully preserved from the hot sun. She was at ease in the tiny room, talking constantly, extending an invitation to Antoinette to visit the court as soon as possible, despite the mourning period.

Standing to one side of them, Ramón Chávez listened in silence. Today he was wearing his dress uniform of green and gold and looked disturbingly handsome. Antoinette wondered if he regretted the escort duty that had brought him beneath her roof again. Out of the corner of her eye she watched his gaze wander slowly around the room, contemplating the clean curtains and the polished furniture, and wished she could read his mind as his eyes came finally to rest on the bowl of flowers in the place of honor on the sideboard. They had arrived late last night by special messenger from Luis Santos, and the enclosed card had expressed a wish that Antoinette would again visit the quinta.

"You must come and see me next week. I will send a carriage for you," Carlota said as she rose to go. Antoinette curtsied and clasped the rather thin hand outstretched toward her, where a huge opal ring from the Esperanza mine at Querétaro glowed with a dull fire. Green eyes, suddenly alert, searched Antoinette's face. "We have met before—I am sure of it."

"Yes, Your Majesty—at Miramar. Why, it must be all of six years now. I was on holiday with my father."

"Miramar, of course." Carlota's thoughts dwelled for a moment on the castle overlooking the Adriatic where she had shared so many happy times with her beloved Max, and her eyes grew moist. "Yes, we must meet again soon. It will be pleasant to talk over old times, and it will do you good to get out of this graveyard of a house. Do you ride?"

"I used to—at home."

"Alas, the countryside is now ravaged by bandits and

rebels, but I'm sure Major Chávez could arrange an escort for you. Could you not, Major?"

"If the señorita wishes."

"Good, that is settled. Now I have a personal errand to attend to. You may return to the palace, Major. I will not require you to accompany me."

"It is not wise to ride through the streets alone, madame," Ramón Chávez returned, closing with her as she reached the carriage door.

"Are you suggesting the people would harm me—their Empress?" Carlota demanded. "Help me in and then return at once." The authority in her tone defied further argument.

A swirl of blue velvet, a hand uplifted in a farewell gesture, and she was gone, leaving Antoinette standing in the courtyard and feeling suddenly unsure of herself again.

"It was sweet of her to come, wasn't it?" she said at length.

A brief nod. He was still staring after the carriage, obviously displeased by the Empress' determination to continue her journey alone.

"She knew your father well. She has a kind heart—a pity La Guadalupana cannot help her."

"Who is she?" Antoinette asked in puzzlement.

"It is the shrine of the Virgin of Guadalupe on Tepayac Hill," the major returned. "Many times in the past months she has gone there to pray for a child."

"But they have a son now," Antoinette said.

"Don Maximiliano and the Empress have adopted Augustín Iturbide, for all the good it will do them." The words had bitterness and anger in them. Augustín was the grandson of the onetime Emperor of Mexico, Augustín de Iturbide. Antoinette's father had mentioned the adoption in one of his letters, and she had thought then that it was a shrewd move. Her companion apparently thought otherwise.

"You are too hard on them. They want only to please the people," she began indignantly.

"There is only one way to do that, but having given up the chance of the Austrian throne to come here, I can't see the Emperor retiring gracefully from this country too, can you?"

"Is that what you want?"

"He is a good man but weak, relying too much on Bazaine and others like him. He has been betrayed by men he trusted. First Napoleon, who withdrew badly needed troops, then Franz Josef, who takes all his money, and now with Carlota ill . . ."

"Why do you say that?"

"It is a rumor. She has headaches, blackouts, depressed moods. No more than most women, you are about to say. Perhaps you are right, but at this moment when he badly needs her counsel, all she can think about is a baby. Nothing else matters to her."

Antoinette stepped back from him, pale and puzzled.

"I don't understand you. How can you talk this way and still serve them loyally?"

"Because they have my respect. In their own way they have done their best to be accepted, and failed, but the fault is not entirely theirs. My people will never accept a foreign ruler, no matter what name he bears. I know this. Perhaps I can persuade them to accept it before it is too late."

"Are they in danger? Could Juárez really regain control of the country?" Antoinette asked, appalled.

"I am not a prophet and I don't live my life more than one day at a time. Tomorrow—quién sabe?" He shrugged his shoulders. "Carlota may have her baby, born on Mexican soil—now that would be a marvel."

"I shall pray for her."

"Yes, do that." The sardonic twist to his mouth told her he had faith in neither God nor man. His dark eyes appraised the skirt and blouse she wore with mild surprise, as if he were only now aware of her appearance. "For a while in the sala I found myself imagining what life must have been like for you in France. You were glad of some company, I think."

"It has been lonely here," Antoinette admitted. "I kept my promise and did not go back to the attic until yesterday, but I have not been able to touch my father's sketches again. I think it will be a long time before I can do that. I was trying to clean his books when you arrived. What must she have thought of me, dressed like this?"

"She is an intelligent woman. No matter how you looked, she would see the real person, as I did on the journey here."

"Have you fully recovered from your head wound?"

"Perfectly, thank you."

"If I were to offer you coffee, would you refuse?"

"I must, but this time with regret. Doña Antoinette, the last time I was here, I did not mean to be rude or upset you by refusing your hospitality. I needed time to think."

Antoinette's gaze searched the sunburned face before her in surprise as she asked, "Why?"

"Surely that should be clear after our conversation at Luis' quinta. I may be an officer of rank and a man of property, but in some quarters my company is not always considered—shall we say—desirable. With the present troubles few French officers like their wives or daughters to associate with someone like myself. Among my own kind, mestizos and indios, it makes no difference, but you are the daughter of a French general."

"You were his friend."

"And as such I have done all I can to ensure that your stay here will be comfortable. You do not have to endure my company out of gratitude."

"How ungallant you are." Tiny blue sparks flashed in Antoinette's eyes, and there was color rising in her cheeks. "What a poor opinion you have of womanhood. Just now you gave me the impression our journey together had shown you I am neither weak nor feckless. I take pride in my judgment—" She broke off, expecting a reminder of her totally wrong character assessment when they first met, but he said nothing and merely smiled in that way of his that told her nothing. She heard herself say, recklessly, "I had not noticed you applying this illogical trend of thought to Doña Mercedes."

"Why should I? She is Mexican and has different values."

"And she understands you."

I find Major Chávez a difficult man to understand—her words to Captain Martínez were still clear in her mind, as was his answer: *Very few men understand him, women never do.* Except, perhaps, Mercedes Santos. Only a woman who knew and respected him for what he was, loved him deeply and passionately, perhaps even blindly, would have given him into the care of Coatlicue.

Ramón Chávez considered the taut, unsmiling face staring up at him. In flat-heeled shoes she barely came up to his shoulder. A strong breeze caught at her loose hair and dragged it across her face until she pushed it back with a gesture of annoyance.

"Mercedes is too selfish to understand any needs other than her own," he answered quietly. "Why did you mention her?"

"Because—because you are her—novio, are you not?" Antoinette did not want to intrude into his personal life, but his question gave her no choice.

Her words brought a mocking gleam to his eyes. "I see Soledad's imaginative tongue has been at work again. Luis Santos has been my friend for many years, and Mercedes is his sister. There is nothing more to it than that, on my side at least."

But far more on hers, Antoinette thought, remembering the long, clinging kiss before his departure from the quinta. Then who was the woman who had given him the amulet he wore about his neck?

"Will you accept the Empress' invitation to Chapultepec?" he asked, moving out into the street. His horse was tethered to a heavy brass ring set in the stonework, for the house had no stable like others nearby.

"I would like to, but . . ."

"You feel it would not be proper under the circumstances. This I understand, but you will find her a difficult woman to refuse. She was right, it would do you good, and I have the feeling you will not be unduly troubled by a few narrow-minded people. On the day my father died, my mother put on her brightest dress to follow the coffin to its final resting place. For hours afterward, she walked in the woods behind the hacienda, reliving days spent there with the only man she had ever loved. She did not inflict her grief on others, but so great was the love she felt for him, she died not two months later—her heart broken. Wear black if you must, Doña Antoinette, so that others may know of your suffering. They will give you sympathy without understanding, words without meaning. Is this what you want?"

What did she want? Over the past days Antoinette had found herself growing more confused. She had come to Mexico City with one purpose in mind, to find out the truth about her father's death, but to know the details now, she knew, would not bring her comfort or satisfaction—only the capture and death of the man called El Padrino could do that. An eye for an eye had been her father's favorite biblical quotation. She would remain long enough to see the fulfillment of those words.

"You promised to show me my father's grave. I think I could see it now. Will you tell me where it is?"

"It is not far from here, in the Ángel d'Oro churchyard. Your father used to go to church there whenever possible. But do not attempt to go there alone, allow me to take you. I will not intrude on your privacy."

"Did you arrange for the funeral?"

"Sí. There was no one else. Afterward I had his things packed away and the house closed. Notification of his death is probably waiting for you in France. You know how long these things take. There was a will leaving money and some land to you, but that is now in the hands of a local lawyer. No one knew that you were on your way."

"Could I ask you to see to it for me?"

"I have already seen him and asked him to get in touch

with you should he require your signature on any documents. I believe there are a few to sign."

"Then I will sign them. The money will be useful, although I have enough for my stay here, but the land— no, I don't want it. Sell it, give it away, I don't care."

"You may feel differently after a while. You might even decide you like Mexico."

"Stay here? So that when the Juaristas overrun the country they can take it away again and make a mockery of my father's death?" Antoinette's expression became decidedly stubborn. "No, Major Chávez, I will have nothing to do with any land. I gladly give it back to this heartless country."

FOUR

A formal invitation arrived three days later. Antoinette's hand shook with excitement as she drew out the plainly printed card to read:

El Gran Chambelán de la Emperatriz tiene la honra de invitar al orden de Su Majestad al Señorita Antoinette Dubec para la tertulia que tendrá lugar en el Castillo de Chapultepec el veinte y tres de junio de 1866 a las siete de la noche.

"Will you go, señorita?" Soledad asked, watching her face expectantly. "La Emperatriz has taken a liking to you —she will make sure you meet many people."

"Yes, I will go. What do you think of the Empress? Do you like her?"

The woman shrugged noncommittally. "She is not bad —for a gringa."

A gringa—an outsider! Antoinette winced inwardly. Carlota, herself—they were both foreigners and as such had no place in Mexico. She had begun to venture out-of-doors in the afternoons, walking in the small alameda nearby or sightseeing and shopping in the marketplace. She made purchases of material, china, kitchenware, a warm woolen rebozo and a pair of embossed leather sandals. Soledad accompanied her on all these occasions, nodding approval over a purchase or exploding into a torrent of Spanish if she thought the price too high. To her surprise Antoinette found the people friendly and extremely helpful, smiling not unkindly at her faltering attempts to make herself understood in their language and prepared to wait patiently while La Française made up her mind. If they resented her presence among them, they did not show it openly.

Reclining in the carriage sent at Carlota's request and escorted by two French officers of the Guardia Imperial, Antoinette felt as though she were royalty herself. The Empress' own regiment comprised mostly foreign soldiers formed for the protection of their majesties' persons.

As the sun dipped in the sky and they approached Chapultepec, they passed age-old haciendas and convents and rich pastureland where groves of oranges flourished. The castle was built on a hill some two and a half miles from the capital, high enough to give a magnificent view of the surrounding countryside. It towered over the giant ahuehuente trees and acacias that covered the cliffs like something out of a fairy tale. Through the window Antoinette glimpsed the snowcapped volcanoes in the distance and a huge lake bordered by cyprus trees, before the carriage swept through the gates and she was admitted to the court of Maximilian and Carlota once again.

The guests were assembling in a suite of rooms that appeared to stretch the whole length of the building. As she stepped through the main doorway Antoinette glimpsed at least five rooms, all communicating by means of folding doors. Furniture of the very latest design graced each room, and the walls were hung with silk drapes in delicate pastel shades to match the curtains at the windows.

A multitude of uniforms paraded before her: Mexican and Belgian, French Chasseurs d'Afrique, and the Foreign Legion. Crinolined, bejeweled ladies chattered in small groups, the Mexican ones easily distinguishable by a bevy of stout duennas hovering in the background. These surroundings were so familiar she had declined to bring Soledad. Here, she could hold her own without a chaperon.

She saw the uniform before the face as an officer

pushed his way through the throng of people toward her —the dark-green trousers with their gold stripe and the jacket with the fringed epaulettes of an "Elite" regiment. On the collar the initial "C" in gold thread identified him as one of the Guardia Imperial.

"Good evening." The voice was familiar, and tonight it held warmth, as if Ramón Chávez were pleased to see her. As surprise kept her silent he took her hand and touched her fingers to his lips and then he stepped back and allowed his gaze to survey the slender figure in black velvet, with the dull-red rubies glowing at her throat and from her ears. "I look forward to the day you wear that white dress again," he said, offering his arm. "Come, let me introduce you to a few people before we find ourselves something to drink. Not everyone is here yet, and their majesties will not appear until the last guest has arrived."

As he escorted her through the rooms, stopping to introduce her and converse with fellow officers and their wives, Antoinette was acutely conscious of their last conversation relating to her mourning attire. Most people afforded her words of sympathy, but their phrases came parrot-fashion, repeated time and time again, totally without meaning. She was disturbed more than shocked, and angry that the death of one more French soldier aroused such little concern.

"Death to the gringos," she said quietly as they stood drinking a glass of Hungarian red wine together by an open window that looked out onto a sea of sweet-smelling flowers, and Ramón Chávez looked at her with a slight hardening of his expression.

"Whatever made you say that?"

"I heard it yesterday from some children. They were chanting it like a revered hymn. Is that what they teach in the churches now? Death to the foreigners? Long live Juárez?"

"Aren't you using the words of children—and that's all they are—as an excuse to alienate yourself from something you are beginning to find increasingly attractive?

When I saw you the other day, I found that La Française looked surprisingly at home."

"Soledad has looked after me like a maiden aunt, I don't feel an outsider with her, but La Française, la gringa—that's what I am, isn't it? An interloper."

"Only if you persist in thinking of yourself as one. Come with me, there is something I want to show you."

His hand was beneath her arm, guiding her swiftly through the open windows and down the steps into the garden. He came to a halt as tall cyprus trees began to close in all around them, and Antoinette saw they were on the edge of the lake she had glimpsed briefly from the carriage. Bright red flowers grew at her feet, and the murmur of the wind in the trees above joined harmony with the whisper of the water against the bank. It was a place for lovers, hauntingly beautiful, peaceful as no other place she had known before. Not even the château where she had been born and which she loved above all, came near to instilling such contentment in her.

"My country is at times harsh, its history has been bloody and barbaric, but as with all things, the bad can be made bearable with a small amount of good. Close your eyes. Don't you feel how alive this place is with the ghosts of Montezuma and his warriors stealing through the trees? Can't you hear the sound of La Malinche laughing as Cortés chases her down to the water? I can't believe you have no imagination."

"I have a great deal. If circumstances were different I don't think I would ever want to leave Mexico," Antoinette answered quietly. In the swiftly gathering darkness it was easy to be honest with him, to admit how deeply his country had affected her in less than one short month.

"You don't have to go back, not yet anyway. The Empress is delighted to have a new face at court, and only yesterday Luis Santos asked after you. Did his flowers please you?"

The unexpected question made her blush as she realized he had known all along who had sent her the bouquet.

"It was sweet of him to think of me."

Ramón bent and plucked a flower and held it out to her with an elaborate flourish.

"Permítame, La Florecita."

"You called me that once before." His fingers brushed hers as she took the delicate bloom and slipped it, with sudden bravado, into the neckline of her gown. She was aware of the sudden intimacy that sprang unbidden between them and sent her heart racing madly. "What does it mean?"

"Ask me another time when we are alone together, but not about to be interrupted," Ramón answered with a soft laugh, and swung about to acknowledge the two figures coming down the path toward them.

"Ramón, so you are here," Mercedes Santos said, and came immediately to his side, linking her arm through his with a possessiveness that made Antoinette immediately step back.

"Their majesties have arrived"—Luis came up behind her—"and Colonel López is looking for you."

"Then I must not keep him waiting or he will be telling tales to the marshal," Ramón returned dryly. By his tone it was apparent he disliked the commander of the Guardia Imperial, Miguel López, as much as Bazaine, to whom the former was related by marriage. "With regret, Doña Antoinette, I must leave you with Luis. Perhaps we can continue our conversation after dinner."

"Not if I have my way," Luis chuckled, but Ramón had already turned on his heel and been swallowed up in the shadowy half-light.

"Has Major Chávez been transferred to duty here?" Antoinette asked as they reentered the castle. On the far side of the room he was talking to a portly blond man with a short fair mustache whom she took to be Colonel Miguel López. They were both unsmiling and preoccupied, and she felt that a cloud had descended over the pleasant interlude in the garden. Would they ever resume their conversation?

"He has been assigned to temporary duty with the

Empress' regiment by Don Maximiliano himself. It is a great honor, don't you agree, Mercedes?"

"The Emperor knows those he can trust." Mercedes Santos' eyes considered the scarlet petals against Antoinette's white skin, and a malicious smile deepened her full mouth. "How—sweet." The words were an insult, and the words that followed were a warning not to trespass on another woman's territory: "But I feel I should offer a word of advice, Doña Antoinette. In Mexico unattached young women do not take evening strolls with attractive men."

"She was only with Ramón," Luis protested good-humoredly.

"Exactly, and you know how easy it is for Ramón's charm to be—shall we say—misconstrued?"

Antoinette's polite smile masked the anger mounting inside her at the insinuation.

"Like you, Doña Mercedes, I have recently suffered the loss of someone very dear to me. At such a time I am sure neither of us would entertain any intention of plunging into a romantic entanglement." She had the satisfaction of seeing Mercedes' lovely face whiten and she continued coldly, "When we were interrupted"—she laid heavy emphasis on the word to show her arrival had not been welcome—"Major Chávez and I were discussing whether or not I should remain in Mexico for a while—nothing more."

"You must miss your friends at home. You will be leaving us soon then?" Mercedes raised a jeweled hand to wave at someone across the room, making it apparent she was growing bored and wished to move on.

"No, I have decided to remain for at least another month," Antoinette returned. Luis' face registered instant pleasure, while his sister's betrayed something near to alarm. After a moment Mercedes made an excuse to leave and joined a group of French officers and their wives on the far side of the room.

"Are you really going to stay?" Luis asked in a low voice.

"Major Chávez has spoken of some money and land in

71

my father's will and something about papers to be signed. I shall have to remain until that matter is settled, and I must confess, after tonight I no longer feel in a hurry to leave."

"You are susceptible to a handsome man after all."

Antoinette blushed under his close scrutiny. After Mercedes' insinuation it was clear what was in his mind.

"What woman isn't?"

"Then you stay to be with Ramón?" There was disappointment in his voice. "I had hoped. . . ."

"Yes, Don Luis?"

"If you have the time perhaps you will come to the quinta and dine with me one evening. I could invite a few friends. We will have music and much good wine. If you wish I shall of course invite Ramón."

"For my pleasure or that of Doña Mercedes? Really, I don't understand why I am being continually linked with Major Chávez. He means no more to me than I do to him. We are friends, but that is all."

"It is a relief to hear you say that."

"For the sake of your sister?"

"No, your own. I would not like you to be hurt. Do not misunderstand my motives for talking to you in this manner—Ramón and I are close friends, and we respect each other as men of the world—but since the death of his wife he is an empty shell, and because of my own feelings for you I think you should realize this."

"His wife!" Antoinette echoed. The deeper, more personal implication behind his words was lost on her.

"She died the year the French expeditionary force came to Mexico," Luis continued. "For months Ramón shut himself away at his hacienda, and when I saw him again he had changed completely. He never speaks of her and in five years he has never become seriously involved with a woman. The army is his whole life. That is not to say he does not enjoy their company. He is muy guapo, after all, and his brusqueness is the very thing that seems to attract most women. They either want to mother him or replace his wife, and he resents both. He would be a fine catch if he ever met the woman capable of rekindling the fire."

Four years of emptiness and heartbreaking memories! At last Antoinette was certain who had given him Coatlicue. Not Mercedes, but his wife, the woman he still loved and would forever mourn in his own way. Unconsciously her fingers touched the bloodred flower nestled in the warm hollow of her breasts. La Florecita—she would never dare ask him what it meant, for she now knew it had only been a gesture of kindness. Better to have found out now before her foolish fancies began to weave something more tangible out of the simple act.

"Thank you for being so open with me," she said quietly. "As for dinner, yes, Don Luis, it would give me great pleasure to see your home again."

"I was afraid my boldness might have deterred you. Since I last saw you I have been like a lost man, much to the amusement of my sister. Look, their majesties are coming this way."

Luis took Antoinette by the arm and drew her to one side of the room as Maximilian and Carlota appeared in the doorway and began to move down the line of waiting guests.

"The Emperor is quite handsome, isn't he?" Antoinette murmured as they came into view.

As the occasion was informal Maximilian wore European clothes and paused now and then to chat amiably. At thirty-four he stood just under six feet and dwarfed many of his retinue. Only Ramón Chávez, five paces to his left, measured him in height. His hair was fair, almost flaxen, parted in the middle, and his pale complexion had been only slightly tanned by the hot Mexican sun. His long beard and whiskers were carefully parted in the center of his chin in the style of Dundreary. His alert blue eyes were warm and friendly, but his full mouth was weak, and Antoinette was filled with a sense of foreboding as she looked past him to the hard-faced campaigners in the crowd. He was surrounded by so many people. How many used him to their own advantage and mocked his attempts to reconcile himself with the Mexican people? Where were his true friends?

On May 24, 1864, Maximilian von Hapsburg, Archduke of Austria, had stepped from a boat at Veracruz and so fulfilled a legend—Quetzalcoatl had kept his promise and returned. But like Hernán Cortés, who had preceded him over three hundred years before, Maximilian was a man, not a god, and men make mistakes, however good their intentions. He found the people proud and arrogant, despite the fact they were little more than half-starved peasants. The welcome they gave the new Emperor was short-lived, and it was not long before Maximilian realized he had been misled. He was not their choice of ruler, and with the strength of Benito Juárez and his rebels growing daily, he never would be. Instead of being realized, his ambitious dreams were shattered, and the bitterest pill of all to swallow was the fact that in order to become Emperor of Mexico he had relinquished all claims to the throne of Austria. Whether he liked it or not, whether the people accepted or rejected him, this beautiful country with its history of magnificent splendor and violent death was now his home. Cortés had his La Malinche to give him wise council and comfort. Maximilian had his wife Carlota, young and beautiful and as steadfast in her dreams as he was disillusioned. La Malinche bore Cortés a son, but for Maximilian and Carlota there was no heir. It had cost them the throne of Austria. It was soon to bring her to the edge of madness.

There was no sign of it, however, as Carlota caught sight of the French girl in the crowd and came toward her.

"Mademoiselle Dubec. I am glad you have come." She shimmered in a dress of pale yellow, diamonds at her throat and in her hair. She looked exquisite. Her gaze flickered to the handsome caballero at Antoinette's side and her smile deepened until it was almost mischievous.

"You are taking good care of our guest, I hope, Don Luis?"

"It is my pleasure, Your Majesty."

"See to it your pleasure does not deprive me too often of her company," Carlota returned with a soft laugh as she moved on.

Maximilian turned, extending his hand toward her, and she swung around in his direction. It was a signal for everyone to follow them into the banquet rooms, through the last of the communicating doors. Two liveried servants pulled them open, and then a sudden hush descended over the room. From beside the carefully arranged tables three men leaped into the doorway. All had weapons pointing directly at the approaching Emperor and Empress. A woman screamed, and several promptly fainted away into the arms of their escorts. Antoinette's cry of fear was obliterated by the sound of gunfire. She expected to see both Maximilian and his wife hit, but men of the Guardia Imperial had flung themselves in front of the pair to screen them from the deadly hail of bullets. Two uniformed figures toppled over almost at her feet. As Luis grasped her by the shoulders, forcing her to the floor out of the line of fire, she glimpsed Ramón Chávez, blood pouring from a face wound, as he threw himself bodily onto the Emperor. Then chaos broke loose. She crouched on the floor, her face pressed tightly against Luis' ruffled shirt, almost stifled as the mad panic began to clear the room.

"Luis, what is happening?" In her terror, his first name slipped from her lips, and she felt his arms tighten around her.

"Be still—I think the guards have them."

"Who are they?"

"Loyalists, probably. Who else would be mad enough to break into this place? Hey there, you, be careful, do you want to crush the señorita?" he snapped as a portly Mexican backed into them.

Five minutes more of feeling as if the world were collapsing around her, and then she was being lifted to her feet, brushed down, and a glass of wine was being pressed to her lips. After a mouthful she pushed it away.

75

The mass of soldiers and civilians who had converged on the banquet hall to overpower the would-be assassins had wrecked it, and in their rage they had killed two of the three men. The third, bruised and only half conscious, was dragged to where Maximilian stood with a disheveled, wide-eyed Carlota in his arms. All of twenty years of age, he stared defiantly through swollen eyes at the sea of faces surrounding him, swallowed hard, and shut his ears to the threats hurled down on his head.

"He is so young," Antoinette whispered. She clung to Luis' arm, trembling, but determined not to cry. People were gradually returning—whispering, pointing, sobbing. Then, with the realization it was over and they had nothing more to fear, false courage returned with a demand for the harshest penalty to be exacted from the men who had dared penetrate the sanctity of the Emperor's domain.

"No, Max. I must," Antoinette heard Carlota whisper fiercely as breaking free of her husband's arm, she moved slowly across the floor to confront the young insurgent.

"Why—after all we have tried to do?" Her voice shook with emotion. She was shocked, bewildered, yet still trusting. "Why?"

Without a word the youngster threw back his head and spat full in her face.

"No." Carlota waved back the soldiers who had moved threateningly toward them. "If that is his answer, so be it."

Antoinette held her breath as Carlota picked up her skirts and walked proudly out of the room. It was a few minutes before anyone realized she had gone, and then her bevy of ladies-in-waiting ran after her. Marshal Bazaine's voice was heard ordering the guard to be doubled, men to make a search of the grounds. His face was red with rage and embarrassment as he stormed out of the room.

"Ladies and gentlemen, please be calm. The danger is over now." Maximilian looked about him almost apologetically. He seemed perturbed by the incident least of all. "I deeply regret this unpleasantness, which has curtailed such an enjoyable evening."

"The man is a fool," a voice breathed close behind Antoinette and Luis. "He narrowly misses death and now apologizes for the inconvenience to people who couldn't care less whether he lives or dies. They were only concerned with their own worthless lives." Ramón Chávez was beside them, no longer the immaculately clad figure Antoinette had encountered earlier. One sleeve was ripped above the elbow, and there was a bruise just below a bloody bullet furrow that stretched across his left cheek. "You are not hurt, either of you?" The question included his friend, but he was looking at Antoinette.

"No, but you . . ." She fumbled in her purse and found her handkerchief and gave it to him. Blood stained the delicate lace he laid against his cheek. "That bullet was meant for Maximilian. You could have been killed."

"Rather a mere soldier than the Emperor of Mexico," came the humorless reply. "Luis, you must take her home at once, we don't think there are any more on the grounds, but if there are . . . Dios, she has seen enough for one night."

"At once. Come, Doña Antoinette, take my arm."

Luis tucked Antoinette's hand beneath his arm, giving her no chance to argue, and escorted her quickly from the room.

The following morning Antoinette read of the assassination attempt in the French edition of a local paper and shuddered at the recollection of how close death had been. MANY DEAD, SCORES WOUNDED—the exaggerated headline could only incite anger and bring about acts of retaliation, she thought, annoyed at the person who had written such thoughtless words, probably without even having viewed the incident himself.

She had slept badly after her return to the house in the carriage of Luis Santos. His sympathetic voice helped to ease the sickness in her stomach, but she was almost oblivious to his kindness and attentions as he put her in Soledad's care. She was immediately put to bed and given a cup of hot chocolate to help her sleep, but throughout the night she tossed and turned, plagued by nightmares.

The spell of the lake had been rudely shattered, forcing her once again to examine her reasons for remaining in Mexico. Did she want revenge for the death of her father, or was there a deeper implication behind her reluctance to leave—a reason she was afraid to acknowledge even to herself?

She had just finished breakfast when Soledad knocked at her bedroom door to announce the arrival of a visitor.

"Don Ramón has come to see you."

"Show him into the sala, I will be down in a moment," Antoinette replied, jumping out of bed. Pulling on a wrap, she ran a brush through her hair, wondering what had brought Ramón Chávez to her house before nine in the morning.

He was not in uniform this morning, but wore dark-gray trousers and a short jacket over a black shirt. A sombrero lay on a nearby chair. The casual attire reminded her he was not only a soldier, but a disturbingly attractive man whose love for his dead wife stood between them. His face was tired and drawn. The bandage on his cheek contrasted strongly with his bronzed skin. Suddenly she wanted to reach out and touch the wounded place, to offer more than mere sympathetic words.

"Forgive me"—he was looking at her wrap and loose hair—"Soledad did not tell me you were still in bed."

"I had a bad night and overslept. You look tired, Major Chávez. Would you like some coffee?"

He smiled and nodded briefly, and Antoinette called for Soledad to bring some for them both. Reaching into his shirt, Ramón Chávez brought out several lace handkerchiefs, tied together with a piece of pink ribbon.

"I came to make sure you were all right and to bring you these—with thanks."

"But—but there was no need to go to such trouble over one little handkerchief," Antoinette said softly. As she examined them more closely she found in each corner the initial "A" woven in blue thread. They had been chosen with care.

"The gesture was very much appreciated."

"Don't," she said quickly, sudden sparks of anger flashing into her eyes, "don't say 'gesture' like that. It reminds me of something you once said to me—something very unkind. The grand lady and the poor soldier—do you remember? Is that what you thought last night?"

"No, it was not. I did not realize how deeply those words had offended you. They were thoughtless and untrue—time and time again you have proved that to me."

Soledad brought in a tray of coffee and looked from one to the other as if trying to understand why this Mexican officer preferred the company of a gringa to that of Doña Mercedes.

Waiting until she had closed the door behind her, Ramón Chávez said quietly, "I have been given a day's leave because of this," and he motioned to his cheek. "Don Maximiliano was feeling grateful. I thought perhaps you would like to go riding. I took the liberty of bringing an extra horse."

"I would love it." Antoinette's eyes shone at the prospect. "I have been looking forward to it since the Empress mentioned you might arrange an escort."

"No escort, I'm afraid, just me. If that is acceptable?"

"Give me ten minutes to change," Antoinette answered, and ran upstairs, her heart singing like a caged bird about to be released.

The major was in the courtyard when she came down again. She wore the green riding habit and black boots he had seen before, but this time a white silk scarf fluttering at her throat added a touch of brightness to the somber outfit. Soledad had wound her thick hair into a tight knot at the nape of her neck and secured it with a ribbon. Chávez thought she looked flushed and happy, and knew he had acted wisely in seeking her company. She possessed the rare quality of making him feel content whenever she was near. He had not experienced such a feeling in many years.

As they rode through the streets Antoinette was conscious of the curious glances following them, but Ramón Chávez appeared not to notice. His thoughts were elsewhere, his face a closed book to her searching gaze.

"Did—did your wife like to ride?" she asked hesitantly as they turned their horses toward open country.

"Yes." No show of surprise at her question, no softening of the hard features. She felt as if he were deliberately detaching himself from her and from the intimacy they had shared for a few brief moments at Chapultepec. "I suppose Luis told you."

"He only mentioned it in passing."

His eyes flickered over her face almost sardonically as he drawled, "You once told me you rode like a man, Doña Antoinette. Shall we see how true that boast is?"

Not waiting for an answer, he dug his heels into the flanks of his horse, and it leaped away from her in a sudden burst of speed. By the time Antoinette had recovered from her surprise, horse and rider were plunging down the slopes of an arroyo, almost out of sight. She had seen enough of his horsemanship to know she could not outride him, nor did her mount have the necessary speed to overtake his, but she managed to close the gap as he forded the stream and urged the huge black stallion up the cactus-covered bank. There were barely ten yards between them as he swung about onto a plateau of scrub and rocks and barely half that distance by the time they reached the far side and began to gallop toward the wooden bridge that spanned the arroyo some way ahead. He drew rein as soon as he reached it, and she followed suit, breathless from the hectic chase, to find he was smiling broadly.

"You do ride well. I didn't expect to be caught so easily."

"Do you feel better now?"

"Why do you ask that?"

"I too have the habit of riding away my sad moods."

"Do you find me that predictable today?"

"You are worried, aren't you? Is it because those men managed to get into the palace unnoticed?"

"You are very astute," he remarked as they moved off

again at a more leisurely pace, "or was I less in control last night than I realized?"

"I saw it in your eyes when you looked at the Emperor." She fell silent, wondering if she had gone too far.

"War has come to Mexico as it did in the United States —brother against brother, father against son, friend against friend. There can be no middle road, yet there are still some of us who try to find one. What does a man do when he has to choose between his conscience and his country?" Ramón's face showed how deeply disturbed he felt.

"Surely the answer is between the man and God," Antoinette returned quietly.

"Not for me," came the bitter retort. "God has destroyed what faith I once had in Him. I see I shock you. I'm sorry. Would you mind if we rode by way of Guadalupe? There is something I must do." His manner changed abruptly once again, leaving her lost for words, and she merely nodded.

To the north of the city below Tepayac Hill, stood the shrine of Guadalupe, the sacred place where Carlota forgot she was an Empress and knelt in prayer alongside simple people who prayed as fervently for peace as she did for a child. Rain for their meager crops, a son for Maximilian, freedom from backbreaking bondage, an heir to make the throne of Mexico secure.

Antoinette and Ramón Chávez tethered their horses below the square. As they approached the main doors she covered her red hair with her scarf. He did not follow her inside, but stood to one side, his eyes sweeping the courtyard as if searching for someone. A blaze of candelight greeted her from the altar of La Guadalupana as she crossed herself and knelt in prayer. The contentment of the lake returned. Anger, hatred, fear, none of them existed within her as she lifted her eyes to the brown-skinned face of the Virgin. "I am the Mother of all you who dwell in this land"—the words were written beneath the cape hanging in a silver frame on the high altar. Folded in this same cape, the story went, were roses the

Virgin had left for Juan Diego soon after the Spanish Conquest. When he had unfolded it before his friends, he had found not roses, but the imprint of her face: confirmation of her promise that she would always protect Mexico.

A peasant woman with a blue rebozo pulled tightly over her head rose from beside Antoinette and lighted a candle. After a moment the French woman followed suit. Then, after a brief hesitation she took a second candle and lighted that also.

"Has La Guadalupana given you her peace?" a quiet voice asked, and she found Ramón Chávez directly behind her, sombrero in hand.

"This place has given me peace," Antoinette answered. "Why do you mock her?"

"Don't misunderstand me. Each of us searches for peace in a different way. If she gives these people what they want, a need to believe someone is watching over them, then who am I to judge? Isn't that what you need just now—a feeling of security, someone to love you and take the place of the father you have lost? La Guadalupana is for women like the Empress, clutching at straws as her hopes for a child diminish. This is not for you." He motioned toward the open doorway where bright sunlight streamed through into the gloomy interior and made picturesque patterns on the dusty floor. "Out there is the reality of Mexico, and it is where you belong. Faith in yourself is all you lack."

As she stood silent he took the candle she held and placed it among the many others before the altar. "For your father?"

"No, that one was for you."

"Me!" His eyes flew to her face, startled.

"Without faith life is empty. Without love it is meaningless."

"What a sentimental little heart you have." He gave a hollow laugh and turned abruptly toward the door, saying in a low tone, "God can do nothing for me."

"And Coatlicue?" she asked, following him outside.

"She reminds me to be true to myself, to remember what I am and be proud of it. Your God has left me nothing to believe in."

"And you choose to be without love. How deeply you must have loved her."

A tiny pulse throbbed at his temple as he stared at her, and for a moment Antoinette felt faint as she looked into his dark eyes.

"Whatever I felt died with her. I buried it with the memory of our life together in her grave. I want it to stay that way."

"Did—did you find who you were looking for?" Antoinette asked, quickly changing the subject. What a fool she had been to admit the second candle had been for him. Whatever must he think of such foolishness!

"Sí. Do you see that girl over there by the steps—the one talking to the padre?"

Antoinette's gaze singled out a pretty Mexican girl in a linen skirt and blouse, clutching a dark rebozo around her shoulders. Despite the distance between them, she could see the tears streaming down her face and feel the tumult of suppressed grief as she listened to the priest at her side.

"Who is she?"

"Consuelo Vargas—the wife of the boy they shot this morning."

"Shot!" Antoinette echoed in horror. "Was there a trial?"

So this was the reason he had wanted to get away from the city so early.

"No. Maximilian's Black Flag Decrees allow executions for anyone caught so much as carrying arms against the monarchy, let alone attempting to assassinate the Emperor himself. He was shot"—he glanced quickly at the sun—"an hour ago. She came to the palace last night begging the Emperor to intervene, but he would not, of course. As I had known her husband, I promised to bring her the news myself."

"Poor girl."

83

"Why do you say that? She is only the wife of a Juarista."

"She is a woman who has lost her man." Antoinette was too angered by the callousness of his tone to remember she herself had once hated all Juaristas without exception. "What will happen to her?"

"She will find work, I expect, although it will be difficult now that she has been exposed as having Loyalist sympathies. No one will want to employ her for fear of coming under suspicion themselves."

"I will," Antoinette said in a firm voice.

"She doesn't need charity," came the cold reply, and she was seized with a sudden urge to slap him.

"Charity is something we both seem to be rather short of," she replied scathingly. "As you know the girl, Major, will you please ask her to come to the house this afternoon?"

"I strongly advise against it." His expression challenged her to argue.

"Then I will speak to her myself."

A lean, strong hand circled Antoinette's wrist, holding her fast. The action was met with such a haughty look she was immediately released.

"Very well, I will do as you ask. In what capacity do you intend to use her?"

"We will discuss that when she comes. At the moment I want to give her a roof over her head and a chance to look people in the face and be proud of what she is."

He had spoken that word only a few minutes before. Pride was the cross he bore; he understood its demands and its rewards. Antoinette held her breath as he went across and spoke to the girl, who never once turned to look in her direction. After a few moments she drew the rebozo over her head and hurried away. Ramón Chávez returned accompanied by the priest, who was a fairly young man despite the unruly thatch of gray hair and a face that showed deep concern for the trials and tribulations of others.

"Señorita Dubec, I am Father Ignatius." Her hand was

84

gripped in a firm handshake. "Your offer has taken me completely by surprise. It was most generous of you to give the poor child a home."

"I too have recently lost someone, Father, and so I share her grief. If I can help her a little then I shall be pleased, and I assure you it is not, as Major Chávez thinks, an act of pious charity. Juaristas killed my father, and I hope I am here long enough to see the man responsible brought before a firing squad. However, my feelings for this one awful man haven't clouded my judgment or made me immune to the suffering of others."

"You are very young to be so full of hatred for a fellow human being," Father Ignatius murmured.

"Hate—yes, I suppose I do hate him," Antoinette said slowly. "I could so easily love this country if it were not for him."

"I will pray for you, my child."

Soledad did not like Consuelo Vargas. Antoinette noticed the tension between them from the first day they were beneath the same roof, yet she herself could find no fault with the girl. She was quiet-natured, courteous, and extremely willing to do anything asked of her. Antoinette realized she had been accustomed to a far different life from the one she had shared with her husband hiding in the hills or the one she now had at the house in the Calle de Comerciantes, but she never spoke of it or hinted about what it may have been like. Appalled at the menial tasks Soledad was forcing on her, Antoinette took Consuelo out of the kitchen and made it quite clear she was to be her maid. For days the atmosphere was almost unbearable as doors were slammed noisily behind Soledad's matronly back or she was suddenly struck down with a headache, leaving the younger woman to cope not only with the housework, but also the preparation of meals. All this she did without complaint, her pretty brown face almost smiling at such tantrums. As the days passed, Antoinette found an easy friendship developing between them.

* * *

Consuelo looked up from her mending as Antoinette came into the sala, drawing on her gloves. It was a sunny afternoon, and she had decided to go out for a walk in the nearby alameda. Soledad was to accompany her.

"Are you sure you won't come with us? I'm sure the fresh air would do you good. You haven't been out of the house for days," Antoinette said with a smile.

"Gracias, señorita, but I am quite content. Besides, I want to get on with your blouse. Will you bring me back the extra material I need?"

"Of course. Soledad and I will go to the market on the way home. We will not be more than an hour."

"I will have the señorita's tea ready for her when she returns," Consuelo murmured, and continued with her sewing. But the moment the door had closed behind Soledad and Antoinette, she was on her feet, watching them from the window until they had disappeared from sight through the garden entrance. An hour! If she hurried, it was more than enough time. She felt her heartbeats quicken at the risk she was about to take.

Fetching her rebozo, she cautiously slipped out of the house and hurried down the nearest side street into the crowded market square, where she threaded her way in and out of the laden stalls, thronged with people, until she was sure she had not been followed. Months of living with the rebels in the hills in constant fear of capture had taught her to be very careful. This was the first opportunity she had of seeing her brother alone since the death of her husband, but she would have forfeited the visit rather than risk his being captured by the French. What a prize he would make for them. Pausing to purchase a bunch of flowers, she placed them in the basket over her arm and walked quickly on. If she were stopped by soldiers, or failed to return before Antoinette, she intended to use them as an excuse for coming out after all. Five minutes later, she was knocking on the faded door of a house in the Plaza Domingo.

"Let me in quickly. It is Consuelo," she ordered the old woman who appeared, and the door was immediately opened wide enough for her to enter. The moment she had done so, it was closed and securely barred. Proof her brother had arrived safely, Consuelo thought as she stepped into the back room.

He stood by the window, peering out from behind the curtain at the street, satisfying himself she had not been followed. He was a tall, well-built man in his thirties. He had cared for her since the death of their parents, until war and circumstances had forced them apart. As she entered he turned, and she threw down her basket and ran into his outstretched arms, allowing herself the weakness of tears for the first time since her beloved Paco had died. How good it was to know she was not totally alone.

"How are you, little one?"

"I am well, my brother."

"You look pale and thin." His eyes probed her face intently.

"I miss Paco."

"Sí, I know you do. I do too, but he went against my orders—you know that, don't you? When I heard what he intended I sent men to intercept him before he reached the palace, but they were too late."

"I understand. I do not blame you. He was always headstrong and stubborn, once he had made up his mind." Consuelo stood for a long while with her cheek against her brother's firm shoulder, comforted by the feel of his arms around her, instilled with new courage by their strength. At last she drew away, wiping the last traces of tears from her face, and smiled up into his anxious features. "Do not grieve for me. You must think of nothing, no one, until our cause is won."

"You are my sister. . . ."

"And you are El Padrino. Our people look to you to give them hope for the future," Consuelo reminded him gently. "I am luckier than some women who have lost their men. I have a roof over my head, a bed to sleep in, and food to eat. When I lived in the hills I was not so comfortable."

"What is it like in the house of Señorita Dubec? Is she good to you?"

"Sí, she is very kind. She has lost her father, and I my husband. It has become a bond between us. We are friends. But the other one—the woman from the quinta of Don Luis Santos—she is not to be trusted. Always she tries to make trouble for me, and she watches me all the time."

"Perhaps I should not have asked you to come here." Her brother's voice was suddenly troubled, and he stepped back to the window.

"I will have to go in a few minutes—the señorita will only be an hour. I bought some flowers as an excuse if she returns before me. She will believe me—she is very trusting."

"She is also French and has no reason to love our people."

"Do not worry, I will not confide in her, although at times I must admit I find myself wishing it were possible to talk to her. She is very much alone, mi hermano," Consuelo murmured.

Her brother moved forward and drew her back into his arms, gently stroking her long black hair.

"It will not be long, niña. Very soon Mexico will be free, and we will be together again."

FIVE

Things came to a head on the day Antoinette received two invitations in the post. One came from the Empress Carlota, requesting her presence at the Residential Palace the following afternoon. The other was the expected invitation from Luis Santos, to dine at the quinta. She sat down and quickly wrote acceptances to both and then set about selecting something suitable to wear for the important occasion at the palace. Eventually she decided on a Burgundy silk gown with full sleeves and a ruched skirt. It was not too gay, but not as somber as the black she had worn to Chapultepec.

"The señorita will require me to accompany her to the palace, of course?" Soledad said.

"No, I don't think so. I would like to take Consuelo. She hasn't been out of the house since she arrived. Would you like to come?" Antoinette asked, looking across to the corner of the sitting room where the girl sat sewing. She was extremely clever with a needle and upon finding several yards of material Antoinette had purchased, had asked to be allowed to make something for her. In less than two days she had finished a skirt and almost completed a blouse to go with it.

Consuelo glanced up. If she noticed the malicious gleam in Soledad's eyes, she gave no sign.

"If that is what the señorita wishes."

"Madre de Dios! You will take her with you?" Soledad burst into a stream of torrid Spanish, her features working furiously. "Don Luis sent me to look after you. It is not proper that *she* should—a Juarista's woman. How do you know she is not a spy for them? Why else should she come into the house of a gringa? She and her kind hate you, señorita. You are a fool to trust her. She is dirt. See, I spit on her."

"That's enough." Antoinette's eyes blazed at the outburst. "Don Luis did send you here to help me, but only until I could make other arrangements. If you feel so strongly about Consuelo, perhaps you should return to the Quinta Santos."

"And leave you with her? Already people are whispering behind your back. La soldadera and la gringa."

"I refuse to listen to any more. Please pack your things and leave at once."

As Soledad flounced away, muttering vehemently under her breath, Consuelo put aside her needlework and looked at Antoinette with troubled eyes.

"You cannot send her away. She was your friend before I came. I must go. She is right—I will only bring you trouble."

"Do you want to leave?"

"No, I am happy here. He judged correctly—you have a kind heart."

"Whom do you mean?" Antoinette asked, her pulse beginning to race.

"Major Chávez."

A kind heart. At that moment it was a lonely heart, for she had not seen him in over two weeks. How strange she should miss him when she well knew she could never mean anything to him. With a smile she took Consuelo's hand and squeezed it reassuringly.

"Stay as long as you wish."

Antoinette's invitation to the palace was not, as she had expected, to spend the afternoon riding with the Empress. She was shown onto the terraced lawn where Carlota sat sipping iced orangeade and watching her ladies-in-waiting playing with a small boy whose copper curls immediately identified him as Augustín Iturbide, the adopted heir to the throne of Mexico.

"I'm afraid I misinterpreted Your Majesty's wishes," she said, looking down at her riding habit as she was invited to sit down and partake of a cool drink.

"It was my intention for us to ride together, but in a few short hours so much has happened." Carlota leaned back in her chair, pale and obviously troubled. "I must leave Mexico and my beloved Augustín and my husband within the week. If we are to survive here, I have to go to France, to plead with that unspeakable monster Napoleon." Her voice shook with suppressed anger, and there was a wild look in her eyes that startled Antoinette. "Not only does he withdraw all his aid and leave us to the mercy of Díaz' rabble, but now he has the insolence to write and tell us there will be no more money for Mexico. No money indeed! Doesn't the silly little man realize what harm he is doing? We have already spent eight million francs from our own private purse, and many of my husband's loyal Austrian officers are paying their men out of their own pockets. I am at my wits end, and so is the Emperor. My poor Max, he feels he has been stabbed in the back. He accepted the throne of Mexico with the backing of France, and now we are alone, friendless, deserted by the very man who persuaded us to come to this country. Sometimes I wish we had stayed at Miramar."

"Oh no, Your Majesty, never say that," Antoinette exclaimed. "You have many friends here both among the army and the Mexican people. When he sees how much this country means to you, Napoleon will not be able to resist giving you all you want."

"If only I could believe that would be so."

"You must convince him." Antoinette broke off, coloring. "Forgive me, it is not my place to tell you what you must do, but I know how deeply you love the people and the land."

"And you . . ." Carlota's eyes rested thoughtfully on Antoinette's flushed cheeks. The light had died now, and she was once more composed, smiling. "My first impression was that you hated Mexico and could not wait to go home. Now I hear you have settled comfortably in your father's house, have engaged a duenna, and are much sought after by a certain handsome caballero. Have you no wish to go back to France?"

"Yes, of course. At least I think I do. I must confess I am not unhappy here. I went to see my father's lawyer the other day to sign some papers and settle the matter of a piece of land he owned. I have more than enough money to remain here if I wish."

"And the land?"

"I gave it away—at least, I asked Major Chávez to see to it for me."

"So you are still bitter. What a pity! I regret having to leave when everything is becoming so interesting."

Antoinette wondered what implication lay behind those words. Secrets were impossible to keep in Mexico City, and she suspected the Empress delighted in receiving all the local gossip.

"I am not sure I understand Your Majesty's meaning," she said demurely.

"Come now, haven't you been pursued by that good-looking Luis Santos since the moment you arrived?"

"I would not put it that way. He has sent me flowers and called on me from time to time, but he is no more than a friend. As a matter of fact he has invited me to dine with him the day after tomorrow."

"I too was invited, but alas, I have had to refuse," Carlota sighed. "Have you accepted?"

"Yes. I am looking forward to it."

"I am glad, I like the young man. He comes from a good, stable background. Let me offer a word of advice, my dear, and please do not take it unkindly. I have nothing against Major Chávez personally, you understand, but he is a soldier. No woman will ever fill his life so completely as the army. I have heard of his interest in you—or is it the other way around?"

Antoinette was so taken aback she could only stare at the Empress in silence. The incident of the candle at Guadalupe, together with court gossip linking his name with hers, must surely be the reason why he had not visited her since that day.

"I—I like the major. He was the first person to befriend me here in Mexico," Antoinette returned defensively, and knew Carlota was not deceived.

"He is a man who has great regard for others, but very little for himself. He is probably impossible to live with, which is very likely the reason why his wife ran off and left him." Carlota rose to her feet, holding out her arms toward Augustín, who was running across the lawn toward her, totally unaware of the incredulous expression on Antoinette's face. "Come here, little one, and let Mama kiss you before you go inside for your nap."

Carlota's devotion to the child was only too apparent as she bent and gathered the copper-haired boy against her breast, smothering his face with kisses until one of her ladies gently but firmly prised them apart and led Augustín away; but Antoinette neither saw nor heard anything as she stared blindly after the retreating figures, still stunned by the Empress' revelation.

It was almost dark by the time Antoinette and Consuelo returned to the house. The latter, having noticed her mistress' pale cheeks, inquired if anything was wrong.

"No. I am a little tired, that's all. I think I will lie down for a while." Antoinette hesitated, conscious of a pair of dark eyes on her. "Consuelo, did you know Major Chávez' wife?"

"Sí." A flicker of something in their depths. Was it contempt? Surely not. "Once they had a house here in the city."

"Was—was she very beautiful?"

"Sí. But it was a cold beauty, like a flower one can admire but not touch," Consuelo returned, and then quickly turned and hurried into the kitchen as if afraid of more questions. Antoinette went upstairs with the definite feeling she knew much more than she was willing to reveal.

An hour later Antoinette changed into her blue traveling dress and slipped out of the house while Consuelo was preparing dinner. She had never been out before without a protective duenna, but tonight she was experiencing the desire to be totally alone. Asking directions from the flower woman at the corner of the street, she purchased a large bunch of asters and marigolds and determinedly set out for her destination.

The church of the Ángel d'Oro was in a narrow cobbled street some fifteen minutes walk from the Calle de Comerciantes. Antoinette drew aside her skirts to avoid the outstretched legs of a ragged lépero sprawled across her path and almost walked into an oxcart in her efforts to avoid him. As soon as the light began to fade, the streets and squares became transformed, filled with pulque sellers and their fully laden carts, drunks and léperos and street women. She was more than a little nervous as she hurried on. The little church, with its candles burning before the altar, was empty when she arrived. In the swiftly fading light she sought and found her father's grave, set aside from the others in a small corner of the churchyard. Someone had erected a rough fence around it, and on a piece of wood in the place of a headstone were carved the words ADOLPHE DUBEC— SOLDAT DE LA FRANCE. Tears blurring her vision, she knelt to lay the flowers below the cross and say a silent farewell to her father.

She had been prepared for this to be an upsetting moment, but her mind was a turmoil of conflicting thoughts as she hurried homeward. Her father had loved Mexico, yet all it had given him was a six-foot plot of land hundreds of miles from his homeland, where no one cared about the death of another French soldier. The magnetism of the country held her too. It bound her to an empty house in a strange country, her only companion the wife of a dead Loyalist, one of the people who were responsible for the murder of Adolphe Dubec. Once again she found herself wondering what she was doing here with people who were not her own. They even regarded her with suspicion, since Carlota, their Empress, had shown an interest in her welfare. She knew she should go home, but it was a dreaded thought. The house would be unbearably lonely now, and she had no one to turn to for comfort or guidance. Utter desolation descended on her like a black cloud.

As she turned into the Calle de Comerciantes the thunder of horses' hooves filled her ears, followed by the sound of sporadic gunfire, and through blurred vision she saw a dozen or more soldiers and rurales turn the corner. Ahead of them ran three Mexicans. People fled for their lives to avoid being trampled underfoot as pulque barrows were overturned and horses mounted the pavements in pursuit of the fleeing men. The screams of women mingled with the shouting of the soldiers. As they passed, Antoinette flattened herself against the wall. She glimpsed two desperate-faced boys barely out of their teens and a third who looked no more than twelve.

"Halt or we fire." The order in French rang out harshly behind them, and when it was ignored, a hail of bullets sprayed the ground around them. It was a miracle she was not hit. Before her horrified gaze one man fell, blood streaming from a head wound. His companion did not even slow down, but the youngster spun around and seized Antoinette by the arm, trying to force himself behind her.

"Señorita, por Dios, help me. They will kill me," he pleaded. Dirty hands clawed at her arm; the upturned face was wet with sweat and grime and fear. She felt revulsion and pity combined and instinctively stepped in front of the trembling boy as some of the soldiers drew rein before her.

"Il est mort." One of them, a sergeant in the Foreign Legion, turned over the fallen man with the toe of his boot before rounding on Antoinette. "Stand aside, woman, or you will be hurt too."

"Don't you dare lay a hand on me or this poor child. You brutes! Riding him down like an animal. Is this what the French soldier has become—a killer of children?" Her scornful tone and the fact she addressed them in French took the soldiers momentarily by surprise. Defiantly she stared into the hard faces confronting her, at the rifles aimed at her body, and sensed the indecision her outburst had caused. Then a horse and rider materialized out of the shadows, and a Mexican officer dismounted beside them to take command of the situation.

"Where is he? If you have allowed him to escape I'll have every one of you confined to quarters for a month." The harsh voice of Ramón Chávez was unmistakable, and Antoinette almost cried with relief.

"Thank goodness you are here. Tell these men to stand aside and let me pass, Major," she said quickly.

"It is you who must stand aside, señorita, and give us the boy. Be quick now, before my patience is exhausted, and I order them to take him," the officer returned curtly.

"He is only a child—" Antoinette began, horrified, and got no further. Ramón Chávez snapped out an order. She was seized by the nearest soldier and swung away from the wall with such force that she lost her balance and would have fallen had she not been grasped by the outstretched hands of his companion. Bitter reproaches died on her lips as she saw the boy pull a knife from inside his shirt and lunge toward the major, his face a mask of hate. He was cornered, desperate, and extremely dangerous. His opponent neatly sidestepped, tripped the wild-eyed youngster, and brought the butt of his pistol crashing down on his head.

"Take him away. I'll question him later."

"Yes, Major. What about the woman, sir?"

"I'll deal with her. Get him out of my sight. He turns my stomach."

Antoinette suddenly found herself released and pushed unceremoniously out of the way. As she leaned back against the wall, fighting to regain her reeling senses, the soldiers loaded the unconscious boy and his dead companion onto two horses and rode off. From the far side of the street curious faces peered through the windows at the last two remaining figures and watched the tall Mexican officer catch the woman by the wrist and propel her forcibly along the street and into one of the houses.

"Let me go—you—are hurting me," Antoinette cried out. She was bruised, panting, fighting against the painful grip on her wrist. "I am not one of your soldaderas to be treated in this fashion."

"You are lucky you were not killed, you little fool!" Ramón Chávez pushed her away with a contemptuous gesture. Obviously the insult was not lost on him, and they faced each other in the courtyard like warlords about to do battle.

"The indiscriminate way your men were shooting, I could have been hit—others too."

"You could also have been ripped apart with the knife that murderous little thug was hiding. I've no doubt he would have used it on you had you not been softhearted enough to take pity on him."

"Nonsense, he was only a child. No more than twelve."

"He is fifteen, and the two men with him were his brothers. Faces of saints and hearts as black as pitch."

"He—he didn't look that old, but what does it matter? Twelve or fifteen, how can you justify riding him down or shooting his brothers in cold blood. I saw it. You can't deny it. It was disgusting! You ordered it—you who profess to care so much about your people. You are as inhuman as the men who did it. How could I have been so wrong about you? Anyone who could act so cruelly has no heart, no compassion, no feelings." She spoke recklessly, part of her mind still lingering at the lonely graveside at the church of the Ángel d'Oro, part of her shielding a frightened child. Her mind was closed against the more pleasant interludes she had experienced with him over the past weeks.

In the half-light she saw Ramón Chávez' face grow taut with anger and his eyes begin to blaze. The long barely healed wound on his cheek made him look almost menacing.

"This concern of yours is most touching, but unfortunately it does not help the two old people who died tonight after being tortured to reveal where they had hidden their life savings. The owner of a wineshop and his wife, both over seventy. The woman was first, the husband later, after she had died. They were poor, they had no money and they said so. God knows how many times they must have said it, but they were killed anyway, and your innocent-faced fifteen-year-old was the one who wielded the knife and enjoyed every moment of it." The words were hurled at Antoinette with a violence that robbed her of all speech. She not only heard but felt his fury and knew it was deserved. She half turned, a rising nausea in her stomach, but a hand closed over her already bruised wrist, dragging her back until his furious features were barely inches from her own—white, shocked, ashamed. "So I have no heart, eh, chica? No feelings! This I must show you is not so."

Like a tight band around her body his arms held her a helpless captive against his chest. His mouth locked on her in a kiss that combined bitterness and desperation and shocked her to the very depths of her being with its passion. She had no strength to fight, no will to resist the burning kisses that bruised and burned her mouth. As abruptly as she had been seized she was released, left to lean weakly back against the fountain and tremble at the secret she could no longer deny as the street door slammed shut behind Ramón's departing figure.

The courtyard was suddenly flooded with light as a door opened behind Antoinette, and Consuelo stood there with an oil lamp. Conscious of her tear-streaked face, Antoinette slipped past her and went into the sala, where she stood in the middle of the room shaking from head to toe.

"Is the señorita ill? I heard a noise outside—a fight perhaps? Madre de Dios, you are shivering. Shall I prepare a hot bath?"

"Yes, in a moment. Some—some men"—she balked at using the word "murdered," remembering Ramón's description of what had taken place—"killed an old man and his wife. The soldiers caught up with them outside the house. It was horrible."

"And you saw it. Poor niña, no wonder you are upset," Consuelo murmured sympathetically. As Antoinette turned to look at her she saw something else in the girl's eyes and realized the maid had been a witness to the argument with Ramón.

"You heard us. Were you spying on me?" She knew the suggestion was ridiculous the moment she had made it, but the remembrance of those undignified moments filled her with shame.

"I was concerned for the señorita's safety, but when I saw she was with the major, I knew I had nothing to fear."

"How can you say that when you—you saw how he treated me. Like a . . ."

"The word is soldadera, señorita. Do not be afraid to say it to me, it is nothing to be ashamed of. A camp follower—I was one. I went with my husband wherever he went, no matter how dangerous it was, because my place was by his side. Someone from your world cannot comprehend what it is to follow a man in order to be with him and tend his wounds, heal his mind after a battle, mend his soul with love that knows no boundaries and no shame. I have none for what I was. If Paco were alive now I would be with him still." She broke off, and for the first time since Antoinette had seen her at the shrine of Guadalupe, bright tears glistened in the liquid brown eyes. "You were unfair to the major. It has been a long time since he has looked at a woman the way he looks at you."

"You knew him before you came here, didn't you?" Consuelo's outburst had sobered Antoinette and made her realize how deeply the girl had suffered.

She nodded.

"I was raised in his village. I too am a mestiza. I attended his wedding. His wife ran off with a French officer a few months after the expeditionary force arrived in Mexico. The major followed her. There was a duel. He killed her lover and then gave her to the French army with his compliments. He did not see her again until her death. She was killed in a Juarista attack some months later. It is true his bitterness has led him to make love to other women without love in him, but with you it could have been different."

Antoinette's encounter with Ramón was still vivid in her mind on the night she went to dine at Luis' quinta. Despite the cordial atmosphere that prevailed she found it impossible to join in.

"So here you are. I was beginning to believe Doña Isabel's singing had sent you rushing home." Antoinette looked up with a smile as Luis Santos sat down on the seat beside her, his brown eyes alight with amusement. She had slipped away to the sanctuary of the garden immediately after an excellent dinner, leaving the other guests in the sala. "Are you not finding the quinta as entertaining as on your last visit?"

"Forgive me, Luis, it was rude to leave, but the garden is so beautiful in the moonlight—" She broke off, remembering the lake at Chapultepec with the moon about to rise over the water, and Ramón plucking a bloodred flower for her to wear. She hated the memory because she found it impossible to put him out of her mind. "Did anyone notice me?"

"No, they are either asleep or fawning over my attractive sister. It is time I found her another husband."

Antoinette looked at him in astonishment, but found he was perfectly serious. Somehow she could not imagine Mercedes Santos being made to marry any man not of her choice. She quickly checked the first indiscreet question that rose to her lips and asked instead, "Have you anyone in mind?"

"Several eligible men—one a widower, but a man of good background and with a will to match that of Mercedes. She needs someone she cannot dominate. Lately I have found her becoming almost unbearable. Sí, I think it is definitely time she remarried."

"But will she? I mean—she might object."

"My dear Antoinette, if your father had selected a husband for you, would you have married him?"

"Yes, I suppose I would."

"Then as Mercedes' brother and the only remaining male in the family, the responsibility of finding her a suitable husband must be mine. She needs security and a home of her own, especially now. . . ." He did not finish, and Antoinette looked at him curiously. "Come, let us walk and enjoy the moonlight."

"Alone, señor, without a duenna?" she mocked softly, and Luis drew her to her feet with a laugh.

"In my own home I can make the rules or break them. Sometimes I just bend them to suit my convenience. Are you glad you came tonight?"

"I have been looking forward to it. What a pity the Empress could not be here. I saw her the other day, and she was so disappointed at having to refuse your invitation. Did you know she is going to France to see Napoleon?"

"And beg for more money? Sí, it is the worst-kept secret in the city. I feel sorry for her. I have a great sense of foreboding—something I cannot explain. With her gone and Don Maximiliano at loggerheads with Marshal Bazaine, he has no one he can trust implicitly. It is not good for a man to be alone. Will you come and visit my quinta more often, Antoinette? Like the Emperor I am very much alone."

"Why, yes, if you wish. May I bring Consuelo with me next time? For some reason she was reluctant to come tonight. I think she is shy."

"Ah, yes, Soledad told me about that one. You are not being very wise, niña. Consuelo Vargas will bring you nothing but trouble. You know her background?"

"Major Chávez made sure I did. He too tried to persuade me against taking her into the house, but nothing has happened so far, and I don't see why it should. The poor girl has suffered a tragic loss. I refuse to turn my back on her."

Luis took Antoinette by the hand and drew her against the side of one of the stable buildings. Before she could guess his intention he had bent and gently, but firmly, kissed her on the mouth. She was so surprised she remained immobile and unresisting. He drew back with a hollow chuckle.

"Obviously I am the wrong man."

"No! I mean—I'm sorry, Luis, I didn't mean to hurt you, but it was so unexpected. We hardly know each other," Antoinette stammered. How different his kiss had been from the ones Ramón had forced on her.

"Then there is no one else? No man you are perhaps attracted to? Forgive the personal nature of my questions, but I do have a good reason."

"A man—here in Mexico? No, there is no one." She could almost feel the relief that swept over him and was seized with shame at the blatant lie.

"I'm glad. He told me it was that way, but I wanted to hear it from your own lips," Luis muttered, pressing another kiss against her cheek and then her neck.

"Luis, I don't understand. Please stop." Antoinette's hands held him at a distance. She had come to regard him as a friend, but nothing more. Her denial of any involvement had obviously prompted him to reveal deeper feelings she had known nothing of. "Who told you I was free? With whom have you dared to discuss me?"

"Don't be angry, chica. I had to know if there was a chance for me before I spoke, so naturally I mentioned the way I felt to Ramón. He understood perfectly."

Antoinette did not know whether to be shocked or angry at his confession. In the darkness her cheeks burned with confusion.

"You discussed me with Major Chávez! When?"

"This morning, as a matter of fact. He stopped by to tell me he is heading the Empress' escort to Veracruz. I must admit I knew you had been seeing him over the past week and I was beginning to wonder if you found him—interesting."

"You sound as if you have been talking to the Empress. She too gave me a lecture on my choice of friends. I was under the impression I am old enough to see whom I please when it pleases me."

"Now I have offended you." Luis' voice was contrite. "That was not my intention. You see, I wanted to be sure your heart was free before I asked you to be my wife."

"Your wife!" Antoinette murmured weakly. She hardly felt his arms about her or the touch of his lips against her hair. This was beyond her wildest imagination. "Oh, Luis —I didn't realize. . . ."

"When I first saw you, all dusty and disheveled from the trip from Veracruz, I told myself you were the woman who would one day become the mistress of my home."

"But—but I don't love you," she protested. "I could not marry you. It would not be fair."

"Love, chica? We are talking of marriage, not love. My kind of marriage. Here in Mexico a man chooses the woman he knows will make him happy and grace his house. Love, if he is lucky, will come with time. You above all women in my life over the years are the only one I have ever considered marrying, because I know we are right for one another. Love could happen for us, I feel it. Already it is close for me. I have only to be near you to know this. You are very quiet. Have I upset you?"

"No. I am honored by your proposal. . . ."

"But you are young and dream of a handsome man to sweep you off your feet. Am I not young and handsome? I am rich. You will have everything you want—a fine house, your own servants, as much freedom as you desire. I would not impose on you the restrictions most Mexican women have to endure, for once you bore my name I know you would never dishonor it." Passion gave depth to the quiet voice coming out of the darkness. Antoinette could not see his face, but she knew every word he spoke was from the heart, and his sincerity made her hate the way she had lied to him. There was another man in her life and always would be, regardless of the fact he was not aware of her as a woman. "Nor would I wish to keep you from your native land. We could go to France together often."

"Luis, please stop, my head is reeling." Antoinette clutched at his sleeves with trembling fingers, and immediately she was drawn into the circle of his arms. She felt very safe cradled against his chest, secure from the deceitfulness of her own thoughts. He was so sweet, the kind of gentle, understanding man any girl in her right mind should rush to marry, and yet she knew that they were not meant for one another.

"You have not refused me," Luis murmured hopefully.

"Nor can I accept you. You were right, Luis, I have always thought I would marry for love, which is why my father never raised the subject of marriage. He knew that only my heart could dictate to me."

"Then don't answer me now. Stay in Mexico. Let me show you how perfectly matched we are, or could be. It is such a small thing. Will you agree?"

"I don't know. I want to stay, but I don't want to give you any false hopes. If I remain it will be with you as my friend—as now—nothing more until I can think clearly about your proposal and decide. That is not such a small thing to ask."

"Rather than risk losing you I will agree to anything," Luis returned.

"Is this why you are so anxious to get Mercedes married?" Antoinette asked, anxious to draw the conversation away from herself.

"Two women in the same house would drive me insane. Of course, I want to be alone with you. Mercedes has plagued my life for too long, now it's time for someone else to deal with her tantrums."

"Surely you need not look far," she said meaningfully.

"Who are you thinking of—surely not Ramón? No, he is not prospective husband material for my sister. He has been hurt too much in the past to be caught again."

"When you told me he had been married, you forgot to

mention his wife ran off and left him. Consuelo told me of a duel. Did you know of that too?"

"Yes. I first met Ramón a few months before his wife left him. They were living in Mexico City. He was not in the army then and he preferred to remain at this hacienda at Val Verde and raise horses. If it had not been for her, I don't believe he would ever have left it. Since her death he spends all his spare time there. The place is run by an overseer, and there is an aged grandmother still living there. He adores her. She is his one link with the past. I think I told you I had once seen him in a murderous rage—that was the night before the duel. After that he disappeared for over a month. When we met again he had accepted Don Maximiliano's invitation to train a regiment of Mexican cavalry. He never mentions his wife, and I never ask. Old wounds are better not reopened."

Then what of Coatlicue?' Antoinette wanted to ask. Why should he wear the amulet of a woman who had betrayed him? Did he love her still, despite her treachery, or was it a reminder of what they had once shared—a lasting monument to the agony he had suffered?

All the way home Luis' proposal filled Antoinette's mind so that when she first saw the horse tethered outside she did not fully comprehend the implication. Paying off the coachman, she opened the gate and had stepped inside before realizing to whom the big black stallion belonged.

He stood in the sala, a glass of wine in one hand, talking to Consuelo. At the sight of Antoinette in the doorway he quickly finished his drink and picked up his shako. The maid began to apologize for not hearing her mistress come in.

"Will you make some hot chocolate for me to take up to bed?" Antoinette asked, waving aside her excuses. "Perhaps the major would care for some before he leaves."

"Thank you, no. I had no intention of being here when you arrived," Ramón Chávez returned. His eyes appraised her dress of Burgundy silk and the dull-red rubies glowing at her throat. A smile tugged at the corners of his mouth. "I trust you enjoyed your evening?"

Consuelo glanced at them both, then quickly left the room, being careful to close the door tightly behind her.

"It was most enjoyable." Aware of his gaze following her, she poured herself a glass of sherry and relaxed in the nearest chair, forcing herself to remain calm beneath the scrutiny of his dark eyes. The wound on his cheek was almost healed, she thought, unlike the wound she could not see. There was tension between them, and she could feel it.

"Did you accept him?"

She gasped at the audacity of the question.

"What business is it of yours, Major Chávez?"

"After all the good advice I gave Luis he was certain to propose tonight. I see no reason why you should have refused him."

"Then I suggest you know less about the workings of a woman's mind than you profess to," Antoinette returned coldly. "To discuss me with Luis was an insult in itself. To presume I would accept his proposal of marriage shows how little you know me. Just what did you tell him to make him feel I was—was free? Attracted to him?"

"Did·I do that? I merely set his mind at rest about our relationship. Certain gossip had reached him, and he felt there might be a mutual attachment. Of course I denied it immediately, as you would have done, and told him you cannot stand the sight of me. I gave him no details, you understand—I simply said what he wanted to hear."

"You had no right. I will not have my private life discussed like some snippet of gossip in the marketplace." Antoinette was appalled by his arrogance.

"My apologies, señorita. It will not happen again." His smile mocked her. "You must be tired. I will leave now."

As he pulled the shako firmly down over his thick black hair she stood up and put down her glass, suddenly remembering he was going away.

"Luis mentioned you are going to Veracruz with the Empress." She tried to make her voice sound unconcerned. "Do you travel with her to Europe?"

"No. But I shall be away long enough for you to give some serious thought to Luis' offer. Think it over very carefully. He is a good man."

"I have no intention of accepting him. I don't love him," she said simply, and his brows came together in a deep frown.

"Love! What does a child like you know of love?"

She flushed at his scorn, her aching heart longing for him to reach out and take her in his arms so that she could show him how quickly she had grown into a woman. Instead she said, "Unlike you, Major, I know nothing of love or the heartbreaks it can bring, but perhaps one day I will meet a man who will teach me and then I will be able to answer your question."

"Be careful he does not break that trusting little heart into a thousand unmendable pieces," Ramón returned. He stood in the doorway, undecided, Antoinette thought, whether to go or stay. His eyes locked on her face until she felt herself begin to tremble. Was he remembering those wild kisses also, wanting to hold her again? Ruthlessly she quashed the impulse to soften her attitude. He did not deserve it after the way he had treated her. To tell Luis she detested him, to discuss her as if she were a servant—it was unforgivable.

"I consider your intrusion into my personal affairs most detestable, Major Chávez. Will you please go."

She did not sleep at all that night, and early in the morning when she heard the sound of bugles heralding the departure of the Empress and her escort for Veracruz, she turned her face into the pillows and wept at the foolish pride that had forbidden her to admit she had come to know not only love, but the heartache of a love denied.

SIX

On July 26, 1866, the Liberal army of Benito Juárez was becoming such a threat in and around Monterrey that French troops operating there were evacuated. Saltillo was abandoned on August 5, Tampico a day later, and the troops were pulled back to reinforce the garrison at the small mining town of San Luis Potosí, which was now the headquarters of the French army. Three days later a regiment of Chasseurs d'Afrique under the able command of Colonel du Priel attacked and severely defeated a group of rebels at Noria de Custodio. When the battle was over more than eighty men lay dead upon the field, and French pride was for the moment appeased.

With Monterrey evacuated and Chihuahua in their hands since March, the Liberals began a determined gathering of their forces around the Imperialist stronghold of Durango. They were aided by a large number of Indian guerrillas, whose hit-and-run tactics upon the supply trains running the gauntlet into the besieged town caused havoc and chaos, and eventually succeeded in cutting all communications between the French and their headquarters.

Antoinette read the reports of the victories and defeats with mixed feelings. War had come to Mexico, but not yet to Mexico City, where life continued as usual. She found it hard to imagine men fighting and being killed in some other place with a strange-sounding name. Since Carlota's departure she had spent most of her time riding with

Luis, who came to the house more frequently as the weeks passed. He was teaching her to speak Spanish, which she practiced whenever she went out to shop. The days seemed endless—hot, stormy days that frayed her temper and made her want to go home to the sanctuary of the château in France. For over a week she stayed at the Quinta Santos, and gradually her disposition improved. Luis made her laugh when her thoughts began to stray and occupied her mind with tales of family history. She loved him for it—yet it was the kind of love one has for a brother or a very close friend. Although she guessed Mercedes resented her presence at the quinta, Luis' sister rarely let her feelings show. Antoinette wondered how quickly the polite mask would have shattered had she heard Luis reeling off the list of prospective husbands he was compiling. He even went so far as to discuss them with Antoinette and ask for her opinion, but she wisely declined to comment, much to his amusement.

On the day she returned to the house in the Calle de Comerciantes the newspapers were full of speculation on fresh victories for the French forces, since Marshal Bazaine had recently returned from France. Many of them predicted the war would be over by the end of the year.

"Has the señorita a moment to spare? Father Ignatius is downstairs and would like to speak with you." Consuelo stood in the doorway of the bedroom, her eyes on the lace shawl around her mistress' shoulders.

Slowly Antoinette put away the present Luis had given her before they parted, trying not to show the hurt she felt at Consuelo's cool tone. There had been an indefinable rift between them since Ramón Chávez had last visited the house. Whereas before that night she had been almost a friend, now she was only a maid, polite and reserved and totally indifferent to any attempts to breach the gap between them. Antoinette realized her short spell away had not improved matters and shrugged briefly.

"Very well."

She took tea with Father Ignatius in the sala and learned of an outbreak of smallpox that had descended on some of the outlying villages. La viruela! A contribution first brought to the country by Hernán Cortés and his men, she was told with a tight smile. The padre was collecting for the poor stricken victims. Money for medicine, clothes, and blankets. Immediately Antoinette's sympathies were aroused. Calling for Consuelo to help her, she went upstairs to the unused rooms, to the store cupboards full of linen, and took out all but the bare minimum required for her own use. Then she went down to the kitchen to sort through the huge larder.

"No," Father Ignatius protested as she reached for her purse. "I cannot take money after all this."

"Then you must let me know what else you require, and I will do my best to see you have it. Can you send someone to me with a list?"

"If it is possible to spare anyone. La viruela strikes more fear into people's hearts than the devil himself. I have few helpers."

"I am sure the señorita could spare me to come with you, Father," Consuelo said. "She has little need of me here."

Slowly Antoinette nodded, not showing her concern at the request.

"If that is what you want, Consuelo. Have we somewhere to put these things, Father?"

"Sí, I have a cart outside," the priest answered, gathering up an armful of blankets. "You will be rewarded for such generosity, Señorita Dubec."

"I want no reward, only peace of mind, and at the moment it seems God is unwilling to give it to me," Antoinette replied quietly, following him out into the street. A small wooden cart with a mule harnessed to it stood near the gate. It was almost empty.

Father Ignatius turned on her with a troubled frown and laid a gentle hand on her shoulder.

"So you still hunger for the death of those who killed your father. I will pray to God to deliver you from this thirst for revenge before it destroys your happiness—perhaps even your life."

Two days later Consuelo returned to the house. She looked as though she had not slept at all during her absence, and the enmity between them vanished as Antoinette led her into the kitchen and poured out two cups of freshly made coffee.

"You see, I am managing quite well," she said cheerfully.

Consuelo's eyes flickered over the two red blisters on one arm where Antoinette had burned herself on the huge oven while attempting to do some baking. A faint smile touched her tired features.

"How are things with Father Ignatius? Did you bring a list?"

"Sí." The girl produced a piece of paper and proceeded to reel off a variety of items. "We need everything, señorita. I shall not be allowed to come again."

"Not come—why? Who is there to stop you?"

"There is a small French garrison nearby. The soldiers are afraid the fever will spread to them, and they have set up a roadblock. No one who goes in after tonight will be allowed out until the fever has gone. Father Ignatius has moved on to another village, only a few miles from my own. The sickness is worse there. He has only indios and myself to help him and hardly any medicine."

"Is there no doctor at the garrison?"

"Sí, but the village lies on the edge of rebel-held territory. The soldiers fear not only la viruela, but the Juaristas too. Why should they care if a few Mexicans die? It will be less to fight against in the end."

"So much for their promise to cure the sick," Antoinette answered in disgust. "Have the rebels no doctors with them?"

"One has already been to help us, but he had to leave when the roadblock was put up. Father Ignatius will not allow him to come back for fear he may take the sickness back among his own men."

"He is right of course. If it should spread . . . But that does not excuse the French. Their actions were unforgivable. Give me a list, Consuelo, and let us see how full we can fill the cart again."

"We, señorita?"

"Why not? I will be of more use with you. Oh, Consuelo, when we come back, please, please, teach me to make tortillas."

The village of Río Verde lay twenty miles southeast of the capital on the road to Puebla. The cluster of whitewashed houses grouped around the small square, with its fountain where the women did their washing, lay deep in a valley and was backed by rich pastureland and green, rolling hills. It appeared to be a prosperous place, unlike the two villages Antoinette and Consuelo had passed through earlier that day, where the sound of women sobbing from behind shuttered windows had followed them on their way. It had added to the sense of desolation they already felt at the almost total absence of people.

They had successfully filled every item on the list, except for the most vital one—medicine. Antoinette's personal plea to local doctors had met with apologetic refusals. With so much fighting going on in outlying districts, all medical supplies had been strictly rationed by the army, she was told. Not one item could be spared to combat a small outbreak of fever. She fumed for hours over that phrase: "a small outbreak." According to Consuelo it had already claimed more than thirty lives in two villages, and at Río Verde it was worse, with more than half the inhabitants suspected cases.

Most of them were a blend of Indian and Spanish blood, Antoinette thought, looking into the dark, aquiline faces of the men coming forward to help Consuelo from the cart. They treated her with respect, almost with reverence, neither of which they afforded Antoinette. Several men and women drifted out of their homes to watch her climb down, but no one moved forward to help her or to offer to unload the badly needed supplies she

112

had helped to bring. Here she was la gringa—an outcast, unwanted. Ignoring the hostile faces, she grabbed an armful of linen and hurried up the steps into the church Father Ignatius had turned into a hospital. The sick lay in rows on the floor. Only a few had beds, the rest lay on straw pallets attended by village women. She remembered how close they were to rebel-held land and wondered how many of the people before her were not only sympathetic to Benito Juárez, but had fought for his cause and sheltered his men in their homes.

"Doña Antoinette!" Father Ignatius was hurrying toward her, his face blank with amazement. "Child! What are you doing here? Didn't Consuelo tell you we are surrounded by troops and not allowed to leave?"

"She mentioned the roadblock, yes."

"That was yesterday. This morning we found all the access roads guarded by soldiers. Their orders are to keep us here until the fever has abated."

So that was why they had not been challenged by the silent men two miles outside the village, Antoinette thought. They were prisoners!

"Consuelo and I have brought you everything you asked for except the medicine." She forced a brave smile to her stiff lips. There was no turning back now. "We tried hard to get even a little, but the stores have been requisitioned. What can be done without it?"

"Isolating the sick." Consuelo put down the bundle she carried and came up to them. "That's what can be done."

"She is right," Father Ignatius said, nodding. "This is not the first time I have encountered smallpox. Over the years I have discovered that if we can get the sick to new, clean surroundings, then we stand a chance of saving most of them. It has worked in the past—it could work here, with God's help."

"Try telling that to the legionnaires by the roadside," Consuelo broke in bitterly. "See if they care how many die. The life of a Mexican is cheap compared to that of a Frenchman."

"I too am French," Antoinette said between stiff lips,

"and at the moment very ashamed of my countrymen. Father Ignatius, is there nothing we can do? If we could move from the village, where would we go?"

"There is an abandoned camp about three miles south of here," the priest replied. "The soldiers used it as quarters many years ago, but when the troubles began they deserted it. You passed it on your way here. I was going to turn it into a hospital and a school for the local people."

"Have you bought the land?"

"No, Doña Antoinette, it was given to me—by you."

She looked at him puzzled.

"Me!"

"Indirectly. The land once belonged to your father, I believe. You asked Major Chávez to dispose of it for you. When he told me of your ideas on how to use it I was most impressed. Your concern for us all then—and now—will never be forgotten. But why the surprise? Did he not tell you the transaction had been completed?"

"No, I—I have not seen him for some time," Antoinette stammered. Her head was reeling. So that was how he had disposed of the land. A present to Father Ignatius—in her name. First he tried to marry her off to Luis, then he presented her as a kindhearted benefactress to the poor. "Can we not reach this place?" she asked at length.

"The soldiers will not allow us to pass."

"Have you talked to them?"

"They will not listen and they are prepared to use any means to prevent us from leaving."

"I will try to reason with them—it is your land after all," Antoinette said determinedly.

"I cannot allow that. It is too dangerous."

"Wait. There is a way if you are truly serious about helping us, señorita." Consuelo was staring into Antoinette's face, scrutinizing it, as if trying to decide whether or not she could be trusted.

"I am here, am I not? As much a prisoner as you," she retorted angrily.

"But not as likely to get yourself shot if you show yourself to the soldiers, as I most certainly would be. I am known to them."

Her words chilled Antoinette. They were almost an admission that she was still with the Juaristas—perhaps even a spy, as Soledad had said.

"I forbid you to use Doña Antoinette in whatever it is you have in mind," Father Ignatius interrupted.

"You are outnumbered, Father. The señorita may not like what I am, but I believe her first concern is with the sick, why else would she have come here?"

"I could always be a spy," Antoinette returned, keeping a tight rein on her temper. Suddenly Consuelo had taken on new stature. The people gathered around them were watching her closely as if expecting—yes—leadership.

"Then if you are not shot by your own side, you will most certainly be shot by mine. We are wasting time. For the present we both have the same objective—do we join forces, señorita?"

"Very well." Antoinette nodded slowly. She was not in a position to refuse, and even if that were possible, she knew she could not desert the people she had come to help. "What is it I must do?"

Consuelo turned to the nearest man and spoke swiftly in a tongue that sounded like a mixture of Spanish and Indian and was totally alien to Antoinette's ears. By the time she had finished talking they were nearly alone in the church as men, women, and children hurried off in different directions.

"We must be at the camp before it grows dark." Consuelo considered the fever-ridden figures a few feet away, her brown eyes filled with compassion. "Soon they will have a chance to get well. Julio will bring you a horse, señorita. You will take the south road. Half a mile along it you will see a narrow arroyo. Follow it toward the hills. It will bring you to where the soldiers are, but from such a direction that they will think you are lost—and that is exactly what you will tell them."

"And how will that help evacuate the sick?" Antoinette asked. She recognized the fact that Consuelo was not the quiet, submissive girl she had grown accustomed to over the past weeks and for a moment she rebelled at the flow of orders.

"You will see in good time. What you must do is most important. You must hold the soldiers in conversation for at least ten minutes. Please, ask no more questions, just trust that there is no other way."

Half an hour later Antoinette found herself riding along a narrow cart track away from Río Verde and wondering if she had taken leave of her senses. As she reached the top of a hill and looked back, she could see great activity going on in the square. It appeared that every cart in the whole place was being assembled before the church. For what purpose, she wondered? And then she knew. The soldiers guarding the road ahead were to be ambushed—that was why all the able-bodied men had been conspicuously absent as she left. She was a decoy! She was filled with a combination of anger and fear—the fear for herself should the deception be discovered; the anger for the stupidity of the officer commanding the legionnaires, whose heartless orders had placed his men in their present perilous position. They were French—she was too, but people were dying right in front of her, and somehow nothing mattered but their welfare.

The sun, a red ball of fire as it slowly set in front of her, burned her eyes, and she averted them just in time to see the arroyo Consuelo had mentioned. Carefully she guided her horse over the uneven ground of the burro trail running alongside it, following it through a group of enormous boulders and out onto a grassy prado that bordered a thickly wooded area on one side of her. On the other stretched rich-looking vineyards as far as she could see.

"Qui est là?" A blue-coated soldier stepped out of the trees to her left, a carbine aimed at her body.

"Je suis Marianne Lebeau. Je suis perdue. Aidez-moi, s'il vous plaît." Antoinette's voice shook as she spoke. It gave conviction to her plea for help, and another legion-

116

naire, a sergeant, appeared from the trees and laid a hand across the weapon aimed at her.

"Easy, mon vieux, this is no rebel." The voice was casual, but the eyes that swept over the woman before him were those of an old campaigner, swayed neither by words nor a pretty face and accustomed to relying on instinct. "Lost, mademoiselle? What are you doing out here alone? Where do you come from—the village?"

"What village?" Antoinette knew a bold approach was the only way to deal with this one. Consuelo wanted ten minutes. It would seem like ten years before they were over. "Did you not understand me the first time, Sergeant? I am lost. I am the daughter of a French officer and not accustomed to being accosted like a soldadera or spoken to like a peon. Tell me how to get back to the capital and stand out of my way at once."

The haughty tone and the fierce anger in the blue eyes regarding the two soldiers had the desired effect. The weapon menacing her was lowered. The sergeant even had the good grace to look embarrassed.

"You are heading in the wrong direction, mademoiselle," he replied. "Why have you no escort? It is dangerous to ride in these parts alone. We are close to rebel territory."

"I have seen no one. If I had, I would not have strayed this far. Where is this village you mentioned? I am hot and dusty and would like to rest for a while."

"Not there, mademoiselle—the place has the smallpox. Please, rest with us and I will explain how to get back to the main road."

With a brief shrug Antoinette allowed the man to help her dismount. She still felt he was too suspicious of her, and her heart lurched when he inspected her horse. It was clear the animal had not been ridden far.

"You say you have come from the capital?" She followed him into the trees, to where another soldier sat with his back against a log. Three of them! How many men would Consuelo send?

"No, I did not say that," she returned with a smile. The effort that smile cost her! "I have been to visit the hacienda of one of my father's friends. My horse went lame, and I had to borrow another, which has made me late starting home. If I had not been in such a hurry, perhaps I would not have taken the wrong road, although they all look the same to me. The houses, the people—everything looks the same out here."

The sergeant smiled briefly at the contempt in her voice.

"I know exactly what you mean. Jules, move yourself and let the lady sit down. Are you thirsty, mademoiselle? We have fresh water, and I see you carry none with you."

He missed nothing! Antoinette prayed he would not question her further about her background. She had told so many lies she was beginning to confuse herself. She drank from the canteen he offered, pretending to do so with relish, as if parched.

"Thank you, Sergeant, that was most refreshing." She wanted to be gone from beneath his deliberating gaze, but forced herself to remain still. "May I take the remainder with me?"

"Bien sûr."

When she at last got up, he walked with her back to where the second legionnaire stood beside her horse, knowing he was studying every detail of her appearance. In the fading light, however, with her red hair covered by a sombrero, it was extremely doubtful that he would be able to recognize her again. The swiftly gathering dusk aided the men who converged on them from all sides. Antoinette heard the sound of a muffled groan from within the trees. As the sergeant and his companion spun around, reaching for their weapons, they were borne to the ground and knocked unconscious. She found herself face to face with the man called Julio.

"Well done, señorita." The impassive face broke into a smile. "Do not look so horrified, we will not kill them. All we need is time, and you have given us that."

"Where is Consuelo?" Antoinette asked, mounting her horse.

The man motioned behind them to the cart just appearing on the edge of the prado. It was filled with women and driven by Consuelo.

"The sick ones are following behind. The women go ahead to make the camp ready. They have lamps and food and clean bedding. Father Ignatius has said we must bring no soiled bedding from the village. We have much to do, eh, señorita?"

Antoinette nodded, remembering the dilapidated state of the shacks.

"Yes, Julio—a great deal to do."

Antoinette's first sight of the camp brought tears of dismay to her eyes. The place was a shambles, and only three out of the five shacks were habitable. Bravely containing her apprehension, she dismounted and began an inspection with Julio close on her heels. There was an old stove in one of the places she entered. That at least would enable the sick to be warm and have hot food, she thought with some relief, but the dirt . . .

Consuelo's arrival with some of the village women dragged her out of the depths of despair, and she hurried outside. Soon it would be completely dark, and there was so much to do. Forgetful of the fact that she was an outsider, she assumed instant command.

"First we need wood and plenty of it, to light the stove. We must boil as much hot water as possible and then perhaps we can make at least one of these awful buildings habitable. The floors must be swept and then scrubbed, all the old curtains burned, and the broken furniture moved out."

Women were climbing out of the cart and moving past Antoinette, handing out brooms and buckets and talking among themselves as if she were invisible.

"Silencio!" Consuelo ran up the rickety stairs and stood beside the French girl, her face dark with anger. For several minutes she berated the women in a tone that brought about instant silence. Antoinette caught the words "La Florecita"—Ramón's name for her!—and felt the color rise in her cheeks as each woman in turn stared curiously into her face. How did Consuelo know that name unless Ramón had discussed her with her own servant as openly as he had with Luis?

"What—what did you tell them?" she stammered.

"That they are to obey you because you are Don Ramón's woman and in his absence you speak for him."

"I don't understand. What has Major Chávez to do with these people?"

"Their village is on his land. He is their patrón," Consuelo returned. "His hacienda lies beyond the vineyards."

Don Ramón's woman! Antoinette opened her mouth to strongly deny such an outrageous suggestion, but then changed her mind, realizing that Consuelo had deliberately lied to enable them all to work together in harmony for the sake of the sick. For the moment she would allow the lie to go unchallenged, she thought as she went inside, but only for as long as she remained here.

It took almost an hour to get the first of the stoves working, which flooded the shack with black, choking smoke. When it eventually cleared, it left a layer of thick grime on the already swept floors. Antoinette lost track of all time. She found herself on her hands and knees scrubbing the wooden floors, arranging makeshift beds, or staggering to and fro with heavy cooking pots until every part of her began to ache with the backbreaking work. She had never toiled like this in her life before. Never had her nails been chipped and torn or her hands red and sore from constant immersion in scalding-hot water; never had she worked in such close contact with people who were not of her own social level nor known such pride as the sick ones were carried over the threshold and gently laid down on fresh bedding and fed nourishing soup in the light of the swinging lanterns. Nothing she had ever done in France had given her such a sense of achievement. Sacking was nailed across the windows to keep out the cold, and women took turns sitting beside the old iron stove and feeding it with wood.

"Will the Señorita La Florecita not have something to eat?" One of the women paused beside Antoinette as she knelt on the floor counting the remainder of their precious blankets, holding out a mug of steaming coffee.

"No, gracias. I am not hungry. Where is Father Ignatius?"

"He and Julio have gone to look at the other buildings. Tomorrow we shall clean them too, sí?"

Antoinette nodded, determined not to show how weary she was. She longed to creep close to the stove and sleep, but none of the others gave any sign of being the slightest bit tired, and she was not going to be the first one to rest. Swallowing a mouthful of the coffee, she put the mug to one side, dragged herself up onto legs that felt like lead, and went outside. She found Father Ignatius alone outside one of the other shacks. A light showed from within, and she could hear the sound of a man whistling. It was well after midnight, but work was still continuing.

"It will make a fine school, will it not?"—the priest turned and came to her with a smile—"but first I think we must have a hospital—a good hospital with a doctor and a well-stocked medicine chest."

"I wish you luck, Father, but what chance will you have when everyone is against you?" In the light of the overhead lamp the outline of the buildings looked grim and forbidding. What if all their efforts had been in vain —if she were infected? What madness had brought her here to endanger her own life for people who resented her presence and that of every other French person in their country?

"What am I doing here, Father?" She spoke her thoughts aloud. She was tired, confused. "What is it that binds me to Mexico?"

"Only you can answer that, my child. Search deep in your soul, and you will find the answer."

"God?"

"I've no doubt He has a hand in it. Do you not find it strange that despite the hatred you felt for these people after the death of your father, you now find yourself an important part of their lives? This piece of land you gave away in bitterness has now been given back to them with love."

"But I don't belong."

"If you think that, then there is nothing I can say or do to make you feel otherwise, but you are wrong. If you don't believe me, look into the eyes of the next man or woman you meet and see for yourself."

"They may feel well-disposed toward me now, but when I leave, it will all change. Consuelo lied to them, pretended I was a close friend of Major Chávez, just to get them to work with me. And even she has changed. Here, she is a stranger to me."

"These are her people, and she loves them."

"And I am an outsider."

"Because you wish to be."

"No, that isn't true. . . ."

"I believe it is." Father Ignatius' eyes searched Antoinette's indignant features. "Do not be angry, my child, be patient. Above all, be honest with yourself. The scar left by your father's death has not yet healed, and the line dividing that hatred from the new feeling you have for these people is very thin."

"He died unnecessarily," Antoinette said dully. She could not deny his words, for they were true.

"Many women from Río Verde have lost husbands or sons since Napoleon first sent troops into Mexico. They too have long memories. Are you so different from them or from Consuelo, whose husband was liberated on the very day your father died, only to meet his death before a firing squad less than a month later? Both of you have suffered—let it end there. Stay with us because your heart asks it of you, not in the hope of someday seeing El Padrino led through the city to his execution. His men deprived you of a loved one, but how many men do you think your father's soldiers killed that day?"

"Father, please, I don't want to hear any more." When he talked this way it was impossible not to be moved.

"I am only trying to show you El Padrino is just a man fighting the only way he knows how, to help his people. You think of him as a murderer, but to my people he is a hero."

"Do you, a man of the cloth, condone what he is doing?" she exclaimed, her mind clouding with suspicion.

"As a priest I am against all acts of violence, but each time I hear of his men freeing prisoners or hostages taken by the French, I must admit I go down on my knees and thank God."

Antoinette stared at him in silence for a long moment, then in a quiet tone she asked, "How is it you know so much about him?"

"Moving from village to village as I do, I hear many tales—some to be believed, others . . ." The priest shrugged his shoulders. "If you persist in your desire for vengeance, then I have given you a way to have it. Report our conversation to the authorities, and I will most certainly be arrested. Quién sabe? Perhaps they will be able to make me talk! Are you prepared to have my death on your conscience?"

That night Antoinette slept in one of the smaller buildings wrapped in a blanket beside Consuelo and the other women. In the days that followed they took turns caring for the sick, cooking the meals, and cleaning and preparing more space. Everything that came into contact with the fever victims was burned after use; the women covered their hair and made sure everything was scrupulously clean, and after each tour of duty everyone stripped off and washed in the crude bathhouse Julio had erected behind the building or went down to the river to bathe in the icy-cold water. Clothes were washed and spread out to dry in the sun. Antoinette soon learned never to leave her things out in the afternoon after a sudden rainstorm soaked the only change of clothing she had, forcing her to borrow from someone near her size.

Four people died within the next six days, and one of the women contracted the fever. Another collapsed with fatigue, but gradually it became clear to everyone the isolation was working. La viruela was diminishing, and when she realized this, Antoinette joined the other women and wept openly with relief.

No soldiers came near them, and by the end of a week she had ceased to worry about the sentries she had helped to trick. Sometimes at night Julio took one or two men and slipped back to the village, returning with news and food, for their rations were rapidly diminishing. The soldiers were still guarding a half-empty village, he told an amused gathering. They were too frightened to venture into it to see what had happened, but did not dare to withdraw any men in case the inhabitants tried to leave.

The sound of moving horses awakened Antoinette from a light sleep. It was barely dawn outside, and she reproved herself for sleeping when she should have been keeping a vigilant eye on her patients. She would be alone in the hospital until eight o'clock, when Consuelo would relieve her. She had worked relentlessly, sleeping barely two or three hours a night and undertaking more chores than the other women. Endless cups of coffee kept her on her feet although the strain was now beginning to tell. For a moment she thought she had imagined the sounds—then, more clearly, she heard men's voices and footsteps on the wooden stairs. French soldiers! Getting to her feet in a daze, she reeled unsteadily to the door and flung it open to stare out into the grayness of morning. Soldiers, yes—but Mexican, not French, and pack mules loaded down with sacks of grain and fresh meat, the sight of which made her mouth water. After living on very little else but chicken soup or stew, her stomach ached for a civilized meal.

"Captain Martínez, is it really you?" He was supervising the unloading of the provisions, and she stepped out, eagerly searching for another and experiencing bitter disappointment when she did not find him. Three weeks since he had gone to Veracruz. Was he still there or had he returned with his men?

"Señorita Dubec—you, here? How are you? You have not been ill too?"

"No, just helping Father Ignatius. What a wonderful sight you are! For a moment I was afraid you were French. They tried to keep us from leaving the village."

"Sí, I know. That has all been taken care of. As soon as the major found out what was happening he went straight to the Emperor himself—and here we are—with orders to do everything in our power to see the sickness does not spread."

"It won't, not now," Antoinette answered with a faint smile. "It's almost over. Father Ignatius should have been a doctor, not a priest."

"He was, señorita, many years ago. But after his family was wiped out by this very same sickness he turned to the priesthood."

"So he has been through all this before," Antoinette murmured. "No wonder he was so sure what to do."

"Where would you like us to put all these things?"

"In the small shack behind you—we have turned it into a storeroom. Then you must have some coffee and breakfast. If there is no one in the kitchen, I'm sure you are capable of looking after yourselves. I must go and find Father Ignatius and tell him the good news."

"He was with the major a moment ago," Captain Martínez said, motioning to an adobe hut across the way. Thanking him, Antoinette picked up her skirts and hurried toward the building, which only yesterday had been turned into a well-ordered kitchen and eating place. She tried hard to contain the excitement within her. On the threshold she paused, uncertain of how she would be received after their last encounter. Clustered around the stove, Father Ignatius and three of the village women were already putting out food for the soldiers. Ramón Chávez stood beside the window, his hands resting on Consuelo's shoulders. Her arms were locked tightly around his neck, her face buried against his dusty jacket. His voice, harsh with anxiety, clearly reached Antoinette's ears as she stood frozen, disbelieving, in the doorway.

"You must realize what I felt when I came back and found you gone. I was nearly out of my mind with worry. . . ."

He raised his head, and his dark eyes burned into Antoinette's ashen face, widening with incredulity at the sight of her. The brightly patterned Indian skirt and blouse she wore were creased, since she had slept in them for two nights; the long red hair, uncared for for many days, streamed past her cheeks like tongues of fire and accentuated her pallor. Suddenly the crushing humiliation of seeing him with another woman in his arms, and feeling embarrassed at her own disheveled state, was too much. With an inarticulate cry she turned and ran, pushing past some startled soldiers behind her. Curious glances followed her as she ran blindly toward the sanctuary of the arroyo, stumbling past the place where she usually bathed to a sheltered spot several hundred yards farther on, where she collapsed in a tearful heap and gave way to the flood of emotion that overwhelmed her.

Despite all the days of exhausting toil the longing to see him again had been uppermost in her mind, but now she wished a thousand miles separated them. She lay shivering in the keen morning air, her shoulders racked with sobs, totally unaware of the uniformed figure approaching with the stealth of a mountain cat, until he stood over her, his outline almost menacing against the background of gray sky.

"Why did you run away?" He sounded angry, and she wondered why. She heard a swift intake of breath and a muttered oath as she raised her head and he saw her tearful face. He went down on one knee, stretching out a hand toward her, but she drew back with a deliberate movement that brought a tightening of his lips.

"Run away? Why should I do that? I had no wish to intrude on a private moment, that's all." She lied badly and knew she had not convinced him.

"Intrude on Consuelo and myself?" He sounded genuinely surprised. "You talk as if we were lovers, and that does not become you. Surely she has told you she comes from my village. She has no family, and I have cared for her since she was a child. At one time she was my wife's maid. She regards me as a fond cousin, nothing more."

Hardly that, Antoinette thought, remembering the possessive way Consuelo had clung to him. He frowned at her silence, and she heard the anger grow in his voice at her refusal to look at him.

"Of course I was concerned for her safety—for you both. When you took her beneath your roof I knew she would be well cared for and want for nothing. In return I asked her to watch over you, to help you if you chose to stay on in Mexico, to be your friend. I was furious when I learned she had brought you into danger."

"She didn't want me to come, but I—I had to," Antoinette returned. She wanted so much to believe him —to reach out and grasp the hand still offered. For a moment they stared at each other, and then a look of such intense desire flashed into Ramón's eyes that it shattered the last of her composure. She felt tears begin to spill down over her cheeks. His hands closed over her wrists, imprisoning her despite her frantic attempts to free herself.

"Let me go—please."

It was an entreaty—almost inaudible. The quaver in her voice told him all he wanted to know, and his look of passion was replaced by one of great satisfaction.

"Dios, what a little fool you are! It is time you and I were honest with each other, mi Florecita."

Antoinette's cries of protest rose and died beneath the fierce pressure of his mouth. Her stiff lips parted and broke as if they were no longer part of her, and her brief resistance was stilled as he pressed her back onto the hard earth and the weight of his body forced her to lie still.

"Why do you shrink when I touch you?" Ramón lifted his mouth from hers and stared down at the tears trembling on her lashes, the soft lips bruised by his savage demands.

"Because when you look at me I know you are only seeing another woman to kiss and make love to, or abuse as the mood takes you—as revenge against your wife."

She felt the sudden tightening of his hands about her wrists and saw the sardonic twist to the lean mouth.

"Who told you about her?"

"The Empress first, and then Consuelo told me how she ran away."

"And I've amused myself with many women because of what she did," Ramón answered quietly, "but with you it is different. You have to believe that."

"I can't. I won't. I can't even trust my own feelings anymore. I thought you loved her, and then to learn she had been unfaithful. . . . Oh, please, let me go." Again it was an attempt to move him to pity, but Ramón had no intention of allowing her to go. The icicle was melting. She was flesh and blood now, warm and unbelievably beautiful, despite the dark lines of tiredness around her eyes and the dirt on the side of her face where it had touched the ground. Instead of releasing her he caught her chin firmly with his fingers and turned her face up to his, his eyes blazing.

"So you are not afraid of me, chica, but of yourself. That pleases me."

Bending his head, he took her mouth, exploring it with an expertise that rendered her incapable of any feeling other than the pleasure she experienced from the touch of his lips and the firm pressure of his body against hers.

"How—how long have you known?" She lay breathless, submissive in his arms, her cheeks now flushed with color, her eyes wide with the shame of his easy victory. One kiss and her secret had been torn from her.

"I wasn't sure—you were always so distant. I tried to reach you, but it was difficult for me."

"Because of your wife?" Difficult for him? For her it had been agony!

"Sí. I swore I would never trust a woman again—or

love one, but the moment I met you I realized how stupid that vow was. I tried to stay away, but you were always with me, La Florecita."

"Why do you call me that? What does it mean?"

"'Florecita' means beautiful little flower—a delicate bloom that has flourished beneath the warm sun of Mexico." He rolled over, gathering her against his chest and lying his cheek against hers as she entwined her arms about his neck with a contented sigh. "Poor little one, you are exhausted. Consuelo has told me how hard you have been working."

"It was worth it. Oh, Ramón, we have won. I am so happy and proud to have been here with your people." Antoinette's voice was so low he could hardly hear it. She nestled closer to him, her eyes closing. How tired she was, the last of her strength had drained from her. Ramón stroked the hair away from her face and gently laid two kisses against her heavy lids.

"Sleep, mi vida, I will watch over you."

Mi vida—my life! More than an eloquent speech, those two words told her everything she had ever longed to hear.

SEVEN

Antoinette awoke to find she was no longer by the arroyo, but lying in a corner of the sleeping quarters with warm sunshine flooding through the window onto her face. Several blankets covered her, and on top of them was a familiar travel-stained jacket that immediately brought to mind the events of the previous night. Beside her, in shirt-sleeves and dusty breeches and boots still carrying half an inch of mud on them, Ramón sat with his back against the wall, his eyes closed. A hastily erected curtain had been pulled partly around them, shielding them from the inquisitive eyes of the soldiers and village women who sprawled in small groups talking quietly or sleeping. Privacy for Don Ramón and his woman! Antoinette felt her cheeks begin to burn at the thought. Consuelo had not known how near she had been to the truth.

"Good morning." Ramón's eyes opened and regarded her with such tenderness she immediately felt her heart begin to race. "How are you feeling?"

"I had a wonderful dream." She stretched languidly and was conscious of his eyes following her every move.

"Tell me."

"I dreamed I fell in love."

He leaned toward her until his dark face was dangerously close. Wicked lights danced in the eyes searching her face.

"And was your love returned?"

"Yes—at least I think so—" She broke off, scarlet with

embarrassment. What if she had mistaken a single endearment spoken in the heat of passion to mean more than was intended?

"Mi vida." He said it softly, his lips against her cheek, her forehead, finally her mouth. Their lips met in a kiss that made Antoinette's senses reel. The dream had become reality—she felt the raging fire of her love consuming her as Ramón drew her against him and she knew the intensity of his desire. Oblivious to the world around them, she abandoned herself to his arms and his kisses. She gave herself to love for the first time in her life.

She drew back with a tremulous little laugh, shocked and bewildered by the depth of her emotions. The expression on Ramón's face told her he not only understood, but was experiencing the same inward tumult. Slowly he smoothed back her disheveled hair, kissed her tenderly but lightly on the mouth, and put her from him.

"No, don't go, please." She stretched out a hand as he pulled on his jacket. "There is so much I want to say."

"God did not endow me with the patience of a saint, mi amor," he murmured. "We will talk, I promise, but not now. You have to eat and return to the capital."

"Leave, but why?" She started up in alarm. "You don't want me here?"

"If it were possible, I would never let you out of my sight again, but for your own sake you must go back. I have ordered the withdrawal of all French troops from Río Verde, but I cannot rule out the possibility of patrols coming this way. The sentries you so neatly tricked could not give an accurate description, but I'm not risking your being seen here at all."

"You know about that? It was necessary, Ramón. I wouldn't have agreed to it otherwise."

"I know, but that still doesn't stop me from worrying every time I think of it. Whatever possessed you to take such a risk? No, don't tell me or by the time you have finished I know you will have persuaded me to let you stay. Come now, Consuelo has food for you. She will go back too."

"But there is so much to do here."

"My orders are to remain in this area with my men, not only to help Father Ignatius in any way we can, but to police the back roads and prevent the infiltration of small Juarista bands. We shall be here for some time."

"Is your home in danger? Consuelo said it is not far away."

"My peons will fight if I ask it of them." He drew her to her feet with a smile. "I am lucky in that respect."

"Am I less than one of your peons that I am sent away from your side?" Antoinette asked in a small voice. She was afraid to go, afraid when they next met something would have changed. She did not know why she should feel such apprehension.

"Do you know the meaning of the words 'mi vida'?" Ramón asked with a frown.

"Yes . . ."

"And do you believe I am the kind of man to use such a term lightly?"

"Of course not." Antoinette flushed at the mockery that leaped into his dark eyes at her answer. She knew of an unhappy marriage to a wife who had left him embittered and withdrawn, but of the enigmatic man himself, a mixture of stoic Indian and proud Spaniard, she knew very little. With a sigh of acquiescence she smoothed down her creased skirt and attempted to restore some order to her hair. "Very well. I will do as you wish."

An hour later, having taken her leave of everyone in the camp, Antoinette followed Ramón to the waiting horses. Julio and another man were to accompany her and Consuelo to the edge of the city. She lingered behind the others until Ramón stopped and waited for her to draw closer. As he drew her into his arms and kissed her a soft murmur of approval ran through the onlookers clustered nearby.

"When will I see you again?"

"Soon, chica. Very soon."

"Be careful."

"I have reason to now."

It was strange to awaken in the house in the Calle de Comerciantes instead of in the hospital, and to stretch lazily beneath cool, crisp sheets instead of beneath a rough blanket on a hard floor. For two days she had retired early to bed and slept late into the morning, reveling in ordinary things she had once taken for granted, like regular meals of appetizing food, hot water for a bath, and clean clothes. The air she breathed was somehow fresher and more invigorating. Not only her eyes, but her mind was now aware of the deplorable hardship and poverty beyond her open windows. The experience at Río Verde had been a lesson that had changed her. She longed to return to learn whether the sick were recovering, to listen to the incessant chatter of the women as they washed clothes by the river, to be with the man she loved.

Consuelo's manner was once again polite and reserved, and it took several days before Antoinette found their relationship returning to normal. She knew now that her maid still harbored Juarista sympathies, and her apparent leadership among the village people hinted at a deeper, more dangerous link that she did not want to consider. It passed through her mind that the girl might have used her friendship with Ramón to gain information, and she wondered if she should confide her suspicions about the girl and also about Father Ignatius to him.

The arrival of Luis Santos put all unpleasant thoughts out of her head. She put on a cool dress, and they walked together in one of the small alamedas. She told him of her nursing among the villagers of Río Verde. The shock on his face made her smile as she peered up at him from beneath her parasol.

"Luis, must you look so amazed? I am not a child and I

am not helpless. I did no more than anyone else in such a position. Those poor people were dying, and many more would have died if we had left them in the village."

"Did it not occur to you the sentries could have opened fire?" The tremor in Luis' voice betrayed how deeply anxious her news had made him.

"I must confess it didn't at first—and afterward it was too late, I was in the middle of it all."

Luis glared over his shoulder at Consuelo, following behind them at a discreet distance.

"That girl of yours should be whipped for taking you into such danger."

"I went of my own accord and I have no regrets. I feel I have learned a great deal."

"Yes—you do seem somehow different." Luis opened the gate leading back into the house, and Antoinette stopped for a moment to admire the garden. It was coming back to life again beneath the capable hands of a local man who came twice a week to tend it. "If I were a suspicious man I might believe you were in love. Are you, Antoinette?"

The direct question deterred any evasiveness she might have shown, and she nodded, wishing she could have told this to him in a kinder way. She had been dreading this moment all afternoon.

"I'm sorry. I hate hurting you of all people, you have been so sweet to me and I value your friendship, but yes, I have fallen in love."

"And is that why you refused to marry me?"

"Yes, but until Río Verde I had no idea Ramón felt the same way about me."

"Ramón!" Luis' lips tightened at the name. "Mi niña, do you know what you are doing?"

"Yes," Antoinette returned, with a determined nod. "Please say you understand."

"That is asking too much, but if you are happy—and your eyes tell me you are very happy—then it cannot be wrong." Luis took her hands and with a smile gently pressed a kiss on the back of each. "My blessings on you both. When is the wedding to be?"

"We haven't spoken of it yet, there was no time," she said, with a shaky laugh. "Ramón wanted me to get home as soon as possible."

"Then he hasn't asked you to marry him yet?"

"No." Her hands were still clasped in his, and she felt his grasp tighten at her answer and hastened to add, "But he will—soon."

"Ramón may love you, but you must be prepared to face the fact he may never marry you. He is already married, Antoinette—to Mexico—and she will never let him go."

Antoinette spun around in front of the mirror, and the yards of delicate chiffon in the skirt of the gown she was wearing billowed out about her like a white cloud. So Ramón was married to Mexico, was he? Well, her demanding rival was going to have some fierce competition tonight.

"How do I look, Consuelo?"

"He will have eyes only for you, señorita," the girl replied, and color flooded into Antoinette's cheeks.

"Eyes, perhaps, but where will the rest of him be—with me, or Maximilian, or someone more important?"

"Is there anyone more important for him?"

"I don't know. Perhaps you can tell me," Antoinette said, turning to look at her maid.

"If the major had confided in me, you would hardly expect me to betray his confidence, would you, señorita?"

"No, Consuelo, you would never do that. We both know how good you are at keeping secrets."

A tiny flicker of surprise darted through Consuelo's eyes, and Antoinette knew her meaning had been understood. Picking up her rebozo and gloves, she went downstairs and out into the courtyard where Julio waited in a closed carriage. He had arrived unexpectedly, only moments after Luis' departure, with a message from the villagers of Río Verde, inviting her to return to the village for the fiesta they had arranged to celebrate the end of the smallpox epidemic.

Luis' doleful prediction was forgotten when she arrived at her destination and was immediately surrounded by smiling villagers. How different it was from her first visit when all she had seen were suspicion and sullen expressions.

"This way, señorita."

Julio led her through the throng of people to a long table laid with an abundance of food and wine and decorated with pots of multicolored, sweet-smelling flowers. Torches blazed from every house, illuminating the tiny square beyond and the vivid colors of the women's dresses. Many of them wore the china poblano, a flounced dress of red and white, adorned with ribbons, which had been adopted for festive occasions. Some of the more well-to-do men wore charro suits, with serapes folded neatly over one shoulder. Beside the stone well a group of musicians began to play, and immediately the square was filled with couples eager to dance. Río Verde had come back to life, Antoinette thought as she watched. This was the real Mexico, and she was suddenly an accepted part of it. She was a gringa no longer, but Señorita la Florecita. She smiled whenever someone addressed her as such, conscious of the curiosity behind the friendly eyes that studied her across the table. She scanned the faces presenting themselves before her, expecting each time to find Ramón, but he was noticeably absent.

"The señorita would like some more wine?" Julio was at her elbow, together with a pretty, dark-haired girl holding out her hand for Antoinette's empty glass.

"No, thank you."

"Something to eat then? This is María, my wife, she will fetch you anything you wish. Tonight it is the desire of everyone to please you in any way they can."

"Thank you, Julio. Very well, I will have a little more wine. I see the soldiers are still here."

The man glanced up at the uniformed figures mingling with the crowd and nodded in obvious satisfaction.

"We are well protected now—from everyone."

Antoinette looked at him sharply, but his smiling eyes met and held hers without wavering. Whom did he want protection from, she wondered, the rebels or the French? His village was on the edge of Loyalist-held territory, making it easy for spies to slip unnoticed among them to reconnoiter and gain information. She had discovered how difficult it was to tell one Mexican from another beneath a wide-brimmed sombrero. On a night like tonight with everyone in a gay, carefree mood, there could be any number of Díaz' cutthroats mixing with the villagers, and if anyone guessed, who was there to betray them? After the recent harsh treatment of the people of Río Verde by the French she was sure at least they would not turn informers.

Consuelo, breathless from dancing in the arms of a handsome young man, dropped into a vacant seat beside her mistress, and for a moment her brown eyes studied the slender figure in white. She said quietly, "The señorita is not enjoying herself."

"Of course I am. Whatever made you say that?"

"My people want only to please you tonight, but if they see the same sadness in your eyes as I do, then they will know they have failed. This fiesta is in your honor, señorita. It is their way of thanking you for your help."

"I—I didn't realize," Antoinette said slowly.

"Why should you? Why should the gratitude of mere indios and peons mean more to you than an evening in the company of a good friend like Don Luis? I think you are regretting you did not accept his invitation to dinner, señorita. After all, wine is better drunk from crystal glasses than the rough cups we have here."

Antoinette's cheeks burned with angry color at the girl's insolent tone.

"You were eavesdropping," she accused. "What were you hoping to hear—a tidbit of information for your rebel friends? Do you think I am a fool and didn't realize you are still with them? What do you know of gratitude —you, who spy on those who have helped you."

Consuelo grew quite pale and was visibly shaken by the unexpected outburst and the vehemence in her mistress' voice.

"The señorita is mistaken. . . ."

"If I am, then I apologize gladly, but if I am right, and you, by word or deed, ever use your friendship with Major Chávez to gain information or harm him in any way, I swear I will personally deliver you to a firing squad."

Consuelo's eyes widened, and a faint tinge of color slowly began to return to her cheeks.

"You dare to suggest I would harm Don Ramón?" she demanded in a shaking voice. "It is not I who will be his downfall, Señorita La Française, but you, because you do not belong here."

Antoinette gasped at the cruel words as if she had been struck. As tears welled into her eyes Consuelo leaped to her feet and disappeared amid the dancers, leaving her shaken and stunned. What more proof did she need of the deep, turbulent passion the girl harbored for Ramón?

The gaiety of the fiesta went unnoticed around her as she fought to recover her composure before anyone saw her distress and began asking awkward questions. La Française—that hated name. Consuelo had struck her in her most vulnerable spot and succeeded in hurting her more than she would ever know.

"Buenas noches, Señorita Dubec." Captain Martínez, glass in hand, was smiling at her across the table. "May I fetch something for you?"

"No, thank you." Then, as he turned away, "Wait, Captain, can you tell me where Major Chávez is?"

"Sí, at the hacienda. I left him not an hour ago, busy with paperwork."

"How far is the hacienda?"

"Two miles. He left strict orders he was not to be disturbed, but . . ."—the officer shrugged his shoulders with a broad smile—"I am sure he did not mean you to be included. Can I be of service to you in some way?"

"Yes. I want you to take me to him."

Val Verde, the hacienda of Ramón Chávez, lay in a deep valley off the Puebla road. Situated on high ground, the old, sprawling house looked down on a wide, circular courtyard, well-stocked stables, and the low adobe dwellings of the villagers who lived permanently within the protection of the high stone wall and tended the vineyards that stretched for miles on all sides. The whole place was ablaze with light, despite the absence of people.

"Don Ramón has given everyone the evening off to go and enjoy themselves," Captain Martínez explained as they reined in their horses a few yards inside the main gate. "He will be alone—except for a sentry or two and his abuela."

Antoinette hesitated at the mention of a grandmother. From what she had heard of autocratic Spanish matrons they were often an important part of family life. It was generally impossible to keep secrets from them, and she did not want any more of her private life being discussed in public.

"Doña Chiana is confined to her bed. She will not interrupt," her companion murmured, sensing her train of thought. "You have come a long way to turn back now."

Antoinette nodded and allowed him to help her to dismount—somewhat awkwardly because of her aching back. She was not accustomed to a high Mexican saddle or to riding over rough terrain in darkness. Neither had helped to keep her cool and composed. Her nerves felt ragged, and she was sure she looked disheveled.

A dark shadow moved in front of them to challenge their presence. Captain Martínez replied to the soldier in swift Spanish, and he immediately moved back, allowing them to pass.

"I will remain with the horses, señorita," her companion said, motioning her to continue.

Her feet made no sound as she crossed the courtyard to pass another soldier at the edge of the house and proceeded up the steps. The hem of her white gown trailed in inches of dust, but she did not notice. She had eyes only for the bright lights that burned at the back of the house. Something told her this was where Ramón was working. She moved along the veranda, turned a corner, and found herself only a few feet away from him. His back was toward her as he stepped through the open French windows and leaned against the rail to light a cigarillo. He was casually dressed in brown riding breeches and a matching shirt, his riding boots as immaculately polished as always. It was the attire of a man who had no intention of going out.

"Ramón."

The sound of his name brought him spinning around, his eyes searching the shadows.

"Quién está ahí? Consuelo?"

"No." Antoinette stepped into the light, forcing the answer through stiff lips.

"What the devil are you doing here?" he demanded harshly.

"I wondered why you were not at the fiesta." Where were all his soft words, his tender smiles? Could this distant stranger be the same man who had held her in his arms and conquered her with his kisses?

"I had work to do. I left orders I was not to be interrupted."

"Obviously Consuelo would have been more readily received. I'm sorry I have disturbed you." Antoinette's voice began to tremble as she fought against the impulse to turn and run. "I naturally assumed you would be at the village when I arrived. Was that too much to expect under the circumstances? Perhaps I misinterpreted the way you felt the last time we were together."

"No—there was truth between us." His quiet tone halted her in midair. "But I needed time to think."

"Why? I don't understand. How can I believe you meant everything you said when you talk this way and look at me as if I am an intruder. You were expecting Consuelo, why not me?"

"She has instructions to bring me word on how the fiesta is progressing. As patrón it is my duty to ensure it is a success. As to the other, you must look to your heart for an answer."

"My foolish heart tells me to believe what you say because I love you," Antoinette returned, "but my head is not so gullible."

Her words brought a fierce frown to his features.

"Then be ruled by it and put me out of your life before I break that foolish heart into a million tiny pieces. I once warned you you might meet a man who could bring you only disillusionment—that man is me. I tell you this now, chica, to prevent you from being hurt."

"Isn't it a little late for that?" When he did not answer her she moved across the veranda until she stood directly before him—so close she could reach out and touch the face she loved so dearly—but she kept her hands and her emotions rigidly under control. His reasons for wanting them to part, however important, would not sway her from her resolution to stay. "If you really want me to go, Ramón, then I will, and I will not embarrass you again. But first, put your arms around me and kiss me. Kiss me as you did by the river—then send me away."

Her words brought a deep flush to Ramón's cheeks. For a moment his eyes blazed, but the light faded abruptly, and he turned away from her, saying quickly, "How did you get here?"

"On horseback."

"A foolish journey on a dark night. I trust you were not alone?"

"Captain Martínez came with me. Won't you take me back yourself?"

"It is better I stay here." He ground out the stub of his cigarillo beneath the heel of his boot, not looking at her.

"Are you so ashamed to be seen with me?" She caught her breath, then gave a brittle little laugh. "How silly of

141

me not to realize it. At the village when I was with Father Ignatius it was different, wasn't it? Then, it was a show of gratitude—a facade. Here, there is no need to pretend. This is your home, your land. As you say, you are the patrón and I do not belong. La Française—tonight Consuelo too reminded me of what I am."

"Be quiet—that isn't true."

"Then show me."

He wheeled on her with a savage oath, his fingers clamping down so hard on her bare shoulders that she cried out. His usually impassive features were twisted into an expression of great torment as he stared down into her upturned face, fighting to maintain his rapidly diminishing control. Then his mouth was on hers, and it was as it had been by the river, and she knew she had won!

"You little witch!" Ramón whispered against her hair. "You knew how much I wanted to hold you again."

"No," Antoinette whispered. "I knew how much I wanted you to hold me. Don't ever put me through such torture again, you monster!"

"Lo siento! Come into the house." He stood to one side and indicated she should enter through the French windows. "Mi casa es tu casa."

Since the first day Luis had spoken those words to her and shown her over his home, she had longed to see Ramón's domain. At last her wish had come true. She stood in what appeared to be a study. The walls were lined with books, the furniture heavy and very masculine. A huge armchair before the inviting fire in the enormous hearth was scattered with papers.

"I interrupted you. I'm sorry," she said quietly as he handed her a glass of wine.

"It was well worth it. Paperwork is the plague of my life."

Antoinette allowed her gaze to wander around the room, past the oak door to the staircase beyond. The house was far larger than it appeared from the outside, built by craftsmen who intended it to last for many generations.

"Do you like my home?" Ramón asked, watching her appraisal.

"It looks as if it could withstand a siege," she laughed softly.

"It has withstood more than one in the past. This country was not always so peaceful. These walls have been scaled by Indians, bandits, and peons in revolt, but the house itself has never fallen into enemy hands. I think everyone who has lived here has loved it as deeply as I do and been willing to die in its defense."

"I have never felt that way about anything," she said slowly.

"You French do not have our hot blood," Ramón returned with a smile. "Strangers either hate or love it the moment they enter. What about you?"

"I—I—" Antoinette lowered her gaze before his burning eyes. "I feel as though it makes me welcome."

From beyond the door at the far end of the room came a discreet cough, and Antoinette saw amusement spread over Ramón's face.

"Who is that?"

"My grandmother. Come, it is time the two of you met."

Taking her hand, he led her into the other room. This was not, as Antoinette supposed, a sitting room, but a bedroom. Propped against a mound of snow-white pillows sat Doña Chiana Chávez, Ramón's aged Indian grandmother. A hand beckoned from beneath the rebozo that enveloped her frail shoulders. From the brown, implacable face, a pair of dark eyes, so like those of her grandson, scrutinized the slender figure of the French girl moving to the end of the bed.

"So you came to him of your own free will. That is good." Her voice was remarkably clear and strong. She was not the feeble old woman she appeared to be, Antoinette thought, and the color began to mount in her cheeks at the realization that the whole of her conversation with Ramón had probably been overheard. "Come closer, child. I have been known to snap, but never to bite. So this is the woman you have chosen to share your blankets, Ramón mío. She will not betray you like the other one and she will bear many fine sons even though she is a gringa." Her gaze flickered past Antoinette's shocked features to those of her grandson. "I see pain and bitterness ahead for you both, but your love is strong, it will survive. I am well pleased. My only regret is in not being able to live long enough to bounce a fine baby boy on my knee again."

"Abuelita!" The harshness of Ramón's voice made Antoinette turn in surprise. He was pale beneath his tan, and a tiny pulse beating at the corner of his temple betrayed great agitation. "I want no more of such talk."

"You have always listened to my words. Have I ever been wrong? Has Coatlicue not watched over you as I promised?" Her tone reproved him.

So Doña Chiana had given him the amulet! Antoinette felt a wild surge of happiness sweep through her. At last she was sure he no longer loved his dead wife. She looked at Ramón and found she was under his close scrutiny.

"Do you understand what she has said?"

"Yes, but that isn't why you stayed away from me tonight, is it?"

"No." He hesitated for a moment, then, bending over the bed, he kissed his grandmother lightly on both cheeks. "Antoinette and I have much to talk about, Abuelita. Buenas noches, go to sleep now, it is very late."

A smile touched Doña Chiana's mouth, and she extended her hand to Antoinette, who took it as she bent to kiss one of the waxen cheeks.

"I think you are a very determined young woman or you would not have tracked the wolf to his lair," the old woman said in a low, amused voice. "It is good. The gods look kindly on those who are not afraid to gamble."

"Even a gringa?" Antoinette asked, unable to refrain from smiling.

"On La Florecita—the woman of my Ramón. Go now, I am tired, and may Coatlicue go with you also."

"Come." Ramón took Antoinette by the hand and led her outside, closing the door quietly behind him. Without a word he led her through the study, out into the gardens at the back of the house, and up a grassy slope toward the shadowy outline of a ruined building some two hundred yards away. In the bright moonlight she saw a concerned expression on his face and did not break the silence with unnecessary chatter. She was still feeling a little dazed from her encounter with Doña Chiana. As they drew nearer to the building she saw they were approaching the remains of a temple—an Aztec temple, it seemed, because of a huge plumed serpent's head on one of the upper walls. A flight of grass-strewn steps ended abruptly halfway to the flat top, which towered above them. A solitary night bird sang its lonely song somewhere in the branches of the high trees surrounding it.

"I come here whenever I feel the need to be alone," Ramón said quietly. "This place is very special to me. Perhaps by bringing you here I can show you how important you are to me. I want to share it with you."

"I want to share my life with you," Antoinette whispered. "I love you."

He drew her against him and kissed her beneath the stony gaze of Quetzalcoatl, the plumed serpent.

"Te quiero, mi alma. For so long I've fought against telling you, but here in this place there can be no secrets between us—no holding back of words I know must surely hurt you. No, don't draw away. Let me finish."

"I know what you are going to say." She knew and dreaded to hear it, yet in her heart she had already accepted defeat.

"How could you, mi niña? I have carried these thoughts in my heart and spoken of them to no one."

"You will not marry me because you are already married to Mexico." Luis' words, spoken with the image of his face in her mind. Sweet Luis, who wanted her for his wife and had been refused because she loved another. She heard Ramón's sharp intake of breath, followed by an inaudible oath.

145

"I think I can guess who told you that, but it does not matter. It is true, and that is why I cannot ask you to stay with me. I do not have the right. I want you safe in France, among friends. When this is all over we will be able to raise our children in peace."

"Nothing you can do or say will make me leave you now," Antoinette replied stubbornly. "Other women follow their men—why can't I?"

"You, a soldadera! I forbid it."

"I am not your wife. You cannot forbid it."

"You think not? I will not have you risking your life in this battle-torn country. I will ask the Emperor to send you back home on the first available transport."

"No, Ramón, please," she begged. "Don't have me sent away. Let me stay."

"To plague my thoughts and haunt my dreams as you have done since the moment we met," Ramón whispered hoarsely. He kissed her again, and she moaned softly, half in pleasure, half in pain, at the fierce kisses pressed on her mouth. They told her he would not, *could* not send her away, but still she clung tightly to him as if afraid he might vanish into the darkness the moment she let go.

"Abuelita was right—you are stubborn."

"If I went away, how could I bear you all those fine sons she spoke of," Antoinette teased softly.

"A son." Ramón's voice was suddenly unsteady. "A muchacho with my pride and your stubbornness. Ay de mí, he will be a formidable child. No—no, it's impossible. I can't allow you to stay. It would be madness."

"I shall, whatever you say. If need be I'll follow you wherever you go as a soldadera—I don't care. I'm not ashamed of that title, Ramón, not anymore. I would revel in it if I were with you, sharing everything as Consuelo did with her husband. Until this moment I didn't understand how she felt or how precious every moment is when you are in love. Will you deny me this?"

"If only I could," he groaned. "In this place my father and mother took their marriage vows—promises made to each other in private, with no other living being as witness. Those promises have lasted beyond the grave. I know they are together. I could wish no more for us, mi vida. Here, in the sight of Quetzalcoatl and Coatlicue, my gods and yours, if you will have them, I pledge my love. Whatever the future holds in store for me, it will never die. Te quiero, mi Florecita."

They were silent for a long while, still entwined in each other's arms, dreaming perhaps of the day when they would stand on this very spot again watching their children playing in the sunlight. They would listen to their children's laughter as the young ones chased each other around the ruins beneath the watchful gaze of Quetzalcoatl.

"It will be good," she murmured.

"Sí. It will be very good," Ramón replied.

"Will you take me back to the village?" She drew away reluctantly, but still held tightly to his hand. How strong he was!

"And dance with you for the rest of the evening. It is time for others to share my happiness."

Antoinette felt a hundred eyes on her and saw satisfaction on the smiling faces as many hands reached out to help her dismount upon her return to the village. She was the woman of Don Ramón and she had brought him from the hacienda to join in the celebrations. Her absence was forgiven.

"Welcome, Ramón, we had almost given you up." Father Ignatius shook hands warmly with the new arrival, his eyes questioning as they passed over Ramón's shoulder to where Antoinette stood. A woman brought them all wine, and they moved to a quieter spot beside the church.

"As you can see, I have been persuaded to forget my work," Ramón answered with a smile. "Salud, Father!" He drank and then turned to Antoinette, and the look in his dark eyes immediately brought a telltale flush of pleasure to her cheeks. "I give you a toast. To peace in

Mexico and to us, querida. I pray we do not have too long to wait."

"That sounded as near to a proposal of marriage as I could ever expect to hear," the priest said slowly, as if he could not believe it. Antoinette wondered why the suggestion was so strange to him.

"Have you some objections, Father?" She was aware of Ramón's eyes narrowing at the cool edge to her voice. He sensed a hostility he did not understand.

The priest did not respond to her frosty gaze and shook hands with Ramón again, congratulating him in such an enthusiastic manner that curious onlookers began drifting toward them. Antoinette was glad when he moved away. His presence still disturbed her, and she stared after him, her brows drawn together in a deep frown.

"What is it, chica?"

"I'm not sure. He worries me. I could be wrong, but I think he has Loyalist sympathies."

"He cannot take sides, he is a man of God."

"Now he is, but he has not always been a priest. Perhaps he finds it difficult to remain neutral. You did not hear how he spoke of El Padrino."

"The two of you have discussed him?"

"One night at the hospital I was given a lecture on how to turn the other cheek. Father Ignatius feels I should learn to accept the death of my father and try to understand El Padrino's fight for freedom. He thinks I should even feel sorry for the other men who died that day and the wives and mothers who lost loved ones."

Ramón put down his glass and moved close to her, his eyes intent on her face.

"And that is beyond you?"

"No, on the contrary. After being in close contact with these people I find it very easy. I wish I didn't."

"You have greatly changed since the day you first arrived in my country. You are trapped, my darling heart. Mexico will never let you go now."

"And you?"

His lips on hers provided the unspoken answer, and she melted into his arms, oblivious to the sea of faces about them.

It was past two in the morning before Antoinette tumbled into bed. It seemed that her head had scarcely touched the pillow before she was rudely awakened by someone hammering on the outside door. Minutes later as she closed her eyes again and blissfully prepared to continue dreaming of her future with Ramón, Consuelo came into the bedroom and gently but firmly shook her by the shoulder.

"Señorita, wake up. Captain Martínez is downstairs with a message from Don Ramón."

Immediately Antoinette pushed all thoughts of sleep out of her mind and struggled into her wrap.

"What time is it?"

"Almost noon, señorita. You have slept the sleep of the dead for many hours."

Pausing only to run a comb through her hair, Antoinette hurried downstairs. Nine hours' sleep and it felt as if it had only been nine minutes.

"Good morning, Captain. Forgive my disarray, but I appear to have overslept." She extended a hand to the waiting officer with a warm smile. "Please sit down and allow me to have Consuelo bring you some refreshment."

"Gracias, señorita, but there is no time. It is I who must apologize for disturbing you, but the major gave me orders to see you before I leave."

"Leave?" Antoinette echoed in a hollow tone. "What has happened? Where are you going?"

"None of us knows, not even the major himself. At first light this morning he received orders to move out. He is on his way to see the Emperor at this very moment."

Antoinette opened her mouth to ask why he had not come himself and then realized the foolishness of her question. Ramón was a soldier, and his orders would always come first. She would have to get used to it.

"What is the message you have for me?" she asked.

Captain Martínez handed her a thick envelope and then stepped back with a salute.

"I must leave at once, señorita. Is there any word you wish me to take back to the major?"

Antoinette hesitated, then shook her head with a sad little smile.

"No, at least none that can be conveyed by word of mouth. He will understand. Thank you, Captain Martínez."

With trembling fingers she tore open the envelope and extracted the single sheet of paper. Ramón's note was short and precise. His handwriting was firm and clear, betraying none of the haste in which he had written:

> Our orders have changed, we pull out in an hour. The enclosed is part of me, as you are. Wear it close to your heart until we are together again. I love you.
> Ramón.

The enclosed article lay at the bottom of the envelope. The hard metallic object glinted in the sunlight as she drew it out. She heard Consuelo's startled gasp from the doorway. On a slender silver chain the head and shoulders of Coatlicue spun before her blurred vision. The amulet had been neatly cut in two. *The enclosed is part of me. . . .* Ramón's words leaped up at her from the letter.

"Is it possible? Dios, could I have been so wrong?" Consuelo whispered. Antoinette looked up at her, not understanding, to find the Indian girl's eyes riveted on the charm. "I have been blind and jealous. May God forgive me. I did not think you could love him, even when he brought you back from the river that day asleep in his arms, and I saw the look of happiness on his face."

"You were jealous because you love him," Antoinette said between stiff lips.

"I love him as I would a cousin, but I am not in love with him," Consuelo returned, and there was no denying the sincerity in her voice. "We were very close when his wife was alive. I suppose he found me easy to talk to and

I was glad, because it is not good for a man to bear his troubles alone. When she ran away and was killed, part of him died too. You have brought him back to life. I regret I did not think you capable of it and I am afraid I made him doubt it too. That is why he wanted to send you away."

"No, Consuelo, he never doubted me. It is true he wanted me to return home, but I refused. My place is at his side wherever he goes, and as soon as he sends word where he is, I intend to join him."

"Last night when I saw you together, I felt that was how it would be. Perhaps it will be better if you dismiss me."

"Where would you go?" Antoinette no longer felt any anger toward the girl. Ramón's gift had brought her close to him, and the joy of feeling near him even in his absence was something no one could take away from her.

"Why should you care, after all I have said to you?" Consuelo stared at her in bewilderment. Obviously she had been prepared to be sent away.

"A few days ago your words could have hurt me," she returned, "but not now." She stared down at the amulet in her palm, suddenly unafraid. "Don't you understand? Nothing can hurt me now."

EIGHT

At the end of September Emperor Maximilian left for the town of Orizaba. The court circular reporting his departure attributed the unexpected trip to poor health and stated that his majesty would remain in the more moderate climate and rest. He would be kept in full knowledge of all Loyalist activities by certain members of the government who had accompanied him in an advisory capacity.

Scarcely had the papers heralded his departure than a new headline blazed across the front pages: SONORA IN REBEL HANDS! It seemed nothing could stem the slow, relentless progress of the rebel army, now converging on the capital from all directions. Durango, in the north, was besieged by more than twelve thousand men under General Mariano Escobedo. If that city fell, the way lay open to the Foreign Legion garrison at the mining town of San Luis Potosí. In the south Porfirio Díaz was moving on Oaxaca, his native town, held by the French under the command of a Mexican officer, General Oronas. He capitulated in late October, and the entire garrison of three hundred men, a mixture of French and Austrian troops, was taken prisoner. The news of the battle sent Antoinette into a state of near panic, for she had received a hastily scrawled letter from Ramón informing her he was on his way to Orizaba with the Emperor and she was afraid he might have been sent to counter Díaz' approach. For days she expected bad news, but none arrived, and at last she convinced herself he was alive and well. And then came the shattering news from Europe. Empress

Carlota had become ill after a visit to the pope in Rome. The papers said she had gone completely mad, turning on faithful servants who had been in her employ for years and dismissing them, refusing to eat or drink, and accusing Napoleon of trying to have her murdered. Antoinette felt very sad. In the short time she had known Carlota she had grown to like and respect her. Maximilian had been deprived not only of a beautiful, loving wife, but also of a staunch supporter of his failing cause. La Guadalupana had not smiled on the Empress. There would be no son to sit on the throne now.

The long days of waiting played on Antoinette's nerves. She occupied herself with trivialities like sewing, reading, and shopping at the local markets, but these things filled her mind for a short while only. The rest of the time she would sit at an upstairs window looking out across the rooftops at the snowcapped mountains—at Popocatepetl in particular, the majestic mountain that overshadowed Val Verde. How she longed to go back there, to talk with Ramón's wise old grandmother and show her the proof of his love, which she wore about her neck.

"The señorita is not going out before breakfast?" Consuelo stood in the doorway of the bedroom, amazed to find her young mistress not only out of bed but dressed in her riding habit at eight o'clock.

"Yes, I am. It's a beautiful day, and I feel like a long ride. I will take a small picnic with me, I think."

"The señorita is going to see Don Luis, perhaps?"

A smile touched Antoinette's lips as she pulled on her gloves.

"No, I intend to ride over to see Father Ignatius, perhaps even Doña Chiana."

"That is madness," Consuelo gasped, turning quite pale. "Have you not heard how dangerous it is to ride alone in such country? The rebels are close to Don Ramón's land. He would never forgive me if I allowed you to go into such danger."

"Then we will not tell him. Go and put together some

food, Consuelo, I am ready to leave. No more of this nonsense. I must get out of this house for a few hours or I will go mad."

Father Ignatius was not at the site for the new hospital and school. There were signs of rebuilding in progress, but the place was deserted. As she looked about the kitchen, noting an overturned chair and unwashed crockery, she began to suspect work had been abandoned rather hurriedly, although she could not imagine why. She had seen nothing unusual in the villages she had ridden through. At one she had stopped to ask for fresh water for her canteen and been given it with great courtesy. She had thoughtlessly drunk all the orangeade Consuelo had provided for the journey and was grateful for the supply. The countryside was quiet, seemingly untouched by the war that raged elsewhere, and she fought down a moment of uneasiness at being alone. She was a competent horsewoman, and the revolver she had purchased secretly soon after her arrival in Mexico was nestled safely in her saddlebags. Besides, Río Verde was less than an hour's ride away, and once there Ramón's hacienda was only another mile or so. How silly to be afraid when there was nothing to fear. She had helped to nurse his people—they would not harm her—and she had seen no signs of activity to betray the presence of any rebels.

She ate her lunch on a seat beside the window in the hospital, remembering how she had slept beside Ramón in this very room. It seemed an eternity ago, and her heart ached at the memory. Was he bivouacked on some sunparched waste remembering such wonderful moments also, or were his thoughts too occupied with war and fighting? If they were, how could she blame him? He was a soldier, and in time of war one wandering thought could mean a life lost. One of his men or he himself might be killed for such carelessness.

She had been riding again for well over an hour before

she realized that she was hopelessly lost. Instead of approaching Río Verde ahead, the river wound into a narrow, rocky gorge, the walls of which towered skyward. The gorge, in turn, was dwarfed by Popocatepetl in the background. Puzzled, she reined in and tried to regain her bearings. How could she have gone wrong? She had, of course, traveled from Río Verde by a back route the last time, in order to engage the sentries guarding the trail, but this time she had followed the river, confident it would lead her to the village. Perhaps when the road forked she should have gone left over the shallows, instead of turning right. That must have been her error. Then surely if she continued on her present course and circled left, she must come out behind the hacienda. The gray granite walls closed in around her, and she shivered at the threat they seemed to offer. The sun was dipping low in the sky, warning her she should be turning back if she were to reach the capital again by dark. She hesitated, then urged her horse on determinedly. Surely Doña Chiana would not mind if the future wife of her grandson stayed overnight. If she did—which Antoinette very much doubted—she would seek shelter in the village, where she felt sure La Florecita would be warmly welcomed.

"Quién está ahí?"

The question was flung at her from behind. As she came to a halt, startled, an armed peon rose from behind a boulder and stared at her over the barrel of his rifle.

"I am Señorita Dubec. You must remember me. I was at the village with Father Ignatius. . . ." Her voice trailed off in horror as she realized her mistake. This man was not from Río Verde, nor were the four men rising from cover to confront her. They were hard-faced, suspicious, and were total strangers—all except one! The youngster who halted beside her horse was unforgettable —as was the way he had wrenched her ring from her on the day the rebels had stolen the money box entrusted to Ramón's care. The recognition that dawned in his eyes told her she too had been recognized. His attempt to steal had brought him a sound beating, and no doubt that also was still very clear in his mind.

"La Française." The words were spat at her with unconcealed venom.

"What do you want with me? I have no money, nothing of value." Antoinette forced herself to remain still and speak calmly, suspecting any hasty move would bring a bullet from one of the weapons leveled at her.

"You will make a good hostage, señorita. One French-woman for the two Mexicans arrested yesterday, one of whom was my brother. You will have saved El Padrino the trouble of freeing them himself."

"You—you are El Padrino's men?" Her voice faltered and broke as she spoke the name of the man responsible for the death of her father. She saw the men exchange satisfied glances at the fear she exhibited.

"I see you have heard of him. Vámanos." The boy indicated that she should continue riding.

"Where are you taking me?"

"To General Díaz. He will decide whether we kill you or hand you over to El Padrino as a hostage."

Díaz! Antoinette's head reeled. It was not possible—all reports placed him in the region of Oaxaca, planning to lay siege to Orizaba to force the Emperor to abdicate. Instead he was encamped within striking distance of Puebla, less than eighty miles from the capital. With enough men and a surprise attack he could cut off the city completely, render it helpless and unapproachable from the garrison at San Luis Potosí. If that happened Benito Juárez would once more be ruler of Mexico. A few hundred yards along the uneven road she was abruptly halted and blindfolded with a piece of dirty rag. Her wrists were bound tightly in front of her with raw-hide. She submitted to the indignities in silence, knowing she was helpless to protest and wishing with all her heart she had heeded Consuelo's warning. The reins were taken from her grasp, and she was led for a time—she did not know how long, since it was impossible to tell with her eyes covered. It felt like an hour, but was probably not more than fifteen minutes before she became aware of a growing hubbub of male and female voices. The horse was halted, she was pulled unceremoniously to the ground, and her blindfold was removed. She stood in the midst of an inquiring crowd and she shook as angry faces moved nearer, inspecting her with merciless eyes. A woman with tangled hair came close to feel the cloth of her riding habit and was immediately pushed away by one of her guards.

"This way." The butt of a rifle prodded her toward one of the tents. She was pushed inside, stumbled awkwardly because of her bound hands, and fell onto the heap of blankets on the floor, desperately trying to shut out the taunts and jeers of the crowd outside.

She wanted to cry, but the tears would not come. She moved away from the entrance, fighting the urge to break down or even scream. A shadow fell across her as her young tormentor poked his head through the flap.

"Luck is with you, señorita. Our gracious general is away and will not be back until tomorrow. If you know how to pray, do so. He does not like the French."

Pray, scream—she wanted to do both and could do neither—she was too shocked and frightened by the hopelessness of her position. No one knew where she was!

Throughout the night she huddled on the blankets trying to sleep, to forget the approach of morning, when she would be brought face-to-face with Porfirio Díaz and sentence would be pronounced against her. What if they decided to use her as a hostage and the French refused to give up their prisoners? She would surely be killed then. Ramón, my love, where are you? Her bound hands pressed against the amulet beneath her blouse, and the feel of it against her heart restored her failing courage. She was convinced she would never see him again, never stand beside him in the tiny chapel at Val Verde to take her marriage vows as she had promised she would that night in the shadow of Quetzalcoatl's temple.

She fell asleep as it was growing light and was awakened only a short while later by the sound of loud cheering from outside. Eyes heavy-lidded, she crawled to the tent opening and pushed it aside. A large group of riders had entered the camp. A uniformed figure whose dark, proud Indian features proclaimed him to be none other than General Díaz himself led the cortege. She felt herself begin to tremble. He did not look cruel and was apparently well loved by those crowding around him, but perhaps his benevolence did not extend beyond his own people. She had heard rumors of ruthlessness—there were the captured Imperialist officers who had been shot out of hand. Would she share the same fate? And then she suddenly forgot her own predicament as her eyes came to rest on one of the last riders. The green uniform stood out against the gray daylight and against the serapes of the guerrillas. Capless, dusty, his face drawn and tired, Ramón Chávez reined in his horse and leaned heavily on the pommel of his saddle. She felt sick and faint at the terror that swept through her.

"Ramón!"

His name broke from her lips in an agonized scream. He was a prisoner too! But how? He must have gone to the house looking for her, and Consuelo must have told him of her intention to visit Val Verde. Because of her foolishness he had been captured.

He spun around, searching the sea of faces before him to see her bound and struggling in the arms of the guard who had grabbed her as she tried to run from her prison. His furious features blurred and receded before Antoinette's vision as he pushed his way to her side. Her legs buckled, and she fell half-fainting in the arms of her guard, but she did not wholly lose consciousness. Through reeling senses she heard Ramón's voice raised in anger and she tried to gather herself together long enough to warn him not to antagonize his captors. She wanted to tell him that she was not hurt, only frightened, but no words came —only the tears she had held back throughout the long night.

"Querida, don't cry." Ramón's arms were around her, lifting her, carrying her back into the tent, supporting her as she was deposited gently down on the blankets and her hands were freed. How good it was to feel his strength again. His hands smoothed back her hair, caressed her cheek. Weakly she turned her face against the solid shoulder and wept until she could weep no more. Then she lay spent against him. "Querida, are you hurt? Antoinette, answer me for the love of God. Have they hurt you?"

"No." Her voice was hardly audible. She winced at the savage oath that came from his lips as he examined the red, angry marks about her wrists. "Don't—please."

"When Consuelo told me you had ridden off alone, I came after you at once," Ramón whispered, his lips against her hair. As she lifted her head he kissed her mouth and she felt his concern for her. "Were you out of your mind, my little love? Consuelo tried to warn you."

"I know, I know, but I couldn't stay in that house any longer. Your letter said you were on your way to Oaxaca, and when I heard of the battle I didn't know what had happened to you. I had to believe all our plans would still come true. I wanted to see Val Verde again—your home—my home to be. To be there would have been like being with you."

"Mi alma." His kisses seared her mouth until she turned her face away with a soft cry, too exhausted to resist, yet knowing this was not the moment for them to give way to passion.

"You shouldn't have come after me. What will they do to you? One of them spoke of using me as a hostage to exchange for some prisoners. Ramón, that man—El Padrino—is here."

"I know, little one. So is Díaz, this is one of his largest strongholds. Don't be afraid, I won't let them hurt you. As for me—quién sabe?"

"Don't say that."

"Your safety is my only concern. Díaz is not a monster. If I offer myself in your place, I'm sure he will let you go."

"Don't trust him, Ramón. Don't trust any of them. Mon Dieu, will I ever be forgiven for bringing you into such danger?"

"You have nothing to reproach yourself for. I knew the risk when I set out. Val Verde has been in danger for some while now. My peons have already decided on which side they wish to fight."

By his tone Antoinette guessed that most, if not all of them, had chosen to fight with Juárez, and she gave a distressed cry.

"How could they, after all you have done for them? It is so unfair."

"That is their choice, Antoinette. Don't look so sad."

"But your beautiful home and your grandmother—they cannot be left to the mercy of the rebels."

"Both are well guarded by loyal men who would die before they surrendered either to the enemy. Come now, wipe dry those lovely eyes and be brave for a little while longer." His calm voice soothed her nerves, and she sat back on her heels with a faint smile.

Her face grew instantly cold at the sight of the young Juarista who ducked through the flap, interrupting them without warning. To her surprise a jug of wine and a tray of food were put down before her—the first refreshment provided since her capture. It was a welcome sight.

"Afuera!" Ramón indicated that the boy should leave without giving him a word of thanks. "Don't come in here again."

The boy hesitated, and she got up to catch hold of Ramón's arm, expecting some kind of retaliation for his curtness. He acted like a man in authority instead of a prisoner, and she feared for his safety.

"Don't," she pleaded.

"Señorita, por favor." To her amazement the boy's face was red with what she could only imagine was embarrassment. "If I had known who you were . . ."

"Leave us. We are not to be disturbed. Is that clear?" Ramón snapped. Never, in all the time she had known him, had Antoinette heard his voice so harsh—so close to losing control. As the rebel still hesitated, he swore violently at him in Spanish as he hurriedly backed out.

"Ramón, what did he mean? How can you dare to give him orders?"

"Querida . . ." He moved toward her as if to touch her, but instead he halted a few feet away, his face a mask of indecision.

"Ramón, for pity's sake. What have you arranged with them?" Antoinette asked, suddenly alarmed. He had spoken of exchanging himself for her—placing his own life in danger because of her stupidity. She would not allow him to do that. Whatever awaited them they would face it together.

"Have no fear for your own safety or mine. There is no need. Madre de Dios, why should I have to explain here, of all places? I wanted you in my arms, at Val Verde, on my own ground where I could look you in the eyes and tell you the truth." Antoinette made no answer. Her eyes were locked on his face, bewildered. Ramón's eyes clouded with pain. She saw his hands clench into tight fists at his sides. "Querida, your father's death—it was as I told you when we first met, the result of a rebel ambush, but not at the hands of El Padrino. He was not even there. . . ."

"Don't talk to me of that man. It is my dearest wish to see him caught."

"Antoinette," Ramón said hoarsely. "I am El Padrino."

They stood alone in the tent, in silence, neither of them moving. Antoinette dropped her hands from her mouth, and her fingers clutched nervously at her skirt. Was she going mad? Perhaps she had not heard him properly—she was ill. . . . How could Ramón and El Padrino be one of the same man? This was the man she loved, worshipped. He was no rebel, no murderer. And yet he stood before her, knowing the torment surging through her and making no attempt to restore her peace of mind, her sanity. Her eyes took in every detail of his grim features. The dark eyes, narrowed as they met her accusing gaze; the tight line of his mouth, which minutes before had plied her own with soul-searching kisses—the same mouth that had wooed her with soft words and endearments. "La Florecita"—he had first given her that name as they traveled together from Veracruz and she had first begun to succumb to his dangerous charm. Now it was only too clear why he had tried to be rid of her before she discovered the terrible truth.

"You are the man who killed my father." The words fell from her lips, and she stepped back from him, avoiding the hand outstretched toward her, oblivious of the entreaty in his eyes. "Don't touch me, you murderer."

"Antoinette, for the love of God," Ramón cried. "I have told you the truth. I was not there the day your father died. I would not lie to you, I swear it."

He caught her by the wrist, but she struck out at him, hitting him twice across the face before he released her. She drew back from him as if he were the devil himself.

"You are El Padrino." She forced the hated name to her lips, half hoping he would deny it. He made no attempt to touch her again. The imprint of her fingers stood out clearly against the thin white bullet scar on his cheek.

"Won't you believe me?" His voice was still harsh, but controlled now. How adept he was at concealing his feelings, she thought bitterly.

"Believe another set of lies, meant to deceive me again?" She flung the accusation at him, her lovely face twisted with bitterness and grief. She gained a little satisfaction from the heavy flush that crept into his cheeks. "What an easy conquest I was for you, Señor El Padrino. An unhappy, lonely girl who was only too ready to accept the friendship you so cleverly offered. You made me feel you wanted me, needed me." She broke off, fighting back a rush of tears. No—no weakness now. She would not let him see that.

"Yes, you *are* still a girl. A woman would listen to

reason. Will you not trust me until we can talk together like two sane people?"

"Trust you! You ask too much. I am quite sane now, I assure you—my mind is perfectly clear. I can remember how you tried to make me leave Veracruz and go home. You were not concerned for me, but for yourself. No doubt that same instinct of self-preservation prevailed that night at Val Verde when you again tried to send me away. I thought it was because you loved me. Now I know it was because you were afraid I would find out the truth and betray you."

"And will you?" A tiny pulse throbbed at one temple. It was his only outward sign of agitation. She wanted to scream at his coolness—hurt him as deeply as he had hurt her—but here in this place where he was surrounded by friends that was impossible. She used the only weapon in her power—cold words, with colder intentions.

"I intend to shout it from the rooftops."

"How quickly your love has turned to hate. So be it. I ask nothing further of you, neither your trust nor your understanding. If you wish it to be different, then speak now before I leave." There was no compassion in his tone, no softening of his dark face, no plea for forgiveness for having wrecked her hopes and dreams—her life!

"You murdered my father. There is blood between us— there can never be anything else," Antoinette said in a trembling voice.

Ramón turned away and stood for a long moment looking out across the camp. When he spoke again his voice was distant and like that of a stranger.

"I will speak to General Díaz on your behalf. You must pretend you were lost, then I'm sure he will let you go. He already knows you and I are involved. Say nothing to make him think otherwise."

"Never!" Antoinette did not consider the consequences of a refusal. Every fiber of her being rebelled at the idea of remaining silent and allowing him to go unpunished for her father's death.

"Don't be a little fool!" He swung around to face her, his eyes blazing, and caught her by the wrists. "When you return to the capital you can do as you please. Remain silent or betray me to the authorities, it makes no difference. But for the moment your life depends on your doing exactly as I say. Maximilian ordered me to Puebla with my men when he heard Díaz was moving in this direction. It was Bazaine's idea, of course. Soon the Emperor will be isolated, deprived of all but the bare minimum of troops, and when that happens he will abdicate to save his own neck. The war is almost over, and the time is now right for me to fight where I belong— with my own people. I can't say I'm sorry."

"Hypocrite. You betray your friends, people who trust you." Antoinette's self-control was beginning to crack. The touch of his hands was like a drug numbing her senses, and she hated herself for the weakness creeping through her body. She threw back her head and stared contemptuously into his face. If he drew her close, kissed her, she was lost. The longing to surrender herself to his embrace, to believe in him and the love she knew could never be erased from her heart, was so strong it was physically painful. Her only self-defense was attack. "Liar. You took from me the last person in the world I loved, and for that I will never forgive you. If I were a man I would kill you. I pray to God someone will soon do that for me."

"You would send me into battle with death in your heart?" Ramón sounded as if he could not believe his ears. The grip on her bruised wrists tightened until she had to bite her lips to prevent herself from crying out. Then, abruptly, she was released, and he stepped back from her with a humorless smile. "I will try to ensure that you do not have to wait too long. Vaya con Dios, señorita—go with God. You have made certain I will not."

"Señorita Dubec. I am General Porfirio Díaz."

How long the uniformed figure had been standing over her Antoinette did not know. She had lost count of all

164

time since Ramón had left her alone and she had collapsed onto the ground, weak and trembling and oblivious to everything around her.

"Are you not hungry? Your food is untouched. I must apologize for the way you were brought here—I can see you have been greatly frightened."

She sat up, becoming conscious of a pair of alert black eyes scrutinizing her appearance. She found the ribbon from her hair in the dust, shook it, and secured the loose, tangled mass about her shoulders. She felt cold, but was not shivering; tearful, yet unable to cry. She was an empty shell.

"Yes, I was frightened," she answered at length, when it became obvious a reply was expected.

"Ramón has spoken of you to me and explained your presence in this area. You are a stubborn young woman, but one of spirit, and I like that. You will make him a fine wife, I think, but that of course comes later. Now we have to get you home. He tells me you do not wish to remain in the camp with the other women. I suppose it is natural for someone of your background to abhor our primitive way of life. I hope the next time we meet, it will be under more pleasant circumstances."

Antoinette stared steadily into the placid Indian features, aware of the underlying mockery in his voice and not understanding why he was capable of making her feel so insignificant. He was not a very tall man, certainly not the imposing figure she had been expecting, yet she felt quite unimportant in his presence.

"You seem very sure we will meet again," was all she could say.

"When we take Mexico City, you and Ramón will sit at my right hand at a celebration dinner at the Residential Palace. I have heard good reports of you, señorita, from many sources. That is why you are free to go. You will be escorted to the outskirts of the city, from there you will be able to proceed safely alone. Once again I apologize for the rudeness of these quarters and of my men—good men, but a little lacking in the finesse you

165

are accustomed to. When you are ready to leave, the horses are waiting."

Antoinette's eyes squinted at the strong afternoon sunlight as she emerged from the dimness of the tent. The guard had been withdrawn, and there was a marked difference in the attitude of the people milling about nearby when they glanced in her direction. She was free! The general had deliberately been misled into believing she was to be Ramón's wife and therefore was wholly trustworthy. She felt no gratitude for the lie, only relief at being able to leave and get as far away from him as possible.

Three horses stood a few yards away, and two well-armed men, presumably her escort, were talking to Ramón Chávez—but how different he looked. The green dress of the Mexican Guardia Imperial had been replaced by a dark charro suit. Two bandoliers crossed his short leather-thonged jacket, and a pistol hung from his concho-studded belt. Antoinette swallowed nervously. The legend of El Padrino was no more. She was face-to-face with the reality.

"Colonel." One of the men touched his arm as she halted, and he turned on his heel and came over to her. So he was a colonel now!

"In a while you will be free to wreak what havoc you wish, but for the moment I suggest you contain your hatred of me. There are a hundred eyes on us. Your life will be valueless if they suspect I have lied," he said in a low, fierce whisper as she tried to pull free of the possessive hand he laid on her arm.

"Why did you?"

"I do not share your desire for revenge. Why should I? All I ever asked of you was love and trust—you have neither to give me. You were right when you said there can never be anything between us. I should have realized a woman capable of such emotions has not yet been born."

He was the old Ramón Chávez—the arrogant, cruelly

mocking man she had first encountered in Veracruz—and his attitude hurt her deeply.

"You have your orders, are they clear?" He addressed the two waiting guerrillas. Both nodded and mounted their horses. The grasp on Antoinette's wrist loosened and fell away, but before she could move, his hands clamped down over her shoulders pulling her against him, and for a long, torturous moment she was forced to endure the fierce pressure of his mouth on hers. She appeared to be held in a passionate embrace, and a low murmur of approval ran through the small gathering of onlookers. They could not feel the rigidity of her body, the coldness of Ramón's kiss, or hear the contempt in his voice as he murmured, "That should ensure my woman's safe return to Mexico City. Good-bye, Antoinette."

She did not answer. She could not trust herself to utter a single word.

Tears! What use were tears? They weakened her body when she needed all her strength, caused her head to ache when it needed to be clear, puffed her eyes and reddened her cheeks at a time when she needed to be composed and in full possession of herself.

For two days and a night she had remained closeted in her room, refusing to see or speak to anyone. The effects of the laudanum administered by a local doctor had worn off, and she had come back to the awful reality of loving the man who had killed her father. On the second day she unlocked the bedroom door and admitted an anxious Consuelo to her presence.

"Señorita, you are ill! Let me bring the doctor back." The girl stared aghast at Antoinette's ashen cheeks, the blank look in her eyes, her unkempt hair. She looked like a ghost—unreal and untouchable.

"No. I will be all right." Antoinette sat down in front of the dressing table and held out a silver-backed brush. "Please do something with my hair. I want to go out."

"You are not well enough, señorita," Consuelo protested. Gently she began to brush the tangled red tresses. Antoinette was hardly aware of her touch, as though it fell on someone else. Nothing had been real since the long ride back to the house. For hours she had listened to the ceaseless chatter of her companions as they sang the praises of El Padrino. It seem his identity had not been revealed to her alone, but also to many men and women who held him in high esteem as a nameless, faceless hero. The moment he admitted he was one of Juárez' agents, his double life was a secret no longer. By the time she reached the sanctuary of the house she was reeling with exhaustion in the saddle. She vaguely remembered Consuelo putting her to bed and the arrival of a doctor who gave her blessed sleep for twelve whole hours. Everything before that, however, was still like a nightmare, and she knew it was not yet over.

"When I have laid out your clothes I shall pack my belongings and leave," Consuelo said in a flat tone.

"Why?" Antoinette swung around to look at her. "I have no complaints about your work—only your association with Major Chávez—or should I call him by the name you will recognize better—El Padrino? Is he the reason for this sudden departure?"

Consuelo turned deathly pale, and the brush slipped from her hand onto the dressing table, shattering one of the glass candlesticks there. It was a damning admission of her guilt.

"He—he told you," she stammered.

"It became necessary when he found me. You see, I wasn't just lost as I allowed you to believe, I was a prisoner of Díaz' guerrillas not far from Río Verde."

Antoinette rose to her feet and faced her maid. "You knew who he was all along, didn't you?" she accused, and not waiting for an answer she continued, with mounting emotion in her voice, "Is that why you were brought here—to spy on me?"

"If you remember, señorita, it was you yourself who suggested I come here. The major was not too pleased at first, but afterward, when he saw how—how content I was, he relented and allowed me to stay."

"He *allowed* you to stay?"

"Sí. He would have done nothing to put you in danger. Because of my husband I could have been an embarrassment to you in the eyes of the authorities. Major Chávez did not want that. Now you have made it impossible to stay. You intend to betray him, don't you?"

"Yes." Antoinette did not deny the fact. It was the only course open to her. El Padrino had murdered her father, and she had sworn he must pay with his life. A faint, almost mocking smile touched Consuelo's small mouth.

"You are too late. He has already been branded a deserter. Even now he is being hunted by the Cazadores, but they will never catch him—he is too important to us all. They will not be able to destroy him—nor will you, señorita—and long after you and your kind have left Mexico, men like Ramón Chávez will rule the land, men who care about the peons and the indios and the land and are not afraid to fight, even die, for the right of every Mexican to hold up his head and be proud of what he is. For one such as you who has never had to fight for food, a roof over your head, the right to earn a decent wage, even life itself, what I speak of means nothing. Perhaps one day . . ." She shrugged briefly, her face impassive. "No, you will never want for anything. There will always be a man in your life to provide for your needs, but no man will ever love you as Don Ramón. . . ."

"That's enough," Antoinette cried. Her voice was almost drowned by the loud banging on the main door downstairs. Consuelo went to the window. When she came back she was very pale.

"It is the soldiers who came yesterday."

"What do they want?"

"You were a close friend of the major. It is only natural they should want to question you. This is your chance, señorita."

169

"Admit the officer in charge to the sala and tell him I will be down in a moment."

It was a full fifteen minutes before Antoinette appeared. She had dressed and made herself as presentable as was possible in the short time. A French officer was wandering idly about the room, and seated in a chair was a familiar figure that brought a glad cry to her lips.

"Luis, thank goodness you are here. Oh, I am glad to see you." Bright tears, the first in many days, welled into her eyes as Luis Santos sprang to his feet and took her in his arms. "Thank you for coming. I so desperately need a friend."

"I came yesterday but Consuelo said you were unable to see anyone—that you had been riding and got lost and returned home in a terrible state." Luis held her at arm's length, searching her face with troubled eyes. "Have you heard this ridiculous rumor about Ramón?"

"It is more than a rumor, Señor Santos." The French officer turned in their direction. He was quite young, perhaps twenty-six or -seven, and still noticeably pale, which indicated he was a newcomer to Mexico. He wore the uniform and insignia of the 8th Battalion of the Foreign Legion. From recent newspaper reports she knew that the recently formed 7th and 8th Battalions were composed of Cazadores and that they were based at Querétaro. Was this man in charge of the search for Ramón? She took an instant dislike to the air of assurance about him and the calculating way his pale-blue eyes regarded her. "I think the lady will confirm the fact that Major Chávez is in fact a colonel in the Liberal army—a spy for Porfirio Díaz."

"Nonsense," Luis blurted out, but Antoinette laid a hand on his arm, shaking her head.

"It's true, and there is something else. Ramón is the guerrilla leader El Padrino."

"Madre de Dios, that cannot be."

"Mademoiselle Dubec, I am Captain Simon Laurent. I have special authority from Marshal Bazaine himself to root out all acquaintances of the traitor Chávez and

170

question them, to establish either their innocence or their complicity in his spying activities. You were more than just a friend, were you not?"

Antoinette's expression grew cold at the insinuation. She saw that Luis had also taken offense at the officer's tone. Before she could speak he said scathingly, "You seem to be laboring under the delusion that Doña Antoinette and Major Chávez were lovers, Captain. Allow me to correct you on that point immediately."

"I think it best if I answer him," she interrupted quietly. "You would be correct in assuming the major and I were friends, Captain, but that is all."

"Was it a close friendship?"

"I thought so until I realized he was merely using me. It is obvious you do not know who I am. My father was General Adolphe Dubec. He was murdered by El Padrino, the man you are now hunting. Had I known his true identity I would have informed the authorities immediately."

"My apologies, mademoiselle, that fact I did not know. You have proof Major Chávez and this other man are one and the same? When he is captured we may need you to make a positive identification."

Antoinette nodded. For a moment she faltered in her resolution. Then, mustering all her courage, she quickly but clearly gave a full account of what had happened to her on the day she rode to Río Verde.

"Bien, you have been a great help," Simon Laurent said as she finished. "I do not think I shall need to trouble you again. Just one more thing. The girl who let me in. Is she to be trusted? Had she any contact with Chávez outside this house?"

"Why should she? The girl is my maid—a little on the simple side, but harmless. I only keep her with me because she has no family." Something inside her balked at implicating Consuelo. She avoided the incredulous look in Luis' eyes and hoped her voice did not betray the tumult inside her. "No, Captain, she is of no importance."

From the window she watched Captain Laurent leave the house, stopping to converse with his sergeant in the courtyard. Both looked up at the house, and she stepped back with a gasp that brought Luis to her side. The sergeant with the captain was the same man she had tricked at Río Verde. Quickly she turned away from the window.

"What is it, mi niña?"

"Nothing. I—I think I am still a little shaken."

"Come and sit down. I will get you some brandy."

Perhaps she was mistaken. Perhaps he had merely looked like the other man. She sat in her chair waiting for a knock on the door to tell her she had been recognized, but none came, and after a while she began to relax. Perhaps he had not been the French sergeant from Río Verde after all. For a moment she had had visions of his confronting her with the audacious trick she had played on him, which linked her not only to the rebels, but to El Padrino himself.

"Do you know what you have done?" Luis stood over her, his face troubled.

"Perfectly. I have denounced the man who killed my father." Her voice was not as steady as she would have liked. Even as she spoke she had visions of the Cazadores closing in on Ramón, shooting him down without mercy, and she shuddered. Why did she feel no satisfaction?

"More than that, señorita." Consuelo stood in the doorway behind them, a rebozo over her head and a bundle containing her few meager belongings clutched in one hand. She ignored Luis—her words were for Antoinette alone. "Perhaps you do not yet realize it. If the major had not intervened on your behalf you would surely be dead now. Sí—I was listening," she added as Antoinette opened her mouth to accuse her, "and I thank you for what you told the captain. I wish you had been as generous about Major Chávez."

"Díaz' men would not have harmed me. They talked of using me as a hostage, but it was only talk to frighten me."

"We both know that is not so. You see, the two men captured by the authorities were shot trying to escape. He knew this when he came after you. He knew he had to get you to safety before word had reached General Díaz. He saved your life, and you have rewarded him with a knife in the back. Love! Dios, you are as ignorant of that as you are of everything else."

"I told the captain no more than he already knew. You told me the major had been branded a traitor," Antoinette protested angrily. Why was she allowing herself to be upbraided by a confessed rebel supporter in this ridiculous fashion? She had nothing to reproach herself for.

"What other choice did he have once you had been released to betray him? One day you will learn many things, señorita, but it will be too late. It is already too late for Don Ramón. You have destroyed a wonderful man who worships you. May you live long enough to ask God's forgiveness."

"Get out." Luis was moving toward her, hand upraised to strike her, his handsome face contorted with fury.

"No, let her go." Antoinette sprang between them. "I deserve it. I wished him dead, Luis. Before I sent him away I wished him dead. Dear God, I don't know what possessed me—I was another person. I wanted to hurt him."

His arms were outstretched ready to enfold her, and she went into them, desperate for the slightest offer of comfort. She missed the look of horror in Consuelo's eyes and the hasty sign of the cross the girl made before she turned and ran.

NINE

At the end of November Antoinette was persuaded by Luis to shut up the house in Mexico City and stay at his quinta. As yet it was still untroubled by the growing unrest in the country and it offered her the peace and quiet she so desperately needed. She rode in the carriage he sent through streets crowded with jubilant, celebrating Mexicans. Durango had fallen to General Escobedo! The way was now open to the Foreign Legion garrison at San Luis Potosí. If the officers there capitulated, the south would lie unprotected before the advancing Liberal army. With the withdrawal of Napoleon's troops from Mexican soil, the Imperial cause seemed lost.

Luis was waiting to greet her when she arrived, casually attired in an open-necked shirt and riding breeches. He looked rather hot and dusty, and she noticed a lathered horse being led away as he helped her down from her conveyance. She looked at him questioningly.

"Is there trouble?"

"No, just a shortage of workers. They have been deserting me for the past two weeks. I have less than half my usual working force, and for the first time since the death of my father I am finding out what it is to manage the quinta myself. Forgive such a poor welcome, Antoinette. Will you rest and take a glass of wine while I go and change?"

"Of course." She took his arm with a smile, at ease for the first time in many weeks.

Mercedes appeared on the veranda, looking cool and elegant in a bright yellow dress. For a moment she stared at the new arrival, then returned to her room without a greeting or even a sign of recognition.

"Oh, dear," Antoinette said quietly. "What have I done?"

"Not you. The fault is mine, my dear," Luis answered, giving her hand a reassuring squeeze. "My sister and I have had several quarrels lately—extremely bitter ones, I might add. She wants me to declare openly for Maximilian now that he has decided not to abdicate and is staying on in Mexico."

Antoinette sat down on the couch in the long, low-ceilinged sala and watched him pour out a sherry for her. There was a tenseness about him she had never seen before, and she knew the matter was causing him great anxiety. Poor Luis was caught like so many other people in the middle of a war he did not want and could not condone, yet found impossible to ignore.

"But you cannot do that," she protested quietly. "You like no more Maximilian than you do Juárez."

"That is true. I am of a mind to remain here and fight for what is mine against anyone who tries to take it from me—no matter what the color of his coat is."

His tone disturbed Antoinette. It was so firm, so decisive, and so unlike the lighthearted man she had grown to know and respect.

"Don't grow bitter, Luis. You remind me of—" She broke off and looked away from him, shutting her mind against the memories that came flooding back each time she allowed herself to relax.

"Of Ramón? Is your hatred of him so intense you can no longer speak his name, or does the sound of it arouse memories you would rather keep buried? By the expression on your face I can see which it is. You love him still, don't you?"

"No."

"You may convince others that is true, and I hope for

175

your sake you succeed, but I know differently. I know Ramón and I know you, Antoinette. He owns you body and soul as surely as if he had already taken you upon the marriage bed." Luis stood over her, his brown eyes intent on her face, which slowly flushed with color beneath his fierce scrutiny. Here at the quinta she had once lied to him when he had offered her marriage, and then, only a short while afterward, had been forced to confess the deception. She had brought pain to the one and only person she could now trust and confide in. It would not happen again.

"When I found out the truth about Ramón, I hated him," she said, levelly meeting his gaze.

"Because of your father?"

"Yes."

"And now?"

"Nothing." She shrugged briefly. "I feel numb."

Luis sat beside her, took the glass of sherry from her hand and put it to one side, then clasped both her hands in his and turned her to face him.

"Your association with Ramón has brought you under the eyes of Marshal Bazaine's intelligence agents. That is why I want you here, where I can watch over you. Ramón is free, but you are not, mi niña. Your movements have been under surveillance since the day he changed sides—or should I say declared his true allegiance."

"But—but why? Why does anyone want to watch me? I told Captain Laurent how I felt," Antoinette replied, alarmed by his words.

"I know, but the orders came from Laurent himself. From what I have heard he is not the polite gentleman of manners you met that day. Men he has arrested, women too, have mysteriously died while being questioned about Ramón. These are rumors, perhaps, and without foundation, but there was something in that man's eyes that day he came to your home—the sly insinuation that you and Ramón were lovers. I don't like him, I would never trust him. Mercedes, of course, does not share my opinion. Her friendship with him has provoked more than one argument between us."

"I—I thought she cared for Ramón," Antoinette said slowly.

"For no one but herself. Ramón, hombre guapo that he is, was a challenge. The crushing humiliation she endured when it became obvious he preferred another will never be forgotten. I ask your forgiveness now for the hostility you will encounter whenever you meet. She will never forgive him for rejecting her and choosing you, and I suspect Laurent is the tool she intends to use to soothe her injured vanity. This time, though, she has met a man who could destroy her in the process."

"Luis, you have not spoken of Ramón since that day. Are you still his friend?"

"His choice of leader changes nothing between us."

"He does not deserve your friendship. Has he not placed you in danger also?" Antoinette's voice was noticeably bitter, and he looked at her sharply.

"I think not. Obviously, he has been working for Juárez since we first met, but I never guessed, and never once did he attempt to confide in me. I like to think he kept silent to protect me, knowing what might happen if he were caught or ever forced to reveal his dual role. It must have been an enormous burden for him— one I could not have borne. That kind of loneliness can be endured only by a very special kind of man. He has my admiration and my continued friendship if he ever needs it."

"You are offering protection to the man who killed my father in cold blood."

"Antoinette, no, how can you say that?" Luis protested, alarmed by the coldness creeping into her face.

"Before you protest his innocence let me remind you it was you who told me how my father died at the hands of El Padrino. You told me in this very room. And there is something else." From her purse she took a folded piece of paper and held it out to him. He saw that her hand was trembling. "My father used the attic room to store

177

his sketches. I found them the first day I arrived, but Ramón took me away before I could look at them too closely. Open it, Luis, and you will know, as I now do, why he was so anxious for me not to examine them. I found that only yesterday." He obeyed her in silence and stared down at the sketch of a man dressed in a combination of the uniform of the Mexican Chasseurs and the irregular dress of the Liberal army. One man, but two conflicting uniforms. The roughly etched features bore a startling resemblance to those of Ramón Chávez. Antoinette tore her eyes away from the drawing to look at Luis. "My father knew who El Padrino was—this is the proof. He and Ramón played chess together in that house. I believe he killed my father to keep him silent."

"This paper is proof your father may have suspected Ramón, but that is all."

"Not for me." Antoinette almost snatched the sketch from him and pushed it back into her purse.

"Destroy it," Luis insisted, but she stubbornly shook her head.

Alone in her room, however, she took it out again and spread it out on the bed. Ramón's eyes seemed to follow her as she wandered restlessly to and fro. The likeness of him was so good it was almost like having him in the room with her, silently mocking her futile attempts to forget him.

That night she deliberately took great care with her appearance. Dressing for dinner, she chose the black gown she had worn to Chapultepec, adding a fichu of white lace to cover her shoulders and a necklace of pearls to grace her throat. Before she went downstairs she tore the incriminating sketch in half and threw the pieces onto the grate. She was searching for some matches when Luis arrived to announce an unexpected guest, distracting her from the task.

"Mercedes had already asked him, I could not refuse," he said tight-lipped as Antoinette stared in dismay at the uniformed figure standing at the bottom of the staircase talking to Luis' sister. Suddenly she was glad she had destroyed the drawing—she had found it too late to harm Ramón, and it could only have been used as a source of speculation and controversy. She had the feeling the man below her would have gained great satisfaction by parading it before his superiors, demanding to know why her father had not made his suspicions public knowledge. She herself was haunted by the same question. And why, when he had successfully rid himself of the one person who could have destroyed him, did Ramón not return to the house and burn the last remaining evidence against him? It was a question to which she could find no answer. Unless . . .

"Antoinette, are you all right? You have grown quite pale." Luis was staring at her anxiously. After a moment she nodded and took his arm, allowing him to lead her downstairs.

"Mademoiselle Dubec, this is an unexpected pleasure," Captain Laurent murmured, raising her fingers to his lips. His hand was icy cold, and she barely suppressed a shudder. "I had of course heard you had left the capital."

"From the men you set to watch me, no doubt. I cannot imagine why you did such a thing. I find your actions unbecoming in a French officer, even in such difficult times," Antoinette returned coldly.

"In difficult times one is inclined to adopt extreme measures. You have not denied you were a friend of the traitor Chávez."

"Why should I? I was taken in like everyone else."

"Of course she was. Poor Antoinette, like so many women before her, fell under Ramón's deadly charm," Mercedes purred cattily. She wore red again, as on the first occasion Antoinette had visited the quinta, and she stood close to Simon Laurent with the same possessive air she had displayed with Ramón that day many months before.

Luis must have felt the tremor that ran through Antoinette, for he said quickly, "Will you take a glass of wine, Captain? The grapes are from my own vineyards, naturally. I think you will find it to your liking. Mercedes, ring for Tomás and tell him to bring two bottles of the 'Eighty from the cellars."

"Your hospitality is most gracious," Simon Laurent returned, following them into the sala. "I can think of nothing better than a full-bodied wine and a good dinner after a hard day—except perhaps the company of a beautiful woman." His pale eyes were on Antoinette again. Their intentness unnerved her. "You had a lucky escape, mademoiselle. I should not have enjoyed implicating you in Chávez' treason."

Antoinette thought otherwise, and her hand trembled as she took the glass of sherry Luis offered, her mind full of the many unpleasant rumors associated with this man.

"I take it I am no longer under suspicion?"

"You never were, mademoiselle," Laurent returned with a smile. "I was merely baiting a trap for Chávez. No matter how you felt toward him, I was sure he would try to see you again. I have it on the best information that you were of great importance to him. Did he not lie to General Díaz in order to have you released?"

"I see no reason to repeat what I have already told you, but yes, he did. Under the circumstances—after I had discovered his true identity—he had little choice but to remain with Díaz and his men. My death would have solved nothing."

"That is not quite true. We were holding two rebel prisoners, and you could have been used to bargain for their freedom. I was in no doubt El Padrino held you in very high esteem, but not high enough it seems. No matter, after today I have the feeling he will show himself. And I will be waiting."

"You seem very sure of yourself." Luis sat on the arm of Antoinette's chair, the firm pressure of the hand that covered hers warning her to remain silent lest she betray herself. "When a beautiful woman fails to have any appeal for him, what possible inducement could you provide?"

Simon Laurent savored his wine for a long moment and

studied the color through narrowed eyes until Antoinette felt the urge to scream at the prolonged silence.

"This morning I had Val Verde razed to the ground and the village too. There was a fight, of course, but I had expected resistance and I took more than enough men to deal with a rabble of ignorant indios. Those who remained alive afterward, fled into the hills. By now Chávez will know what I have done."

"You destroyed that lovely old house. . . ." Antoinette was too shocked to continue, and Luis' arm slid around her shoulders comfortingly.

"What of Ramón's abuela?" he demanded coldly.

"The old woman? An unfortunate mistake—I did not realize she was bedridden and could not leave the house. No one answered my repeated demands to surrender, and when we were fired upon, I assumed all the occupants to be hostile."

"You killed Doña Chiana too?" Antoinette fought down a rising nausea at the picture his words conjured—of the hacienda consumed by fire and Ramón's aged grandmother trapped in the flames. "What kind of animal are you?" The warning pressure of Luis' arm about her shaking shoulders was ignored. Even Mercedes, who had just rejoined them in time to overhear the news, stood stunned and silent. "Any one of the villagers could have told you she was an invalid if you had bothered to ask. Mon Dieu, I have been ashamed of my countrymen many times since I came to Mexico, but never like this. Have the French sunk so low they now murder helpless women and children? The villagers were harmless."

"They were Juarista sympathizers, mademoiselle."

"They were protecting their homes and that of their patrón," Antoinette protested angrily. As she spoke, Ramón's words were clear in her mind: *Both are well guarded by loyal men who would die before they surrendered either to the enemy.*

"And who are you protecting, Mademoiselle Dubec? Why should you concern yourself with a few peons and an old woman? An Indian woman known, I might add, to have entertained Benito Juárez himself beneath her roof."

"Doña Antoinette did not know that," Luis snapped. "She feels as I do, that the measures were not justified, even to trap Ramón into coming out into the open. Take care, Captain, he idolized his abuela. You have destroyed more than just his home and those of a few peons."

"Exactly." Laurent offered his empty glass to Mercedes, who filled it without a protest, despite Tomás' hovering in the background to accomplish such tasks. "That was my intention, Señor Santos. I am sorry you do not agree with my actions, but as one who has so far watched only from the background, you cannot expect your opinion to carry much weight. Of course if you wish to speak of this to Marshal Bazaine or the Emperor, I am sure they would be glad to receive you. The latter spoke of you only the other day and mentioned that he wished you to accompany him to Querétaro. He feels a definite stand and a solid show of force will bring Juárez to talk of peace. He has need of your support—and you have need of mine."

Antoinette watched Luis rise to his feet, his face hardening, and prayed he would not allow himself to be provoked by this terrible man.

"Is that a threat, señor?"

"I am a guest beneath your roof, drinking your most excellent wine and about to eat at your table. It would be most discourteous of me to insult my host. Shall we say I am trying to warn you of the dangers of nonalliance? Your powerful name could influence many others to Maximilian's cause. When the war is won and Díaz and Juárez dangle by their necks in Mexico City as a warning for all the stupid cochons who have followed them, that will be the time for loyal men to be rewarded."

"Don Maximiliano can give me nothing. I have everything I want right here," Luis said stubbornly.

"He can give or he can take away," Simon Laurent returned meaningfully. "The choice is yours."

"Luis, it is very hot in here, I would like some air." Antoinette got up from her chair, giving Luis no chance to refuse, and she moved across to the open French windows. He was at her side as she stepped out into the garden and leaned weakly against the nearest tree. Without a word he gently helped her to a seat and sat down beside her, drawing her head against his shoulder. It was several minutes before she could stop trembling.

"Luis, don't anger him. He talks as if he has unlimited power. Don't allow him to destroy everything you love," she pleaded.

"He is well on the way to doing that already. I mean you, mi niña. He was watching your face, as I was, when he spoke of his plans. You were more upset than you should have been."

"Of course I was upset." Antoinette closed her eyes and sat very still, the image of Doña Chiana still uppermost in her thoughts.

So this is the woman you have chosen to share your blankets, Ramón mío . . . she will bear many fine sons . . . pain and bitterness ahead for you both, but your love is strong, it will survive. . . .

How that prophecy had haunted her dreams. She had believed every word, cherished the thought of the fine sons she would one day bear Ramón. She had visions of them playing at Val Verde, growing up to look like their father, inheriting his fierce pride, his love of his country and his heritage. With a soft cry she clutched at Luis' sleeve. Would the pain never end?

"Help me, Luis. Tell me what to do."

"You must help yourself. Your life may depend on it."

"How?" She raised her head. In the lights from the house her face was a white, anguished mask.

"You have to convince the captain that Ramón means nothing to you, and I don't mean with words alone."

"Do you mean I should go away—back to France?"

"I doubt if he would allow you to reach Veracruz. No,

you must stay and show him in another way—by agreeing to become my wife."

"That is out of the question." Antoinette would have drawn back from him, but he held her fast. She fought against the desire to relax against the solid shoulder and accept the easy way out he offered. It would be a loveless marriage, for her at least, but they would share respect, and his name would protect her.

"I will not stand by and watch you being hounded. There is no need to announce a wedding date, simply the engagement, to refute the rumors linking you with Ramón. As soon as it is safe to do so, I will release you. You have no choice, Antoinette. It is the only sensible thing to do."

"Sensible! How can you talk so calmly of being sensible when you know this madness will not stop with our betrothal."

"I realize that. We will announce the news tonight, and then I will tell Laurent I have decided to go to Querétaro with Maximilian. He will not dare to speak out against either of us once I am at the side of the Emperor. Trust me, querida."

"Luis. Oh, Luis, how can I agree to such a lie?"

"I cannot help you if you refuse. No one can." Luis took her face in his hands and kissed her very tenderly on both cheeks. "Love has always eluded me. Passion I have regarded as a weakness, but with you I have grown to know both. How you tremble, my dear. Am I such an ogre? I will never take advantage of your plight, but I shall pray each day for you to grow used to having me around so that when I give you your freedom you may not want it. Will you do as I ask?"

Mutely Antoinette nodded and instantly felt the tension go out of his body. His hands fell to her shoulders, tightening as he bent toward her. She realized his intention and tried to move back, but he held her fast as he kissed her long and lingeringly on the mouth. As he drew back, she heard a soft movement at the windows and realized they were not alone. She knew he was aware of it too.

"Tomás is waiting to serve dinner, Luis." Mercedes stood watching them; Simon Laurent stood at her side, his face impassive. At the sight of her brother kissing the French girl two spots of bright color had risen in Mercedes' cheeks. "Doña Antoinette seems quite recovered now. Will you come in?"

"Yes. And you must pour wine for us all," Luis declared, tucking Antoinette's arm beneath his, "and then I shall give you a toast. Your rather pointed insinuations have altered our plans, Captain Laurent. Doña Antoinette and I had no intention of formally announcing our betrothal for at least another four weeks. However, we have discussed it, and I believe it will put a stop to these ridiculous rumors once and for all."

"A toast! Your betrothal!" Mercedes almost choked over the words. "Luis, are you out of your mind? I have never know you to be so blind. You know she is Ramón's woman and has been since the first day she came here. Simon knows it, every gossipmonger in the capital knows it. They will tell you La Florecita belongs to Ramón Chávez."

"Watch your tongue. You are my sister, not my guardian. Must I remind you, you remain here only so long as you remember your place? I first spoke of marriage to Antoinette at Chapultepec. She accepted me a week later, but we kept silent, mainly out of consideration for you. She wanted you to grow to accept her, to like her. I see how foolish we both were to put your selfish needs above our own. Now I am considering my future wife. I demand you show her due respect—or leave my house."

"Señor Santos, you have taken us by surprise. You have the good wishes of us both. Does he not, Doña Mercedes?" Simon Laurent murmured. "Do not be angry with her, not on such an auspicious occasion. Mademoiselle Dubec, please accept my most humble apologies for any embarrassment I have caused you. If only you had confided in me earlier . . ."

"I accept your apology," Antoinette replied haughtily,

extending her hand. His pale eyes, as he bent low over it, probed her face and were as cold as death.

By the end of December two-thirds of the country was in the hands of the Loyalists. Guadalajara in the north was evacuated on the twelfth, and the French headquarters at San Luis Potosí on the twenty-third. The Cazadores were withdrawn to reinforce Puebla. The man who rode beside Porfirio Díaz into the open town was Colonel Ramón Ruy Chávez.

Luis' refusal to have any newspapers at the quinta was a vain attempt to spare Antoinette's feelings, but the news continued to come from the outside, brought by Simon Laurent on his frequent visits, or by the officers he invited to dine beneath Luis' roof. He treated the house as if he owned it, and Mercedes reveled in his apparent power over her brother. Antoinette watched and listened with growing apprehension. Luis had declared for Maximilian, but how long could he endure the facade, as he entertained men he detested? All this to protect her from suspicion. It was more than she should have demanded from any man, yet when she approached him he merely smiled and told her not to worry, that the war would soon be over. Yes, the end was in sight, she realized, but Maximilian would not be the victor. When he was deposed, what would happen to Luis, who had gone against his better judgment for her sake?

Long after you and your kind have left Mexico, men like Ramón Chávez will rule the land, men who care about the peons and the indios and the land and are not afraid to fight, even die. . . .

Those were Consuelo's words, spoken with bitterness and anger behind them. She had been right. Men like Ramón were winning the war—men who cared. But Luis cared too, for his land, for his home, and for her. If only he had not cared so much for her . . .

On the pretense of wanting to begin assembling her wardrobe for the supposed forthcoming wedding, Antoinette announced her intention to return home. She overcame Luis' objections to her being alone by agreeing to take Soledad back as her maid and duenna. The woman had been attending her stay at the quinta and seemed to have forgotten the unpleasant quarrel over Consuelo that had resulted in her dismissal. Mercedes voiced her intention of taking up residence in their townhouse in a few days to help Antoinette choose the material for her wedding gown. Since Luis' harsh words on the night of the announcement, she had gone out of her way to be pleasant to the other girl. Antoinette found that having her as a friend was more of an ordeal than if they had remained enemies.

"I shall bring Mercedes to the capital myself," Luis murmured as he escorted Antoinette to the waiting carriage. "The little minx is up to something. Do you know she is telling everyone we are planning to be married before I leave with Maximilian next month?"

"Luis, no! Why should she do that?"

"I'm not sure, but I'll wager Laurent put her up to it. Perhaps he's hoping Ramón will come to the wedding—" Luis broke off at the intense pain that flashed into her eyes. "Forgive me, niña, that was a thoughtless thing to say. He is still with you then?"

"Don't torture us both, Luis. I want so much to forget him. What is wrong with me that I cannot love such a wonderful man as you?"

A wry smile touched Luis' mouth. His gentleness and understanding never failed to amaze her. He knew her thoughts were constantly of another man, but he never reproached her or showed how much she hurt him by drawing back from his kisses.

"Perhaps if I had been at Veracruz the day your ship arrived, we would be married by now. Still, it isn't too late—but we will talk of that another time." He kissed her on the cheek, then planted a kiss on the fingers of her left hand, against the coldness of the emerald he had placed there at Christmas. Then he firmly lifted her into the carriage and shut the door.

"The señorita has been at home over two weeks and has not yet found a dressmaker."

Antoinette looked up from her embroidery with a frown as Soledad brought in the afternoon tea. She evidently disapproved of the slowness of the wedding preparations. She was becoming as insistent as Mercedes, Antoinette thought.

"There is no hurry. A wedding gown is a very special thing."

"And it will take time to make. How can you marry Don Luis when you have not even chosen the material?"

"Contrary to what Doña Mercedes may have told you, Soledad, Don Luis and I have no plans for the wedding to take place before he leaves for Querétaro. We have not yet decided on a date. When we do I promise you will be the first to know."

"You should marry him now. Have you not heard? Marshal Bazaine is arranging transportation for all French civilians who want to go back to Europe. The city will be empty with so many people leaving. Do you want to stay here without friends and with the Juaristas almost on our doorstep?" She paused, then added with a shrug of her shoulders, "Perhaps you have no reason to be afraid of them."

"What on earth do you mean?"

"He will come here, will he not? El Padrino. He will protect his woman."

Antoinette put down her teacup, her eyes darkening with anger. How her heart still raced at the mention of that hated name. Had she no shame?

"I forbid you to mention that man to me again. He is a rebel and a murderer, and I wish to forget I ever knew him."

"But he would not harm you, señorita, would he? He is a powerful man now, at the right hand of Díaz, I have

188

heard. Such importance for a traitor, but a useful person to have as a friend."

"Friend! He is no friend. I rue the day I ever met him."

"As I said, señorita, you should marry Don Luis as quickly as possible and find happiness while you can."

Happiness! Such a luxury was lost to her, Antoinette thought, forcing herself to concentrate on her sewing once again. How the days dragged when Luis did not come to cheer her up. Most afternoons she sat in her bedroom reading or sewing, listening to the steady exit from the city of packhorses, laden carts, and overloaded carriages. A slow but steady evacuation of both Europeans and Mexicans was under way. The withdrawal of foreign troops was almost complete. A Belgian company of 750 men and 35 officers, released by Maximilian, was mustered at Puebla, ready for the long march to Veracruz. The remnants of the Austro-Belgian legions that had avoided capture at the capitulation of Miahuatlán and Oaxaca had also left, despite the fact that many of them had enlisted for a term of six years and had received not only uniforms and training but substantial monetary payments in advance. Their numbers swelled with the addition of over a thousand French officers and more than nineteen thousand men.

On February 5, 1867, Marshal Bazaine placed himself at the head of the few remaining French troops and prepared to leave Mexican soil. Surplus arms and ammunition were thrown into the Vega canal. Livestock and stores were auctioned off. Nothing was to be left for the enemy. After waiting over a week in the vain hope that Maximilian would abandon his decision to go to Querétaro and assume command of the army, Bazaine proceeded from Puebla to Veracruz where thirty French ships belonging to the Compagnie Transatlantique de Paquebots waited to convey him and his men to France. It was the end of one of the most unsuccessful oversea expeditions in French history.

The Imperial Mexican army, which numbered not more

than seventeen thousand men, less than half the number Maximilian had been assured would be ready to fight, was poorly equipped and lacked discipline. As she watched them in the streets Antoinette found herself comparing them to the rebels, who wore no uniforms, but were well armed and dedicated, despite their lack of training. They lacked neither courage nor the money and munitions, that poured over the border from the United States. The apathy of the Mexican soldiers frightened her—they had neither the inclination nor the strength to overcome their enemies.

It was the time for making decisions—something that had never been Maximilian's strong point. In dividing up the remnants of the Imperial army, he entrusted commands to weak, treacherous men who were to betray him at every turn. They were General Miramon, who took control of the infantry operating in the west between Zacatecas and Guadalajara; and General Leonardo Márquez, policing the state of Michoacán and the country comprised within the state of Veracruz. Only General Mejia, operating with the cavalry in the north toward San Luis Potosí, was reliable. The Foreign Legion had now been reduced to a regiment of Hussars under the command of Colonel von Khevenhüller and a battalion of four hundred men under Major Hammerstein. All were Austrians. The Cazadores were also all foreigners.

"Don Maximiliano is a fool!" Luis declared as he walked arm-in-arm with Antoinette in the garden after dinner one night. She winced at the anger in his voice and shut out the memory of another voice that had murmured in her ear at Chapultepec: *The man is a fool!* Ramón had made his opinion of the Emperor quite clear that night after the assassination attempt. Weak and too easily led—she had seen that in him too. Poor Maximilian, how would he accept defeat and probable exile? Poor Carlota, certified insane and shut away behind the protective walls of the Château de Bouchout near her old home in Laeken, unable to give him counsel or comfort.

"I feel so sorry for him," she said quietly. "Is his cause really lost?"

"We shall be lucky to get out of Querétaro alive," Luis returned dryly, and she stopped short with a horrified gasp.

"Then I won't let you go."

"I have made my choice. Perhaps we will win after all. The whole of the army is there now—nearly nine thousand men and fifty pieces of cannon. But the man is still a fool. He could have left with Bazaine and instead he allows himself to be talked into this last great gesture." Luis smiled down into her anxious features. "We leave at the end of the week. I wish you were coming with me, but it is too dangerous. When I come back it will all be over."

When I come back—when—when . . . Antoinette paced the floor of her room long after Soledad had locked up the house and gone to bed. He spoke of defeat in one breath and of coming back to her in the next. She was convinced she was sending him to his death. The lives of two men were now on her conscience. She had sent Ramón away, wishing him dead, and now Luis was going willingly, knowingly endangering himself to protect her. It was more than she could bear. She put her head against the curtained window and wept bitterly.

Sporadic gunfire broke the silence somewhere in the city, followed shortly afterward by a loud explosion. Before long, the night sky was red with flames. Such incidents had grown more frequent since the French had departed, and they no longer greatly alarmed her. Although there were five thousand Imperial troops still protecting the capital, they seemed unable to do anything about the guerrillas who infiltrated their defenses. Such men were accustomed to fighting from ambush, hitting the enemy hard and then disappearing without trace. This manner of fighting was the trademark of El Padrino, and she wondered how close he was when the city was attacked. Soledad's words still troubled her: *He will come back, will he not?*

Would he? Would Coatlicue protect him despite everything?

Go with God, señorita. You have made certain I will not!

Slowly, she sat down at the dressing table and opened her jewel box to push aside the rings and necklaces nestled there. Yes, it was still at the bottom where she had placed it on the morning she had returned from Río Verde. At first she had flung it into the farthest corner of the room, but hours later she had found it and thrust it beneath her other jewelery.

This is part of me—wear it until we are together again.

Fresh tears flooded her eyes.

I know Ramón and I know you, Antoinette. He owns you body and soul as surely as if he had already taken you upon the marriage bed.

Luis had been right, and in admitting this to herself she knew there could be no future for her in Mexico any longer. If Maximilian triumphed she would ask Luis to release her and leave on the first available boat. If Juárez won his struggle, there would be no place for her, a Frenchwoman, in the newly independent country.

A sound suspiciously like the closing of the front gate drew her to the window. In the bright moonlight a shadowy figure could be seen first leaning against the wall, then reeling unsteadily across the courtyard toward the side door. A thief—or a Juarista? Whoever it was, he appeared to be hurt. Fighting down a moment of panic, Antoinette seized the long brass poker from the grate and carefully felt her way down the dark stairs. A low moan followed the sound of breaking glass. He had entered through the sala windows! Her heart was in her mouth as she paused outside the door, wondering if she should go back and try to awaken Soledad, but the woman slept deeply under all circumstances. Besides, what could she do? Bravely Antoinette pushed open the door and stood searching the gloom.

"Who is it? Who's there?"

It occurred to her how silly she must look standing in the doorway brandishing the fire iron. It was no match for the pistol that the intruder most probably possessed. A movement to one side brought her swinging around.

"Answer me. Who's there? Oh, dear God!"

The poker fell from her hand as she moved forward to catch the figure swaying toward her. Long black hair obscured ashen features streaked with blood as Consuelo fell forward into her arms.

"Please lie still and let me clean this wound," Antoinette protested quietly as Consuelo tried to sit up. "You need a doctor to stem the flow of blood. As soon as I have finished I will fetch one."

"No—that is impossible. By now the whole garrison will be alerted and searching for us." The effort to talk was too much for the girl, and she fell back onto the bed, her pretty face contorted with pain.

Antoinette had succeeded in getting her upstairs to the bedroom, where she had the presence of mind to lock the door before stripping off Consuelo's jacket and the blood-soaked shirt beneath. The bullet wound in her side was an ugly sight and made her feel momentarily sick, but she overcame the wave of nausea and proceeded to wash away the dried, caked blood as gently as possible.

"I—I did not mean—you to find me. I thought the house was empty—that you were at the Quinta Santos," Consuelo faltered. "I would—have rested and then gone on."

"Gone where?" Antoinette seized a white petticoat from a drawer and tore it into long strips to use as a bandage. How did Consuelo know of her movements? Was she under the watchful gaze of the Loyalists as well as Laurent's men?

"To Ramón. We were to meet back at Río Verde."

Antoinette's hands trembled as they completed their task. To Ramón! Was he her leader or her lover? She could not bring herself to ask.

"I heard an explosion—and shooting."

"Sí." Consuelo nodded weakly. "We destroyed the

193

arsenal at the Miguel Barracks. Our information was that it was not heavily guarded, but it was a trap. When we tried to leave we were surrounded. Many are dead. Ramón and I were separated, and then I was shot."

Consuelo, dressed in boy's clothes, fighting with the rebels as her husband had done and walking into a cunning trap that could only have been set by Simon Laurent. He had allowed them to accomplish their mission—although Antoinette doubted that the arsenal had contained much of value—then the trap had been sprung shut. Another desperate attempt to capture Ramón, perhaps?

"I cannot stay here," Consuelo whispered.

"You must." Antoinette knew that beneath the thick wadding of bandages the girl was still bleeding badly. She needed expert attention. She was barely conscious. "There must be someone I can go to for help."

"Mi Ramón. He would know what to do, but I will not endanger his life by having him come here."

My Ramón! Antoinette died inside at the thought of fetching the man she loved to the side of another woman. She drew back, gathering up the bloodstained clothes. They would have to be burned before Soledad saw them. And how could she keep Consuelo's presence in her bedroom a secret? She had to be moved. The attic would be a good place, but she could not do it alone. "There is a doctor in the next street."

"Sí, and he will hand me over to the authorities. If that is what you wish, then inform them yourself, señorita. I would prefer that and I would not blame you. Why should you care what happens to me?"

"They would execute you. You know that."

"I have been prepared for death for many months. I would like to be with my Paco again." A faint smile flickered over Consuelo's face. "You must do nothing to endanger your own life, señorita. I do not want the death of a friend on my conscience."

"Friend?" Slowly Antoinette sank down onto the edge of the bed. "We have never really been friends."

"I have always thought of you that way, but I could never tell you because I needed to be free to work with Ramón. I wanted many times to confide in you, but he did not want you involved. That does not matter now—you do not care for him any longer, and he goes into battle like a man possessed of the devil. You took away his desire to live, and I should hate you for that, but I cannot. I too often wish for the peace of death—to be with so many loved ones. . . ." Consuelo's voice trailed off, and for a moment Antoinette thought she had lapsed into unconsciousness, but then she began to speak again, in a tone so low it was scarcely audible. "You said once I loved him and you were right. I have much love for him—the love of a sister for her brother."

Antoinette drew back with a startled gasp. Ramón and Consuelo, brother and sister . . . No matter what Consuelo feared she now knew she had to find Ramón and bring him to the house.

"Consuelo, do you know where Ramón could be hiding now?"

TEN

Number 17 on the Plaza Domingo was a drab house at the end of a bullet-scarred street. Antoinette walked past it to the corner to ensure she had not been followed, then quickly turned and ran up the stairs to knock quietly but urgently at the door. No lights were visible from within. Had she come to the wrong place? Consuelo had definitely said 17. No, this was the house. One trembling hand clutched at the dark rebozo covering the telltale brightness of her hair, the other tightly held the amulet around her neck. Consuelo had insisted that she wear it. "It is well known among my people," she had said. "It will prove you are La Florecita—his woman—and they will not harm you."

She had locked the bedroom door behind her and slipped out of the house as a nearby church clock chimed twice. The streets were deserted, unfriendly, and dark with shadows. She encountered only one patrol and hid in a doorway, not daring to breathe until it had gone past.

She heard the sound of a bolt being drawn back, and then the door was edged open just enough for her to see the face of an old man illuminated by the dim light of the lamp he held. He stared at her suspiciously and mumbled, "Quién está ahí?"

She thrust the amulet out for him to see, watched his eyes study it without a flicker of expression.

"I have come from Consuelo to see El Padrino." The words almost stuck in her throat. "Please, don't keep me out here. Let me in, it is urgent."

"No comprendo, señorita."

"Of course you understand me. Look at what I am wearing and open this door at once."

"Qué pasa, hombre?"

Another voice came out of the darkness beyond him —a voice she knew well—followed by the ominous sound of a pistol being cocked.

"Ramón, tell him to open the door. Consuelo has been hurt." The words tumbled out in a rush.

A muttered oath, and the old man disappeared. The door was swung open wide enough to allow her through. No sooner had she stepped inside than a rough hand covered her mouth and she felt something cold against the nape of her neck. Frozen with fear, she allowed herself to be propelled into a nearby room where an aged woman sat silently rocking in a high-backed wooden chair.

"Be quiet," Ramón warned as he released her, and she obeyed without protest, watching as he cautiously stood beside the window, peering out into the street from behind the partly open curtain. The room was dark with shadows as the old man put down the lamp and went to stand in front of the door. He looked past seventy, but there was something about his stance that told her he would use the ancient pistol in his belt if she made a false move. Ramón came away from the window, muttering under his breath in Spanish. She gasped as he caught her by the wrist and dragged her against him. His face, only inches from hers, was a suspicious mask. "Where is Consuelo?"

"At my house. Let me go, you are hurting me."

"Tell me what game you are playing, or I'll break that pretty little neck," he snarled, and shook her. "Consuelo is not hurt. She is on her way out of the city with Julio."

"She has been shot. She thought I was with Luis and broke into the house intending to rest. Oh, for goodness sake, Ramón! She looked terrible when I left her. I tried to stop the bleeding, but I couldn't," Antoinette cried. "She wouldn't let me fetch a doctor—she wants you. She wants her brother."

The agonizing pressure on her wrist increased until

the pain made her feel quite faint, but he was oblivious to her distress.

"So you know that, do you? I suppose I had better believe you, but if you are leading me into a trap . . ."

"She told me where to find you. For heaven's sake, what can I do to convince you?"

"Nothing." She gave a sigh of relief and stood rubbing her bruised wrist in a miserable silence when he released her and turned to speak to his companions. Perhaps it was just the dull light, but she thought he looked somehow older. The expression on his brown face was more cruel than any she had ever seen before.

He goes into battle like a man possessed of the devil, Consuelo had said. He looked like a man possessed, but by what? Hate for her, perhaps? She thrust such thoughts out of her mind. While they lingered here, Consuelo could be dying.

"Think what you will of me, I don't care, but Consuelo is your sister. Will you risk her life with your mistrust of me?"

"If it comes to a choice between her life and yours, have no doubt she will be the one to survive," Ramón warned, holstering his pistol. She swayed back from him, her eyes dilating in horror.

"You would kill me?"

"Without hesitation. Why do you look so amazed? We mean nothing to each other. You made that quite clear the last time we were together. I have no reason to trust you or to spare your life if you attempt to betray me. Do you still insist Consuelo is hurt and at your house?"

"Yes. For pity's sake, hurry. I got lost twice trying to find this place. I have been away over an hour."

"Very well then, let us go."

He kept a firm grip on her arm as they hurried through the streets, his free hand never far away from the wicked-looking knife sheathed at his belt. It was the Mexican's favorite weapon—deadly and silent. It was unbelievable that she should be afraid of him, but she was. Afraid of the hard set to his features, the indifference to the fact that his grasp was hurting her. Once he had said he loved her. If that had been true, she had killed his love that last day—her aching wrist was proof of that.

Ramón followed her into the house, closed and securely locked the door, and stood with his back against it, his eyes sweeping the silent kitchen. "Have you no servants?"

Throwing aside her rebozo, Antoinette lighted a lamp and turned toward the stairs, saying quickly, "Only one. Soledad gets up at seven. Consuelo is in my room, but she can't stay there. We must put her somewhere else. I was thinking of the attic. If you carry her up there, I will make up some kind of a bed—" She broke off abruptly, the mention of that top room bringing to mind the sketch she had found there. Remembering it made it easier to harden her heart against his disquietening presence.

"Consuelo—mi niña pequeña." Pushing past Antoinette, Ramón knelt beside the bed, the mask dropping from his face as unrestrained grief broke through. "She's unconscious. Is the bullet still in her?"

"I don't know."

Antoinette watched helplessly as the bandages fell away beneath his competent hands, saw the horror in his eyes as the ugly wound was exposed.

"Yes, it is. She has lost much blood."

"Can we move her upstairs?"

"We shall have to. As you said, she can't stay here. She will need something soft to lie on and warm blankets."

"I'll see to it now," Antoinette answered, but he never heard her. His head was bent over Consuelo, and he held her hands clasped tightly in his. He did not look up as Antoinette left the room.

For a day and a night, while Consuelo tossed with fever in the attic room, watched over and protected by a vigilant Ramón, Antoinette did her best to go about the house under Soledad's watchful gaze as if nothing were amiss. They were the most difficult hours of her life, dogged with frustration, fear, and uncertainty for the safety of the two fugitives. She gave no thought to her own perilous position should they be discovered beneath her roof.

To her relief Mercedes did not arrive to further complicate matters and plague her life with talk of her wedding trousseau. Antoinette retired early to her room on the second day, pretending to have a bad headache, but she did not undress. As soon as she was certain the maid was asleep she crept down to the kitchen to collect the tray of food and drink she had prepared while Soledad had been shopping at the local market.

"How is she?" she asked as Ramón admitted her to the attic and reholstered his pistol. It was always in his hand whenever he unlocked the door, she noticed. He still could not bring himself to trust her. He looked drawn and tired from lack of sleep, and there was a dark shadow of beard beginning to show on his chin, but he refused her offer to rest while she kept watch. He went to sit by the small window with his plate of food while she tried to persuade Consuelo to take a little chicken broth. His knife lay on the floor within easy reach—the sight of it made her shudder. They were strangers—no, more like enemies. For Consuelo's sake he tolerated her, but did not trust her. His eyes followed her every move. Nothing escaped him.

At length she rose from beside the makeshift bed and stretched her cramped limbs. He watched her in silence, his face inscrutable.

"She has taken a little nourishment. When did the fever break?"

"This morning, but it will be several days before she can be moved. That wound could open again at any time. Don't worry, we will not stay longer than is necessary," he added grimly, seeing the alarm on Antoinette's face. "I realize how distasteful my presence is to you."

"Don't! I have no stomach for an argument just now. Ramón, I am worried about Consuelo. She should be seen by a doctor."

"As soon as she is stronger I will get her to one."

"Where will you go? She said you had walked into a

trap at the arsenal. Soldiers will be watching all the roads."

"That is not your concern. If necessary we will hide out in the city, but we will go well away from here. You have too many friends in high places."

Antoinette was not sure whether he meant Luis or Simon Laurent. His contemptuous tone stung her into retaliating, but he waved aside her bitter protest with a curt gesture.

"Go back downstairs. I don't want you here."

Deeply humiliated by the brutal rejection, she gathered up the tray and his plate. He had barely touched his food, consuming, instead, most of the bottle of red wine she had provided. In the light of day she saw there were already streaks of gray at his temples. He had indeed aged during the months they had been apart.

Early the following morning she slipped back up to the attic, anxious to know if Consuelo was stronger.

"You should not be here," Ramón said tersely. "Where is your maid?"

"I sent her out on the pretext of wanting some lace."

"Rather a flimsy excuse, wasn't it?"

"I—I told her it was for my trousseau." Her cheeks bright with color, Antoinette knelt beside Consuelo and tried to make her more comfortable. She looked a little better, but was still unable to sit up unaided.

"Ah, yes, I had forgotten. Congratulations are in order, are they not?" Ramón stood over her, his glittering eyes riveted on the ring she wore on her left hand. "He thinks highly of you—that is a family heirloom."

"It—it isn't the way you think," Antoinette began, but he interrupted her with a brittle laugh.

"I know very well how it is."

"Are you blind, mi hermano?" Consuelo whispered. "Sí, I think perhaps you are. You look at her, but you do not see what I see in her eyes. Forgive her, Ramón mío. I owe her my life."

"Forgiveness! There is none left in me," Ramón said

201

harshly. "Even my best friend puts more faith in a pretty face than in a close friendship. He will pay a high price for his folly."

Antoinette leaped to her feet, her hands clenching into tight fists at her side. She deserved his contempt, but Luis did not.

"You are not only blind but stupid also if you think Luis would turn his back on you. What you are and have done has changed nothing between you. He told me so. Our engagement is a pretense to protect me from being harassed by a man called Laurent—one of Marshal Bazaine's intelligence officers."

"Laurent!" Ramón's eyes narrowed to dark, angry slits as he repeated the name. "Sí—I know him. Why should he be interested in you?"

"Am I not La Florecita, the woman of El Padrino?" She flung the words at him scathingly. "He called me by that name. And how do you think he learned of it? He arrested and tortured people who knew you and had seen us together. Maybe even people from Río Verde . . ."

She watched his mouth tighten into a taut line at the mention of the village. She wanted to tell him how sorry she was about his home and his grandmother, but the coldness in his face deterred her. He was only a foot away, but it could have been a thousand miles.

"Laurent burned Val Verde," she faltered. "He wanted to bring you out of hiding. For several weeks he has had my every move watched, hoping you would come here. I told him you would not, but he seems incensed with the desire to catch you. Luis became so worried he offered me this way out."

"And you suggested how much more convincing it would be if he declared for Maximilian." The cruel, mocking voice hurt her far more than if he had struck her.

"That also was his idea—again to protect me. I begged him not to, but I think he felt he had little choice. Don't look at me like that. Do you think I want him killed? He is the kindest, sweetest person in the world."

"The responsibility for one more death should not unduly trouble you," Ramón drawled, and the insult snapped the thin thread of her control. With a sob she drew back her hand and slapped him with all her might across his scarred cheek. The blow he dealt her in return sent her reeling back against the wall. Consuelo's startled cry rang in her ears.

"Ramón, no . . ." She was struggling to sit up, her eyes wide with distress at his action.

"Lie still, little one. She is not worth your pity."

"You are wrong, so wrong. Oh, dear God, I think I am bleeding again."

Ramón swore as he pushed aside the blankets and saw that her bandages were spotted with fresh blood. Antoinette stood watching helplessly as he redressed the wound, knowing from the desperation in his eyes that he was as afraid for Consuelo's life as she was. Despite the risk they had to get her to a doctor. Neither of them heard the sound of someone on the stairs or heard the opening of the door Ramón had not locked. He wheeled around, his hand coming away from his belt holding the blade of the knife he was poised to throw. A muffled exclamation sounded behind them.

"Hold, amigo, I am alone," Luis declared. "In the name of all the saints, what are you doing here of all places?"

"Consuelo was hurt," Antoinette replied, moving to his side. She saw Ramón's face darken as Luis slipped an arm around her shoulders. "We have to get her medical aid, Luis. Do you have your carriage downstairs?"

"Yes, but Ramón cannot be seen in broad daylight." He looked at the weapon in his friend's hand, and a wry smile touched his lips. "You are in no danger from me, you should know that. I heard a rumor you had been seen in the city, but when I heard voices up here I never thought to find you. It has been a long time."

Antoinette sighed in silent relief as Ramón put away his knife and embraced his friend.

"You have been very foolish, hombre. Maximilian's cause is lost. I don't agree with the reasons for what you have done, but I understand. Very soon, I think, I will kill Captain Laurent, but first I have to get my sister away from here."

"Sister—Consuelo?" Luis echoed, amazed.

"I will explain later," Antoinette said quickly. "Can we use your carriage, Luis?"

"Of course. I will help Ramón, and you will stay here. You have risked too much as it is."

Antoinette felt herself grow quite weak as Ramón's dark eyes fastened on her face. For three days they had been too concerned for Consuelo to dwell on their own personal problem, and she had managed to maintain her composure, but now he was about to go out of her life forever. One kind word, one gesture was all that was needed for her to break down and beg his forgiveness. She waited expectantly, only to have her hopes cruelly shattered.

"You have Consuelo's thanks for your help. I know you do not want mine, but I suggest you accept a word of advice. If you stay in the capital, I cannot guarantee your safety. Have Luis take you to the quinta. Will you do that, compadre? I assure you the place will be left alone by our men. Forget Querétaro—you will die there. We already have men in all the key positions around the town. Once Maximilian enters the gates, he will not leave again as Emperor of Mexico. Some of us have to live to rebuild our country—I would like you to be one of us."

"It is too late to think of myself," Luis returned quietly. "I have to protect Antoinette."

Ramón's eyes gleamed sardonically.

"How proud you must be to wield such power over a man," he sneered, glancing into her white face.

"As proud as you when you lied and deceived my father," she flung back, her temper flaring. "You played Judas well."

"Let it go," Luis muttered, sensing the suppression of emotion inside her. "It can do no good now."

"No, why should I? You are right, Ramón, I don't want your thanks. What I did was for Consuelo. It changes

204

nothing between us. My only wish is that I had found my father's sketch when I first came here. I could have denounced you then and saved myself these past farcical months."

"Sketch?" Ramón looked at Luis questioningly. "What does she mean?"

"Don't you know? Antoinette's father did a drawing of you. One-half of you was wearing Mexican uniform, the other was dressed in the irregular Juarista garb. The implication was very clear."

"And when he showed it to you, you realized he knew your secret. You killed him to keep him silent," Antoinette cried recklessly.

"And what happened to this drawing?" Ramón asked, tight-lipped. "Where did you find it?"

"Here, in this very room. That was why you wanted me out of here that first day, wasn't it?"

"I once gave you credit for being a woman of exceptional intelligence—yet another mistake I made. Dios, do you think if I had cold-bloodedly arranged his death I would have left the sketch here for anyone to find? I had a hundred opportunities to remove it before you arrived. Where is it now? Let me see it." His fists were clenched at his sides, his body taut as a bowstring.

"I—I don't have it," Antoinette stammered. "I destroyed it. Luis thought it would be best."

"How convenient."

"It did exist. I saw it," Luis broke in, "but I don't for one moment believe what Antoinette does. I know you too well. She will come to her senses in time. Be patient."

"It is already too late for both of us." Ramón took out his gun and checked it. The anger disappeared from his face, and it became a closed book again as he contemplated the two people before him. "Consuelo will need clothes. . . ."

It was an order, not a request, and Antoinette blinked back weary tears as she hurried downstairs. He had decided how it would be between them, and she was too proud to fight him. Proud or foolish? She loved him still.

Her body ached with being so close, yet unable to reach out and touch him. She was foolish and proud and stubborn—and she had lost him forever.

As she gathered up an armful of clothes the sound of shouting and voices outside the garden gate sent her rushing to the window in a panic. Soldiers in the courtyard. Soldiers everywhere. Ramón wheeled about as she burst into the attic, gasping for breath.

"Soldiers. There are soldiers outside. Run—save yourself."

He did not move, and she ran to him, grabbing at his arms in desperation.

"For God's sake, don't you understand what I am saying? The house is probably surrounded. Get out through the window. Luis and I will look after Consuelo, try to hide her. . . ."

"I won't leave her," Ramón answered harshly, "nor you. A fight would mean not only my death, but yours too, and I will never bring harm to you." Simple words, yet with so much depth of feeling behind them. His eyes darted around the room to the small window that led on to the roof and was the only means of escape. Escape for him, but not for his injured sister—not without more time. A wry smile flitted across his face as he looked at Antoinette. "In a short while you will have your wish. . . ."

"What are you saying?" She clutched at him more tightly, wanting to shake him out of his composure, make him run before it was too late.

"You wanted to see me dead."

"No—no. You don't understand. I love you"—how easy it was to say the words now—"I always will. Please go. Run now before they are here. . . ." Antoinette's wild words died as she was crushed against Ramón's chest and his mouth claimed hers. For a long moment she enjoyed the exquisite pleasure of his kiss and the realization he had never stopped loving her. His love remained as powerful and steadfast as ever. With an effort she tore herself from his grasp. "No—I won't let them catch you."

He called her name as she wheeled about toward the

door, then started after her, alarm springing to his face.

"Luis—stop her."

It was too late. The attic door slammed behind Antoinette, drowning his words. Turning the key in the lock, she threw it as far as her strength would allow as she ran downstairs, stumbling, almost falling as she reached her bedroom. An audacious idea was forming in her mind. She dared not think of the consequences when she was caught, as she would surely be. For her there would be no escape, but her scheme would give Ramón time to escape and enable him to get Consuelo to safety also with Luis' help.

Snatching up the dark rebozo she had dropped by the door in her haste to return to the attic and warn Ramón, she draped it around her head and shoulders and hurried downstairs. As she appeared in the courtyard, soldiers swarmed through the gate they had forced open and immediately turned in her direction. Her heart in her mouth, she ignored the order to halt and ran through the gardens to the long, low wall at the back of the house. She heard her petticoats tear as she clambered over it and fell onto her knees in the cobbled alleyway on the other side. Fear forced her on despite the agonizing stitch in her side that robbed her of what little breath remained in her body. The longer she remained free, the more time Ramón had, and that was all that mattered to her now. He still loved her! Her cheeks were wet with tears as she struggled on. She had not destroyed his love with her anger and hatred. She was La Florecita again—the woman of Ramón Chávez—and her heart swelled with pride at the knowledge that nothing could ever destroy the memory of the moments they had shared together.

One ankle twisted beneath her and she fell against the wall of a house, crying out in pain as the rough brickwork grazed her arms. Two soldiers close on her heels, were upon her before she could recover her balance. One of them hurled himself at her, knocking her to the ground. A blow across the face rendered her almost unconscious. She was crying incoherently as she was dragged to her feet, and her hands were tied tightly behind her back before she was propelled back toward the house. She had no strength left to resist her captors, who swore at her in French as they pushed her across the courtyard. She was led past grim-faced legionnaires who stared at her, some with open animosity, and taken upstairs to her bedroom, where she found herself face-to-face with—Simon Laurent. . . .

Behind him stood Soledad, and to Antoinette's amazement, Mercedes, her full mouth deepening into a satisfied smile at the alarm on the face of the French girl. At the captain's side was the sergeant she had tricked at Río Verde. By the way he was glaring at her she knew he recognized her as the woman who had supposedly been lost that day. Pleasure registered on his weather-beaten face at the sight of the bruise on her cheek and her bound hands.

"Mademoiselle Dubec." Simon Laurent's voice was dangerously low. "We have come for Chávez. El Padrino if you prefer."

"That man! You are mad to think I would give him sanctuary—he murdered my father."

"You are trying my patience." Laurent turned and snapped out an order to the men behind him. They continued upstairs, rifles at the ready. The sergeant followed, and Antoinette swallowed hard. Ramón had escaped by now—at least she prayed he had. Surely he would not stay and fight? Capture meant death in front of a firing squad under Maximilian's summary execution order. Dear heaven, how could she have once prayed for that to happen? And Luis would be arrested too, as an accomplice, and would share the same fate. The room reeled unsteadily about her as she fought to retain her composure.

One of the legionnaires reappeared. "There is a locked door upstairs. Shall we break it open?"

Simon Laurent wheeled on him, his face contorted by fury. "Of course, you fool!" Turning to Antoinette, he looked so fierce she felt sure he might strike her at any moment. "When you ran out I felt sure it was the woman Consuelo. You are very clever, mademoiselle, but the delay will not be enough. My men are everywhere. Chávez cannot escape. Tell him to come down. Save his life while you can."

"So that you can have the pleasure of executing him? Never! Take him if you can," she flung back, uncaring that her words condemned her. At least Ramón had the same chance he had given her at Díaz' camp. She owed him that much.

Turning away, she sat down on the bed, trying to ignore Mercedes, who advanced into the room, her eyes blazing with triumph. Antoinette wondered what part she had played in all this—and Soledad too, who was standing with hands folded in front of her by the window. The ropes around her wrists were cutting into her soft skin, and the pain was making her feel faint.

The attic door shuddered under the heavy shoulders of many soldiers, and several shots followed. It was a strong lock—they would have had to shoot it off, she thought, waiting for the burst of gunfire that would tell her Ramón and his companions had been discovered. None came. She lifted an anguished face as the sergeant appeared beside Captain Laurent, heard with incredulity and overwhelming relief his words, "There is no one there, but we found these."

He was holding several bloodstained bandages. "There was more than one of them up there, Captain. They got out through a small window onto the roof."

Gunfire from outside interrupted him, shouting from the courtyard, horses' hooves sounding a loud staccato on the cobblestones, more firing, and then a breathless Mexican soldier reeling into the doorway to report that a carriage waiting outside had been driven away at high speed. The driver had been knocked unconscious and two soldiers killed when they tried to stop it.

Antoinette heard and still could not believe the impossible had happened. They were all free—Ramón, Consuelo, and Luis.

"Did you say a carriage?" Mercedes demanded. "That belonged to my brother. Where is he?"

"Surely that is obvious," Laurent returned, and his eyes were cold as he stared at her. "He came here to help his friend escape. His conveyance was conveniently waiting outside, no? Mon Dieu! A few minutes earlier, and we would have caught them all—your traitorous brother included."

"Luis would not risk his life for Juárez' cause. He is for Maximilian, on our side." Mercedes looked almost frantic. She was afraid for herself, not her brother, Antoinette thought in disgust. Quietly she said, "Not for Juárez— for a friend. He would die for Ramón."

"As you will, mademoiselle," Laurent intervened.

She rose to her feet, suddenly afraid. "Of what am I accused?"

"Treason against his Imperial Majesty, Maximilian, Emperor of Mexico. When my sergeant recollected where he had seen you, I knew your so-called betrothal to be a trick to put you above suspicion, and so I called off my watchdogs and set the woman Soledad to spy instead. A slight subterfuge on my part, I admit, but it worked, did it not?"

"Whatever she has told you, it is without foundation," Antoinette retorted. Soledad! Recruited, no doubt, at the suggestion of Mercedes.

"Brave words, but words cannot help you now. I have all the evidence I need. I see I do not convince you. Then let me enlighten you further. First, your friendship with Chávez. Innocent? No. You could have convinced me, but for the drawing Soledad pieced together in your room at the Quinta Santos. You should have burned it. It has already been submitted to the higher authorities who are now considering your case. You knew who he was from the beginning, aided him in his work, even took one of his accomplices into your home as a maid. You have been to his village, nursed his accursed peons, been the center of an attack on three French soldiers. For that

210

incident alone you would be condemned to death. Must I go on? I see you at last realize your position."

At the words "condemned to death" Antoinette had gone pale and swayed back against the wall.

"Perhaps I could intervene for you if you cooperated. A little information could mean deportation back to France instead of death."

"I know nothing," Antoinette replied in a clear voice. Ramón was free to carry on his fight, Consuelo would soon be with a doctor, and Luis now had another chance to reconsider his disastrous decision to side with Maximilian. "I have no idea where they have gone."

"So be it." Simon Laurent motioned two soldiers to position themselves behind her. "Antoinette Dubec, by the power vested in me by General Bazaine, marshal of France, I hereby place you under arrest for giving aid and succor to the fugitive Ramón Chávez, knowing him to be the rebel leader El Padrino, a colonel in the Liberal army of Benito Juárez. Take her away."

The prison, which lay in the shadow of the Residential Palace, was like something out of a nightmare. The tiny cells were overcrowded with frightened, bewildered people who clawed at the bars as she passed, stretching out their hands to the elegant woman in a blue dress and cape who moved past them like a sleepwalker. Antoinette closed her ears to their whining pleas, the oaths and abuse flung at the two French soldiers behind her, knowing that if she allowed herself to look at them, she would lose her sanity. The poor of the city were there, mixed in with insurgents, innocent bystanders who had been arrested for being in the wrong place at the wrong time, convicted rebels awaiting execution, and women who had followed their men into prison rather than be separated from them. She felt sick and could hardly breathe.

"Through here." The sergeant opened a door and stood back for her to enter. Two cells adjoined each other, separated by a large barred grille that offered little or no privacy for the occupants. She could see the boots of a man who lay on the straw palliasse in one of them as Laurent laid a hand on her arm.

"In here, mademoiselle. It is primitive, but you will not be here long. No longer than forty-eight hours by my estimation."

The huge barred door swung noisily shut, imprisoning her in the dark, unfriendly cell.

"What do you mean? I demand to be allowed to write some letters." Antoinette's voice betrayed the fear in her heart, and she saw Simon Laurent's eyes gleam with satisfaction.

"You will be allowed the services of a priest before the sentence is carried out."

"Sentence!" She reached out a hand and grasped one of the bars to steady herself. "What sentence? I have had no trial. Am I not allowed to defend myself against the charges?"

The captain produced a folded piece of paper from inside his tunic. As he unfolded it she saw it bore the official crest of the Emperor.

"This was prepared before I came to the house. You see how confident I was of your total involvement with Chávez. Shall I read the contents to you? No? A brief summary then. It is a document listing all charges laid against you, together with a statement from your maid, who has been a most able spy—she even discovered the small bloodstain you had not managed to wash out of the carpet in the sala. There are other witnesses against you —minor ones, I must admit. But together with my own evidence of what was found today—and the drawing, we must not forget that, must we—there will be enough to have you executed for treason. As soon as I have put my signature on this piece of paper the sentence will be carried out."

"Your signature," Antoinette gasped. "Only the Emperor can sign that, and he will never sentence me to death. I was a friend to the Empress, he will remember me."

"The Emperor left for Querétaro early this morning," came the shattering answer. "If you make it necessary for me to sign this, I will—without the slightest hesitation. Tomorrow all that rabble out there"—he waved a hand in the direction of the crowded cells outside—"will pay the penalty for their crimes. You are lucky, mademoiselle, you have time to reconsider. As I said before, a little information could save your life."

How long she had been lying on the palliasse, Antoinette did not know. It was growing dark outside the single window high above her head, and evening shadows were lengthening across the narrow cell. She watched with dull, red-rimmed eyes, numb, uncaring. She was to die alone and friendless. Dear God, why could it not be her turn tomorrow? The waiting would send her mad. She could not bear listening to those other poor wretches being led out to die and then the ominous sound of the firing squad cutting them down without mercy. The horror of it all overwhelmed her, and she covered her face with her hands and huddled, sobbing on the miserable bed.

"Señorita Dubec, is that you? Answer me, por favor. It is I, Pedro Martínez."

Antoinette rolled over onto her back with a startled gasp. Were her ears playing tricks?

"Captain—it is you!" The face pressed against the bars was indeed that of Ramón's second in command. Dark bruises stood out on his forehead and cheeks; blood smeared his torn shirt. He had been brutally beaten. "Why are you here?"

"I was caught trying to get out of the city after our attack on the arsenal."

"So you are one of them too?"

"Sí. Colonel Chávez and I have worked closely together for the past two years. But you, señorita. Why have they arrested you?"

"Consuelo was hurt, and I hid her in my house. Ramón —Colonel Chávez—managed to get her away when the soldiers came, but evidence that they had been there was found. I was betrayed by my own maid, who was set to spy on me by that terrible man Laurent. Can he really have me executed? Have I no rights?"

"None, señorita, under the Black Flag Decrees of the Emperor. Many of my people have died in the same way. Tell Laurent what he wants to know and save yourself."

"I have no idea where Colonel Chávez is." Antoinette pressed her hands against her mouth as fresh tears began to flow.

"Dios—that you should come to this after all the colonel did to protect you."

"Protect me? What do you mean?"

"Those of us who knew of your association with him were sworn to secrecy. None of us would ever have told how close you were to him. Believe me, the colonel's anger would have been far more terrible than anything these French pigs could do to us."

Antoinette drew a hand across her blurred eyes. The strain had been to much for her—she was beginning to lose her mind. Ramón protecting her after the way she had treated him? Such was the action of a man who loved her!

"But he hates me," she whispered dazedly. "I found out he killed my father."

"No, that is not true. On the day your father and his men were ambushed, he was on his way to Cuenevaca with the Emperor."

"No—no, what are you saying?" Antoinette moaned. "He was responsible even if he did not fire the actual shot. They were his men—obeying his orders."

"Again you are wrong, señorita. The colonel told me of the patrol, led by your father, that was to escort some prisoners from San Luis Potosí to the capital, but before he could work out a plan for their escape, he was ordered to leave with Don Maximiliano, and so I acted independently on the information he had already given me. I had recently been ill, and so it was not too difficult to be excused from accompanying the detail. I led our men, señorita. I alone gave the orders for the attack in which your father died."

The guards came for Captain Martínez at first light the following morning. He was at the head of the long list of condemned. Antoinette dragged herself into wakefulness and pressed herself against the bars as he halted before her cell, pale but composed. He was a soldier. He knew how to die. Would she be as brave when her turn came?

"Forgive me, señorita."

"Yes, Captain." She had no hesitation in giving him peace of mind, wishing she could ask forgiveness of Ramón before it was too late.

She stood dry-eyed at the window, listening to the sound of marching feet, the issuing of orders, the harsh crack of the rifles. As the echo of the volley died away, she slid down onto the straw mattress, shivering uncontrollably. Tomorrow it would be her turn to walk down the long corridor and out into the bright sunlight where sudden, violent death was waiting. . . .

Antoinette did not even bother to get up when Simon Laurent appeared that evening.

"You have not eaten." He was looking at the tray of food left untouched near the cell door. The mere smell of it had made her feel sick. "You are being very stupid."

"I have nothing to tell you. I know nothing."

"Before you swear away your life there is something I want you to see. Come."

"Where are you taking me?" Antoinette asked as he led her out of the dingy cell.

"To show you how unpleasant I could make your last hours if you persist in being difficult," came the alarming reply.

His hand on her arm was too tight for her to pull free. In silence Antoinette allowed him to lead her along several corridors, each one more somber than the one before, until they were descending into the very bowels of the prison. An agonizing scream pierced the silence. It came from one of the cells in front of them. Antoinette stopped, but was dragged relentlessly forward.

"No—I don't want to see." She struggled against his grip, suddenly panic-stricken; her lovely face a mask of fear.

"So you are afraid—that is good," Laurent murmured. Dragging her close to him, he propelled her forcibly through the nearest open door. Antoinette screamed and recoiled back against him, half fainting at the nightmarish scene that confronted her.

Two men and a woman were chained against the far wall. All three had been terribly tortured. As much as the sight sickened her, Antoinette found she was unable to drag her eyes away from the poor wretches, especially the woman, whose breasts and stomach had been terribly branded by red-hot irons from the glowing brazier in the middle of the cell. The heat from it was overpowering, and the fumes seared her throat. She cried out as a swarthy-faced man stepped out of the shadows and drew a pair of white-hot pincers from the flaming coals and then looked questioningly at Simon Laurent.

"Yes, Marcel, show Mademoiselle how expert you are at inflicting great pain. Perhaps it will loosen her tongue."

"No," Antoinette cried out as the man turned toward his helpless victim. "How can you be so inhuman? I can't watch."

"But you will," her companion growled, and thrust her forward. When she tried to turn away, he wound a length of her loose hair around his fist and jerked her head back, holding her fast. The glowing pincers swam before her tortured vision, and she shut her eyes to blot out the sight, but she could not stop her ears against the piercing screams of the unfortunate woman.

"Take me away," Antoinette moaned. "I beg of you."

"So you are begging now—a few minutes more and I think you will be willing to answer all my questions," Laurent murmured in her ear.

"I know nothing of Ramón's activities with the rebels. Can't you understand I helped him and his sister to escape because I love him?"

"Don't lie to me," her captor snapped, and slapped her heavily across the face, grazing her cheek with the gold ring he wore. "I have proof of how deeply you are involved with him. For weeks there has been talk of La Florecita, the woman of El Padrino. That's you, isn't it? You are not only his contact in the city, but his mistress. Confess it now, or do I have to confront you with someone who will betray all your secrets?"

Mutely, Antoinette shook her head.

"You are trying my patience to the limit. . . ."

With a painful grip on her hair, Simon Laurent propelled her out into the corridor, unlocked the door of the cell immediately alongside, and thrust her inside. By the dull light of an almost extinguished wall torch Antoinette was just able to make out two figures sprawled against the far wall. The old man lay inert with his head on the lap of his wife. The last time she had seen them had been at the house on the Plaza Domingo when she had gone to tell Ramón of Consuelo's injury.

"I never cease to be amazed at the strength in a woman's body. These two were arrested yesterday. The old fool died without talking last night, but it took Marcel until this morning to break her."

Antoinette fought down a rising nausea. He sounded as though he had enjoyed the spectacle.

"Look at us, old woman. Look at us, I say. Who is this with me? Do you know her?"

A nod came from the broken woman. Her voice when she spoke was flat and emotionless.

"She is the one El Padrino calls La Florecita. She is his woman. She came to the house."

"Your house—the house where he met his rebel friends?"

"Sí."

"Did she come often?"

"Sí."

"No, that isn't true," Antoinette cried. "I went there only once to tell Ramón his sister was hurt."

"Ah, yes. Consuelo is his sister, isn't she? And your maid. I remember you once told me she was of no importance. Go on, mademoiselle, tell me more."

"I didn't know who she was then—only that her husband was dead. I felt sorry for her."

"So you admit to harboring a rebel sympathizer beneath your roof?"

"Yes . . . yes . . ." Antoinette almost screamed the words at him as her limited self-control began to crack.

"Old woman, did El Padrino's sister ever come to your house?"

"Sí."

"With this woman?"

"Sí."

"Did this woman ever stay with El Padrino—at night, perhaps?"

"Many times." A shrug of the old, tired shoulders. "Why not? She is his woman."

"It isn't true." Antoinette was almost sobbing now. "She will say anything you want her to—you have hurt her so much."

"As I can do with you if I so choose," Laurent gloated. The pressure on her hair increased until the pain brought tears to her eyes. Then, abruptly, she was released. Dazed and trembling, she leaned back against the wall, oblivious to the hot tears streaming down her cheeks.

"Bring what charges you wish against me, I'm sure you have more than enough manufactured evidence to secure my death sentence. I have nothing more to say."

Simon Laurent stepped close to her and ran a finger down the mark on her cheek. She shuddered at the clumsy caress. The intense scrutiny of his pale eyes was somehow more frightening than anything she had so far been forced to witness.

"We shall see. Let us go upstairs where we can talk."

"Please—have me taken back to my cell. I want to be alone."

"Time for that later. Come with me."

She had no choice but to obey, knowing full well he was prepared to use force if she refused. Wiping a hand across her wet cheeks, she followed him and was almost blinded as they emerged from the gloom. In silence he led her to a floor above the main cell block and into a room where a pleasant fire blazed in the hearth and a table nearby was laid with appetizing food. She thought she was hearing things when he said, "There are soap and towels in the other room. Go and make yourself look like a woman again instead of a bedraggled peasant."

Antoinette swallowed the retort that rose to her lips and went into the small antechamber, where she found a bowl of water, towels, and a large piece of perfumed soap and other toilet requisites. She realized his game at once, but the chance to rid her face and hands of the prison grime proved too strong. When she emerged ten minutes later, she was clean and refreshed, her hair combed and swept back from her face, which bore a decidedly stubborn expression as she confronted Simon Laurent, who was seated at the table. His eyes considered her for a long moment, and she was frightened again. Pouring out a glass of wine, he pushed it toward her.

"Sit down and relax, mademoiselle. Drink and eat and then we will talk."

"No."

"Sit down." The invitation became an order, and she slid down into a chair and drank the wine. It was nectar after the filthy water that had been provided in the prison. He filled a plate with ham and other cold meats and placed it before her. Antoinette wished she had the courage to refuse it, but she was ravenous.

"First you frighten me, now you are kind, but it won't work, Captain," she said between mouthfuls.

"Will it not?" Laurent emptied his glass and immediately refilled it. She noticed he was drinking brandy, not

219

wine. "I thought this might give you the chance to reconsider your position. I had hoped the tour would loosen your tongue, but no matter. As you say, I already have more than enough evidence to have you shot without resorting to torture. You are Chávez' mistress, and that is what interests me most. I can make good use of that."

"I am not," Antoinette protested coldly.

"True or not, it makes little difference. More wine? Give me your glass and listen to what I have to say. I am about to offer you your life."

She obeyed and then sat back in her chair, hands locked tightly in her lap.

"What scheme have you in mind now?"

"My file on you is now quite comprehensive," Laurent drawled. The heat from the fire and the large amount of brandy he was consuming were making him exceedingly warm, and he removed his tunic and gun. Antoinette's gaze followed the weapon as it was put to one side. He noticed her interest and laughed.

"That would be most foolish, Antoinette. My way is much easier."

He stood by the fire, glass in hand, watching her until she felt the color mount in her cheeks. He had never looked at her this way before—as though he owned her. In a way he did—he had the power of life and death over her. She was no more than a puppet in his hands. She felt as if those hands were about to reach out and touch her. Dear God—what was to come?

"What way? What are you offering me?"

"A chance to redeem yourself in the eyes of your judges. Your life, freedom when the war is over. Think of it. You will be able to go back to France and forget this whole unpleasant business."

"What do I have to do to receive such generosity?"

"First read this." He produced a folded piece of paper from his breeches and held it out to her.

Antoinette's eyes widened as she studied the contents. They proclaimed her to be a French agent, working first under the direction of Marshal Bazaine and then Laurent himself, dedicated to bringing El Padrino to justice for the murder of her father. In gratitude for the detailed information she had provided through her relationship with the enemy, she was to be personally rewarded by the Emperor. It was signed by Maximilian himself.

"This is a monstrous lie."

"But enough to bring your lover out of hiding, I think. I intend to have copies of this posted all over the city."

"No! He will never believe it."

"There is more. This document he may dispute, but the sight of you free, enjoying the company of the Emperor's officers at your home, coupled with the rumor that I have taken up residence at your house and we have become more than friends . . . What would he believe then? I have heard he is a very jealous man. . . . These Mexicans are so hot-blooded, so emotional. . . ."

The blood drained from Antoinette's face. She stood up so quickly her glass of wine tipped over and the dark-red stain sank into the white cloth. Even if Ramón did not believe the rumor, he would try to get to the house if she were free, and walk into a trap—just as Laurent intended. He was a devil!

"You can't be serious?"

Laurent drained his glass and put it to one side. He was beginning to sway slightly.

"But I am, Antoinette. Come now, am I such a poor catch? Think of what I—and I alone—can offer you. Your life, your freedom. Agree to my terms and I will personally escort you home this instant."

"And remain to seal the bargain." Antoinette spat the words at him contemptuously.

"Of course. Why do you look so shocked? I ask no more of you than you gave Chávez."

"I gave him only my love. He did not even ask for that. He took nothing from me. He is not like you, a torturer of old men and women—an animal."

Antoinette was growing exceedingly afraid and knew by his expression he could read it in her eyes, hear it in her voice. Part of her screamed out to accept his terms, to cling to her life, perhaps gain time to get back to the house, where Ramón might be able to rescue her. But underneath it all, she knew she would not be freed. Laurent hated Ramón; the final insult to her was only part of the humiliation he intended for the man who had eluded him for so long.

"Think of it, Antoinette—clean sheets, fresh clothes, a warm bed . . ." Laurent was close to her, his hands on her arms drawing her against him. She shut her eyes to blot out the hungry gaze that devoured her body. She prayed she might faint and thus escape the hot mouth reeking with brandy that was seeking hers. Sick with disgust, she gathered the last of her strength and broke free of him, backing away until the door was behind her.

"You are an animal. No, I will not agree to your terms. Did you honestly believe I would betray Ramón Chávez in order to save myself? I mean nothing to Mexico—my death will be of no importance to her people—but El Padrino must live; he is needed." Something Consuelo had once said flooded into her mind, and she spoke with reckless courage, her blue eyes flashing with pride as she stared into his cold face. "Long after you and your kind have gone, men like Ramón will rule Mexico. Men who care about the peons and the indios and the land and are not afraid to fight and die for the right of every Mexican to hold up his head and be proud of what he is." How well she remembered Consuelo's scorn. It had hurt her deeply. To her horror she saw it was lost on Simon Laurent, who was smiling as he crossed the room and took up a document and a pen from his desk. And then she knew that even if she had agreed to his terms, she would never have been allowed to return to France. He would have abused her and then, probably, discarded her, leaving her to bear alone the ridicule not only of her own people, but also of the Mexicans she had come to know and respect.

She did not have to ask what he held. The paper

needed only his signature. He signed his name with a flourish and waved the document before her.

"As you say, your life is of little importance. I am after far bigger game. By tomorrow afternoon I shall have forgotten you ever existed. I suppose you would like to see a priest?"

"Yes."

"There is a convent across the square—it is most convenient at times. You shall have your man of God, mademoiselle. May he make your last few hours on this earth tolerable."

Antoinette did not answer or move as he flung open the door and called for a guard to return her to her cell.

"Find Rosita and bring her to me after you have dealt with this one. I am in need of a little relaxation," Laurent told the legionnaire who came in, and his pale eyes gleamed with cruel amusement as they followed her out of the room.

Less than an hour later, the door of Antoinette's cell was unlocked to admit an aged, stooping priest supported by a young nun. It was securely locked behind them, and they were left alone.

"My child, it grieves me to see you in such circumstances. We have come to rectify the matter."

Strong hands closed over her wrists and drew her to her feet. In the shadowy light, with a fair growth of beard on his chin, she had not recognized the face beneath the cowl, but the familiar voice brought a soft cry to her lips.

"Father Ignatius—how can it be?"

"I have come to take you out of this place. Be quick now—take off your dress."

"What?"

The nun was disrobing. From beneath the cumbersome black robes emerged the white face of Consuelo. Even in the dim light, Antoinette could see that her eyes were bright with fever. What madness had brought her here in her condition? Her eyes widened as she saw the dark stain on one side of Consuelo's blouse. The wound was bleeding again.

"Do as Father tells you, señorita, please. There is little time. Captain Laurent is getting drunk in his quarters with a woman friend and will probably not appear until morning, but the guards may change at any time and Father Ignatius could be recognized."

"But if I change clothes with you, how . . ." Antoinette's brain refused to function. Consuelo was hurt—how would she escape?

"I shall take your place, but they will not execute me. Please hurry, everything is arranged. Give me your dress. Now, put on this outfit and be sure to hide all that red hair."

With Antoinette's cape secured over her head and face, Consuelo sank down onto the palliasse as if to pray, making sure her back was toward the door.

"Vaya con Dios, señorita. Make my Ramón happy."

A terrible fear swept through Antoinette at her weak tone. Only with a tremendous effort was Consuelo able to remain upright. She started toward her, but the priest caught her arm and held her fast.

"No, Doña Antoinette, this is the way she wishes it to be."

"But I can't leave her here. She is badly hurt."

"The bullet is lodged too near the heart for me to remove it. She knows she has only hours to live. She has chosen to use that short time to give you life, my child. Have courage, she is in God's hands." Gently but firmly he propelled Antoinette to the door. "Guard! We are ready to leave now." To Antoinette: "Keep your head down and away from the light. Quickly now, someone is coming."

"You did not take long, Father." It was a great relief when only one soldier appeared. As they turned away from the cell, Antoinette trembled, aware that she would never see Consuelo alive again. Her footsteps faltered. She could not leave. Father Ignatius kept her moving determinedly.

"The poor woman has no need of me now, she is with God," he said quietly. Antoinette shivered again. He had said that a moment ago: *She is in God's hands.* He spoke of Consuelo as if she were already dead. "You have a kind face, my son. Will you respect her vigil through this night? She has so little time to prepare herself."

"She won't be disturbed—not until morning."

"Come, take my arm, we have to walk quite a distance," the priest murmured as they came out into the open. Antoinette gulped in fresh, clean air and conquered the awful nausea rising in her stomach at the sight of soldiers milling all around them.

Lack of sleep and the strain of her short but torturous ordeal began to take its toll of her strength. The next hour was a jumble of passing faces, ill-lighted streets, and voices that never registered in her dazed mind. Then, when she thought she could go no farther, they reached the burro-drawn cart Father Ignatius had arranged to have waiting to transport them safely out of the city. Willing hands materialized from nowhere to lift her in among the grain sacks and cover her with blankets. The last thing she felt before lapsing into unconsciousness was the priest's cool hand against her burning forehead.

ELEVEN

The fever that had descended on Antoinette the night of her escape from prison grew worse and raged through her body for over a week. When she came out of her delirium and began the slow return to reality, she discovered she had been transported to the huge, sprawling Juarista camp at Puebla that was managed by Father Ignatius. When she asked for Ramón, she was told he was en route form Querétaro and that she had been issued a safe-conduct pass to Veracruz, where she could take ship for France. She looked at the piece of paper the priest held out to her, and silent tears rolled down her cheeks. Had it all been for nothing?

"You don't have to go. Consuelo gave you the chance to be together again."

"Do you think I don't know who arranged this pass for me? Once my father's death was between us. Now it is Consuelo's. How—how did he take the news of her death?"

"He was full of grief. His words to me were bitter—his sister was all he had left. You had turned your back on him, yet she sacrificed her life for you. He did not want to understand."

"She knew I loved him. I tried to tell Ramón too before he escaped from the house, but it would seem I failed."

"No, he believed you, but he loves you too much to have you remain here and risk death again. If I were you, I would go to him. Without him you are only half alive. Two bodies, but only one heart. Can you live without him?"

"Are you suggesting I become a soldadera?" Antoinette asked, her eyes widening. With an aching heart she remembered her brave words to Ramón at the ruined temple behind Val Verde.

If need be I'll follow you wherever you go—as your wife—a soldadera—I don't care.

"You were willing enough to give up your life for him," Father Ignatius said with a deep frown. "Will you allow pride to destroy the last opportunity you may have?"

"He doesn't want me. . . ."

"He wants you, but he too is proud. You must convince him you will stay at his side no matter what hardships are ahead. Love and cherish him even without a roof over your head, food in your mouth. Bear his children on the hard ground if necessary, but be one with him under any circumstances. For love of him you almost died. For love of you he was ready to risk his life attempting to rescue you. For love of you both Consuelo took your place in prison. So much courage, so many people willing to make enormous sacrifices for those dear to them." The priest took Antoinette's hand and smiled down into her pale face. "Is it all to be in vain?"

"Are you trying to tell me Ramón cared enough to try to free me?" Hope swelled inside her, bringing with it new courage to go on.

"When I saw Consuelo I knew she could not live more than a few hours if Ramón attempted to take her out of the city. With rest and quiet she might have lasted one day, perhaps two, but she was dying and she knew it. She swore me to silence, not wanting to worry Ramón, who was already half out of his mind after you had been arrested. He and Señor Santos managed to get out of the capital. Ramón wanted permission from General Díaz to select some men to make a diversionary attack while he penetrated the prison. It would have been a hopeless attempt for a lone man, and Consuelo realized this. As soon as he had gone, she spoke to me of her plan to change places with you. How could I refuse her what was in effect a dying wish? She was not afraid of death—she welcomed it as a way of being reunited with her husband."

"I know—she once told me—but to have to face a firing squad! Oh, Father, it is more than I can bear."

"No, my child, she was dead when they went to the cell the next morning, as I knew she would be. I am a man of God and I have much to answer for to Him about my part in your escape, but I am also a doctor and I knew the tremendous exertion in moving her from her hiding place to the prison would considerably shorten her time. I met Ramón and his men some five miles outside the city. He had secured Díaz' permission to try to rescue you. It would have been a suicide mission, but he had to do it. By then you were burning with fever and did not know him. Had you seen the look in his eyes when he found you alive and free, you would not ask more questions of me or hesitate to go to him."

Antoinette's fingers strayed to the amulet around her neck—she had worn it constantly since her mission to the house on the Plaza Domingo. When the two pieces were joined they would be one in body, soul, and mind.

"I've never really had a choice, have I?" She forced a brave smile to her lips. "Father, will you ask General Díaz if I may join the other women?"

"You already have. Welcome, La Florecita."

It was the middle of March—three long weeks—before Antoinette was strong enough to travel. She lived with the other women under conditions that were almost primitive as the soldiers moved from one place to another and the soldaderas followed. Under the tutorship of Father Ignatius, her nursing experience broadened. She helped with the sick and wounded and the organizing of make-shift hospitals whenever a new camp was made. She spent many long, weary hours at his side, watching the competent hands of a brilliant doctor trying to patch up bullet-torn bodies and listening to the quiet, soothing voice of the priest giving absolution to the dying. His unruffled calm was often a great comfort to her as the weeks slipped by and they moved closer and closer to Querétaro, where Maximilian and the remnants of the Imperial forces were surrounded and under siege from an overwhelming number of Loyalists.

Querétaro was the capital of the state of the same name. It lay in a valley, within easy cannon range of the hills that sheltered the Liberal army forces under the command of General Mariano Escobedo, a man of blind devotion to the Republican cause. Maximilian had been in residence at the convent of La Cruz without too much harassment for several weeks before the general's cavalry began occupying villages and farmhouses on the outskirts of the town, preparing for the final assault that would forever rid their country of a foreign ruler.

From inquiries made by Father Ignatius on her behalf, Antoinette had learned that one of the cavalry regiments was commanded by Colonel Chávez. From the moment she learned the news she was eager to move on, declining the priest's suggestion that she send a letter informing Ramón of her decision to remain and wait for him. She wanted to be with him and would not be dissuaded.

Walking with the women and children and the carts carrying the sick and wounded in the dust raised by heavy cannon and the reinforcements marching to join up with Porfirio Díaz, who had already invested the capital, Antoinette came one late afternoon to the ruins of Río Verde. The sight of the burned adobe buildings and the bullet-scarred fountain in the middle of the square, where villagers were waiting with water and food for their compatriots, brought tears to her eyes. So many faces were missing—Ramón's abuela, Captain Martínez, Consuelo . . .

A woman came to where she sat in the shade of a tree, rubbing blistered feet and legs that felt like lead.

"Have you come far? Are you hungry?"

Antoinette reached thirstily for the water bottle held out to her, and after drinking her fill, pulled off the dirty scarf covering her hair and poured the remainder over her head as she had seen the other women do.

"Señorita Dubec?"

"I'm sorry—I don't remember you," Antoinette said apologetically. So many people had come and gone in her life over the past months.

"I am María—the wife of Julio. I remember you well, señorita. You helped us defeat la viruela, did you not? And then you came to our fiesta in your white dress and danced in the arms of Don Ramón with such love in your eyes."

"María—yes, I do remember. What is happening here?" She waved a hand toward the gutted buildings. Out of the whole village, less than half a dozen remained habitable. "Will you rebuild?"

"Sí. We have already begun with the church. When it is finished we start on the hacienda of Don Ramón so that it will be ready for his return. Have you seen him, señorita? Is he safe?"

"Yes—at least I believe so. He is at Querétaro. I am on my way there now."

"To be with him. How lucky you are." María sat back on her heels, and for the first time Antoinette realized she was pregnant. "I do not have a man any longer, he was killed at Cuenevaca last month. But I am lucky too. I shall bear him a fine son who will grow up in a free Mexico. Let me come with you, señorita. I am of no use here, and I have two brothers with General Escobedo at Querétaro."

Antoinette nodded, glad of the company of someone she knew even slightly. Refreshed and rested, she followed the other women out of the village the next morning, María walking beside her. It was an effort not to look back, to allow her gaze to wander past the village to the peaceful valley where Val Verde lay in ruins. When the war was over she would help Ramón rebuild it for their children.

Until then, she must keep her eyes fixed firmly on Querétaro.

Maximilian, Emperor of Mexico, had been arrested! The news brought by a troop of soldiers returning from the besieged town spread through the camp like wildfire. Drawn by the sound of wild cheering and shouting, Antoinette came out of the hospital tent, Father Ignatius at her side. Since her arrival there had been a steady stream of Loyalist wounded as the siege moved into its ninth week, and she had been kept very busy. Two of the injured, she discovered, had come from Ramón's cavalry regiment, which was concentrated on the plain west of the Cervo de la Campaña. Each time she bent over a bloodstained newcomer, her heart was in her mouth for fear the face would be his. She was given a severe jolt when among the new arrivals one day she discovered Luis Santos with a bullet wound in his shoulder.

"Antoinette!" He first saw her as one of the women was helping him off with his jacket. "Madre de Dios—am I dreaming? Ramón thinks you are in France."

Indicating she would take over, Antoinette moved to his side, conscious, as she began to clean the wound, of his eyes appraising her appearance. Like most of the other women, she wore a simple cotton skirt and blouse and leather sandals on her feet. Her hair was braided into two thick plaits over her shoulders. The white skin that had once received so many compliments had been darkened by months of marching and living out in the open under the fierce Mexican sun. She was a totally different woman —but still beautiful—still the woman he loved. She saw it in his eyes as she poured a small amount of tequila into a cup and held it out to him.

"Drink this and then rest. We cannot talk now, I have to help Father Ignatius."

She came back to him as it was growing dark, pulling the scarf from her head as she sat down beside him against the door of an old farm building.

"You look tired," Luis said gently.

"I am. Father Ignatius had to amputate some poor man's hand. I've seen him operate before, but it still makes me feel ill. Oh Luis, it is good to see you. Forgive me for such a terrible welcome."

"We both seem to have been very busy since we last saw each other. You decided to stay, then?"

"I'm trying to reach Ramón. I've followed him from Puebla."

"Yes, he told me how you had escaped from prison. Consuelo's death shattered him—that and the fact that he has resigned himself to the fact he will never see you again. You are a wonderful girl, Antoinette. I wish you both every happiness in the world—you deserve it."

She leaned against his shoulder with a tired sigh and was comforted by the arm that crept around her shoulders. Solid, dependable Luis. She would pray for his happiness.

"And you, Luis? Where have you been since that terrible day?"

"I helped Ramón and Consuelo to escape, as you know. I wanted to come back for you, but Ramón almost dragged me out of the city. As he said, if I had been arrested, I could not have helped you or anyone. I wanted to come back, mi niña, believe me—so did he. We rode to Díaz and asked for men and he gave them gladly. If he hadn't, I think Ramón would have returned alone, he was that distraught. My God, how he suffered during that ride back! And then to find you safe and Consuelo in your place . . . I thought for a while he would lose his sanity."

"Have you seen him lately? Is he well?"

"He was yesterday morning. Tired and impatient to finish all this, but otherwise well."

"Thank God. How do you think he will receive me?"

"Like a man unable to believe God has given him a second chance," Luis returned. Antoinette did not mind the mockery in his voice. He had told her what she wanted to hear.

"How I have prayed for the war to end, we have so

much rebuilding to do—Val Verde—the village . . ."

"My home also," Luis interrupted. "Laurent burned it less than a week after your escape. He came to arrest me and found he had a fight on his hands. I could have gone with Ramón, but I wanted to protect my home. In the end my staying destroyed it. But at least I had the satisfaction of killing the swine before I rode away."

"And Mercedes?" Antoinette asked, looking up at him. The shadowy profile of his face hardened.

"She is dead too. You have probably realized she was the one who suggested Soledad should spy on you. She hated you because of Ramón. She was no sister of mine any longer when I learned she wanted you dead. Laurent turned against her too, as I warned her he would. Her usefulness was over. She was the sister of a traitor and subject to the same penalties. She fled to the quinta to warn me of his coming—at least she did that. She was killed as we ran from the house. Only two peons and I reached safety."

Antoinette did not speak. At such a time no words could bring him the comfort he so desperately needed. Ramón's grandmother, Captain Martínez, Consuelo, Julio, and now Mercedes. The list grew longer. How many more would be added to it before Mexico could begin to heal its wounds?

It was impossible not to remember Chapultepec and the glittering assembly of friends who had gathered about Maximilian that night at the ball. Where were the Emperor's friends now? Although he had been afforded many opportunities to leave the doomed city, Maximilian had listened once more to his confidant General Miramon, enduring personal hardship and privations as food and ammunition dwindled and his precarious position became clear to him. General Miramon and General Mejia were to share his ordeal of a trial. The second in command, General Márquez, escaped their fate, for he had left Querétaro on March 23 with eleven hundred men, under orders from his Emperor to muster five thousand men and return within a fortnight to the besieged town. Not one man returned. Another soldier turned coward was Colonel Miguel López. Antoinette remembered him as Ramón's superior officer in the Guardia Imperial. Always a great favorite of Maximilian's—Empress Carlota was godmother to one of his children—he was nevertheless of disreputable character. Betraying the man who trusted him implicitly, he had proceeded entirely on his own initiative to one of the Liberal army camps, where, for the sum of fifty thousand pesos, he was prepared to sell his royal master. It was even rumored that he had relieved certain officers of their posts, thus enabling a group of Loyalists to enter the town and arrest Maximilian early on the morning of May 15, without a single shot being fired. Such examples of cowardice and desertion from the Imperial cause only served to strengthen the desire of the people that the Emperor be delivered to them for judgment.

Antoinette kept her own council on the subject as she went about her daily duties. The men and women she was with accepted her as one of them because she was El Padrino's woman, and she wanted to say or do nothing that might jeopardize her position. On the day Luis left camp to return to Querétaro, the verdict was pronounced on Maximilian and his two generals. The trial had lasted two short days. The verdict on all three—guilty!

"I wish it could have been different," she said as she walked with Luis to his horse. "Do you think Carlota will be able to understand?"

"For her own sake, I hope not. She had her faults, but I think she loved him. Mexico has been a cruel mistress to them both." Gently drawing her into his arms, he planted a kiss on each of her cheeks. "Are you staying here or going back to the capital?"

"I will wait here for Ramón."

"Then your patience should be rewarded soon, mi niña. Some of our men are pulling back from Querétaro and moving to join General Díaz outside the capital. I shouldn't be surprised if Ramón were among them."

"He doesn't know I am here."

"Sí, he does." Luis was smiling as he swung himself into the saddle. The happiness in her face helped to ease the pain in his heart. "I sent word to him yesterday."

Antoinette hardly slept that night. She lay beneath her blankets outside the hospital tent staring at the starry sky and thanked God and Coatlicue for watching over her. The Christian god and the pagan idol—her God and Ramón's. They both belonged to her now, for his world was hers. Coatlicue lay in the warm hollow of her breasts—what comfort the amulet had brought to her during the long, arduous months.

I see pain and bitterness ahead for you both, but your love is strong, it will survive.

It had survived and now it was even stronger.

Morning found her busy in the hospital with Father Ignatius, but her mind was elsewhere. At the first sounds of horsemen riding into the camp, she ran out into the sunlight, her heart racing. She pushed her way through the women crowding around the travel-stained riders, kissing, embracing, lifting up children to the men, welcoming home the first free Mexican soldiers. She saw Ramón dismount from his huge black horse and start toward her, but she could not believe it—even when she went into his outstretched arms and saw the love in his eyes. She felt the great strength of his arms, which would from that day hold and protect her, and surrendered to the caress of his lips against her hair and face. Still, she could not believe that all the obstacles keeping them apart had finally been overcome, until at last his mouth was on hers and the ground moved beneath her feet to convince her.

They were married that evening, their hands entwined, their bodies touching as they stood together before the main campfire. Two solitary silhouettes in the flickering flames. Around them a hundred or more Juaristas sat quietly watching and listening to Father Ignatius reciting the marriage service. El Padrino and La Florecita—it was a good match, despite the fact that she was a gringa. She had chosen to stay with her man—to die with him if necessary—and that made her no different from any other woman sitting close to her man by the fire or making love in the darkness of the tents beyond.

The bells of Querétaro echoed through the still night air, their golden notes pealing out over a free land—a free Mexico. They rang for the living and the dead; the old and the new; for Maximilian under sentence of death, and Carlota, so many miles away in Belgium; for the day-old son of María and the father who would never see him; for Antoinette and Ramón, entwined in each other's arms. . . .

Two bodies, but only one heart. Joined now, never to be separated again.

*The irresistible love story
with a happy ending.*

THE PROMISE

A novel by
DANIELLE STEEL

Based on a screenplay by
GARRY MICHAEL WHITE

After an automobile accident which left Nancy McAllister's
beautiful face a tragic ruin, she accepted the money for plastic
surgery from her lover's mother on one condition: that she never
contact Michael again. She didn't know Michael would be told
that she was dead.

Four years later, Michael met a lovely woman whose face he
didn't recognize, and wondered why she hated him with such
intensity . . .

A Dell Book $1.95

A love forged by destiny—
A passion born of flame

FLAMES OF DESIRE

by Vanessa Royall

Selena MacPherson, a proud princess of ancient
Scotland, had never met a man who did not desire
her. From the moment she met Royce Campbell at
an Edinburgh ball, Selena knew the burning
ecstasy that was to seal her fate through all eternity.
She sought him on the high seas, in India, and
finally in a young America raging in the
birth-throes of freedom, where destiny was bound
to fulfill its promise. . . .

A DELL BOOK $1.95